Life Swap

Abby McDonald graduated from Oxford University with a degree in politics, philosophy and economics – and a penchant for teen pop culture of every kind. An entertainment critic turned full-time author, she now lives in London. She is twenty-four years old. Of Life Swap, she says, "I wanted this book to explore what feminism can mean to a new generation of teenagers. Through their exploits, Tasha and Emily learn to make conscious decisions about their futures; they discover different sides to their personalities – and feminist identities – despite social pressures and expectations. Claiming that kind of autonomy is one of the most powerful things a young woman can do."

Visit Abby online at www.abbymcdonald.com

Life Swap

Abby McDonald

WALKER BOOKS

This is a work of fiction. Names, characters, places and incidents are either the product of the author's imagination or, if real, are used fictitiously. All statements, activities, stunts, descriptions, information and material of any other kind contained herein are included for entertainment purposes only and should not be relied on for accuracy or replicated as they may result in injury.

First published 2009 by Walker Books Ltd
87 Vauxhall Walk, London SE11 5HJ

2 4 6 8 10 9 7 5 3 1

Text © 2009 Abigail McDonald

The right of Abigail McDonald to be identified as the author of this work has been asserted by her in accordance with the Copyright, Designs and Patents Act 1988

This book has been typeset in Sabon

Printed and bound in Great Britain by Clays Ltd, St Ives plc

British Library Cataloguing in Publication Data:
a catalogue record for this book is available from the British Library

ISBN 978-1-4063-1900-2

www.walker.co.uk

For Elisabeth—an amazing critique
partner, and an even better friend

Tasha

This is *so* not a good idea.

I'm barely five minutes into my first class of the semester when it hits me just how bad an idea this is. Sure, it's not "getting into the hot tub with Tyler Trask while the cameras are rolling" bad, but then what is? I would have to search the world for the people who decided Crocs were a cute shoe concept before I found an idea as bad as *that,* but taking my semester-abroad placement at Oxford University when I barely scrape a B minus. Way up there on the dumb-ass rankings.

". . . By now, you'll all be familiar with the basic texts on the reading list . . ."

I glance down at the dense two-page list they included in my exchange information pack, full of titles like *Political Innovation and Conceptual Change,* and have to remind myself to breathe. I only arrived in England a couple of days ago, but apparently hell waits for no girl, even if she's suffering killer jet lag.

". . . And we've got a new face with us. Natasha Collins, welcome."

My head jerks up, and I look around to find the group staring at me. Instead of the packed, anonymous lecture halls I'm used to back home, I'm sitting in a dim, wood-paneled room, one of a group of just ten students balanced on battered couches and overstuffed armchairs.

"Would you like to introduce yourself?" Professor Susanne Elliot asks, her salt-and-pepper hair falling around a face that, back home, would have been Botoxed into oblivion.

"Umm, sure," I begin. "I'm Tash—Natasha," I correct myself. I keep forgetting, Tasha is no more: the version of myself I left giggling and drunk in that hot tub. "I'm here from UCSB for the semester."

"UCSB?" Elliot repeats, frowning. Yup—definitely no Botox.

"University of California?" I explain hesitantly. "I go to school in Santa Barbara."

"Oh." Elliot seems surprised. She shuffles her papers, searching for something. "We don't usually exchange with that university."

"It was a kind of last-minute thing." I begin to pick the clear varnish on my thumbnail and ignore the amused looks my classmates are exchanging. I don't know why they have to be so snobby about it. I mean, sure, it's not Stanford, but the UC system is totally second tier!

"Santa Barbara," the professor repeats. "And what were you studying there?" She looks over her thin wire-rimmed glasses at me.

"I'm . . . undeclared." My discomfort grows. Technically that's not quite true, but if I'd told the Global Exchange crew what my classes were, they'd have put me on some kind of international blacklist and branded me unfit for study.

"Well." She pauses. "Welcome to Oxford. I'm sure you'll find Theory of Politics very . . . interesting." She moves on to talk about research-paper schedules, but I catch the slight smirk all the same.

Sinking back in my seat, I sneak a look at my classmates. Dressed in an assortment of preppy sweaters, Oxford shirts, and neat jeans, they look totally at ease: nodding along and exchanging familiar smiles, but then again—they would. They've all spent the past year and a half bonding over dusty library books and term papers while I was five thousand miles away, blowing off classes to hang at the beach and shop. I may have a great tan and awesome bargain-hunting skills, but somehow I don't think those will count for much here.

". . . So I suppose that's all. Any questions?" Professor Elliot looks at us expectantly.

I had plenty. *What the hell am I doing here?* for a start and *Why didn't I just go volunteer in Guatemala like my mom suggested?* I'd been so focused on getting out of California, I hadn't really thought about what would come next.

"I have one." The sporty blond girl beside me raises

her hand a little. "Will we be starting with power theory or basic ideological distinctions?"

I blink.

"I thought I'd leave that up to you. Everyone?"

They all pitch in with enthusiastic suggestions while I smooth down my denim skirt (which is officially three inches shorter than anything my classmates probably own) and wish for the twenty-eighth time since my flight landed that I could take it all back. Not the "leaving the States" part, of course. That was a given. I mean, Christmas in L.A. was bad enough (with Mom and the stepdad alternating their silent treatment with plenty of "we're so disappointed in you" lectures), but when I got back to school, the gossip was worse than ever.

So what could I do? I didn't want to just drop out of college. I may have chosen keg parties over studying and put more thought into first-date outfits than any of my papers, but I'm no quitter. And more than that, I couldn't stand the symbolism—if I dropped out, it would look like it really had all been my fault. Ever since Tubgate, I'd been walking around with a smile on my face, pretending I was cool with what they were saying. The whispers. The tabloid lies. Dropping out altogether would be like admitting I felt dirty and ashamed, and there was no freaking way I would give them all that satisfaction.

So even though the semester had already started, I begged the exchange program, calling that stuck-up administrator every day until she finally broke down and told me that they'd had a mix-up with some girl at Oxford who still needed a spot. And although I didn't meet their oh-so-high Ivy League grade requirements, she could let me go if it was a straight swap: my classes for hers, my roommate for her dorm. School hadn't even started back over there, so I wouldn't miss a day. Nearly three whole months in England. Perfect.

But now I'm stuck in a room full of people who were probably high-school valedictorians instead of spirit-squad captains; I'm struggling to even follow the intro talk, let alone the classes themselves, and I have to ask myself . . .

Is this really so much better?

By the time our not-so-welcoming welcoming talk is over, I've made a mental note to buy a "Beginner's Guide" to political theory. According to Elliot, I have three days to prepare my first paper, which will then be offered up to my classmates for discussion. Three days! *National Geographic* shots of feeding piranhas flood my mind, and I add yet another note to my schedule: find out where the library is. Somehow, I don't think my usual tactic of cribbing from Wikipedia and the fruits of Google will cut it with this crowd.

Pulling on my fur-trimmed parka, I follow the other students out onto the icy main quad. It turns out that Oxford University is a collection of a couple of dozen separate colleges, scattered across the city. I'll be living and studying in Raleigh College: a group of sandstone buildings set back from the riverbank. I walked around the campus yesterday, and this place is totally gorgeous. Dorms, dining hall, and an old chapel are arranged around these tiny cobbled courtyards, and there are neat lawns and gardens all around. It's pretty for sure, but in this weather, I can't help wishing they'd added heating to the sixteenth-century stone cloisters. Even my favorite Uggs can't keep me warm in this.

Speaking of which . . . the way my classmates are treating me is giving the weather competition in the sub-zero stakes. Snatches of their conversation drift back to me in the cold wind, but nobody so much as acknowl-edges my existence.

"Coming to Hall later?" one of the boys asks, push-ing back his floppy dark hair.

"No, I've got to revise for my collection," a brunette girl answers, her hair fixed in this weird semi-back-combed ponytail. I'd find it easier to understand if they were speaking Spanish, thanks to my core language require-ment and four years of high school *"Me llamo"*-ing, but right now I'm clueless.

"I'm thinking bin bags for the Bop on Friday," the athletic blond adds. OK, so I'm being tactful here; by "athletic," what I really mean is butch. Cropped hair, baggy sportswear, and if that doesn't paint a clear-enough picture for you, she has a rainbow badge on her bulky backpack. Hey, I'm not judging. I just don't see why a same-sex preference has to go hand in hand with complete fashion backwardness. I mean, look at Portia de Rossi: a hot wife and an *Elle* subscription. It can be done!

"Or maybe—" They duck through an archway into what I think is the mailroom, the old wooden door slamming shut with a hollow thud. I don't try and follow. There's only so much cold shoulder I can take, and besides, I know for sure I won't have any mail. I'll be lucky if my parents send a single card, such is the shame Tubgate brought upon my family—or so my mom says. They're so mad, they're probably redecorating my bedroom as a playroom for my new baby sister-to-be.

Suddenly weary, I weigh the choice between noodles and whatever sludge passes for cafeteria food here. Pulling my jacket tighter, I head for my dorm, squinting against rain now falling in cold slices. I can't take sitting alone in the huge, portrait-lined dining hall again, and at least Ramen will keep me a size four. Tripping up the bare stone staircase, I heave open my door and collapse onto the bed, ready to wallow.

Damp shoes off, sweatpants on, and Joni Mitchell playing low. There. I'm set. Let the wallowing commence.

But just as I'm about to curl up under the covers and wish myself across the ocean, I take a closer look around. Back in Santa Barbara, I share a place with Morgan—it's tiny but in this fun block with other students, super-close to the beach. Here I'm living in a single dorm room; wait, make that a prison cell. Faded gray carpet, a hard twin bed . . . I get up and slowly take it all in.

The plain walls are totally clear except for a color-coded study schedule and reading list—pinned to the board so perfectly, she must have used a ruler to arrange them. The desk is set with a sheet of notepaper and two pens at precise right angles. And the nightstand—home to the universal "goodie drawer"—holds only a container of vitamin pills, a pocket pack of Kleenex, and a small dictionary.

I sink back down on the bed, this time in disbelief. I think of my own apartment, overflowing with junk, clothes, and noise, and then look again at this temple of order and precision.

Emily Lewis. Just what kind of freak are you?

Emily

"... And I was like, 'No way,' but she says, 'Hell yeah,' so we totally started grinding in the middle of the dance floor! Uh-huh ... No ... Totally! And, like, he was all crazy jealous ... Ha! No, totally!"

I shut my eyes tightly, but when I open them, I'm still here: staring at a wall full of foreign photographs while my new flatmate continues her fascinating analysis of modern sexuality.

"No. Way!" she squeals, perfectly audible even in the next room. "Omigod, I can't believe you let him do *that*!"

With a sigh, I swing my legs over the side of the bed and survey the task awaiting me. I'll need cleaning supplies for a start, and some kind of flat edge to scrape the debris off the walls. She probably used Blu-Tack to keep all this up, and I know what kind of grease marks that will leave. Warming to my project as Morgan keeps up her steady stream of "like" and "totally!" in the next room, I methodically begin to peel the layers of magazine clippings and photographs away, bringing order to the chaos until pale cream walls are revealed beneath, soothing and cool.

"Hey, Em!" Morgan pushes the door open without knocking. She's cocked her head to trap the phone on her shoulder, halfway done painting her nails a violent shade of raspberry. "We're heading out to eat—wanna come?"

"It's fine." I shake my head quietly. "I need to unpack. But thanks."

"Sure, cool." Morgan shrugs, but she doesn't leave. Instead, she turns to the huge vanity mirror, finishing her nails and then starting on a fresh coat of mascara. Her blond hair has platinum highlights and is twisted into loose ringlets that fall halfway down her back, shining synthetic and bright against her pale-blue tank top. With the tan and careful makeup, she looks only half real— like some kind of perfect doll. And she's not the only one. This city seems to be home to some sort of junior Stepford experiment.

"No, she's staying." Morgan's voice drops as she turns back to the phone. "No . . . uh-huh . . . no, she's kinda quiet. I know . . . she's *cleaning*."

I ignore her hushed comments and keep working until she leaves, settling into a blissful rhythm of lift, wipe, repeat, and then unpacking my own things, a warm breeze rippling the curtains and a familiar pop song drifting up from the apartment downstairs but nothing else to break my peace. And, at last, my new room is neat and clean, Natasha's many belongings tucked away under my bed, my clothing and study materials in their place.

There.

I pause for breath, regarding the order I've magicked out of thin air and teen-girl offcasts with a warm glow of satisfaction. I can't concentrate when things are out of place. Everything else about the exchange may be a monumental disaster, but this mess I can control.

My own phone begins to ring, not with the heavy rap music that Morgan's cell has spewed forth a dozen times already today, but a normal beeping tone.

"Hi, Elizabeth." I collapse onto my crisp new bedding and notice a stain on the ceiling I'll have to deal with later.

"Santa Barbara? Emily, have you lost your mind?" My elder sister doesn't waste time with "How was your flight?" pleasantries, her disapproval echoing clearly down the line from England. "It's not even Ivy League! What possible use could it be to waste three months in a school for beach bums and party girls?"

"It's not my fault," I argue, kicking my bare feet in the air. I may as well get in a few toning exercises with the criticism. Constructive use of all available time, that's the key. "Professor Tremain forgot about my application. He didn't send it until after the deadline, and by then all the good universities were booked. I was lucky to get this place at all. They've already started term." I gave silent thanks for whatever slutty prank had sent Natasha fleeing to England. Morgan had babbled about hot tubs and TV stars when I first arrived, but I'd been too jet-lagged and bitter to pay much attention.

"Lucky?" Elizabeth exclaims. I hear the sound of pans clattering and picture her in her sleek granite kitchen, whipping up a three-course meal after a fifteen-hour shift at the hospital. "You shouldn't have gone at all. Your second year isn't time to slack off, you know. It's when you should be going to extra classes, getting involved in student politics and debate."

"I know." I'd heard this all before. Elizabeth was repeating my father's lecture practically word for word.

"So why jeopardize everything by disappearing?" Elizabeth switches from disapproval to exasperation as a kettle hisses. "I don't understand."

"It's not such a big deal." I neatly avoid the question. "Study-abroad programs are a legitimate enrichment activity. It'll show I'm resourceful and adaptive to change."

"Of course they are." Elizabeth sighs. "But what possible enrichment are you going to find in that place? It's hardly Harvard."

Harvard. Just the mention of it burns. I'm supposed to be there right now, walking through neat red-brick quads to seminars on international relations and political philosophy, surrounded by the most brilliant minds in the country. I had it all planned out, right down to my study schedule and lecture list. The pamphlet is in my suitcase, tucked inside a travel guide to Boston my father gave me for Christmas. I suppose I won't be needing them now.

". . . Will you? Emily?"

"Hmmm?" I blink out of the reverie.

"I was saying that it's not too late; you could come home. Go back to Oxford."

"But my place is taken already. The other girl is there."

"We'd be able to work it out, I'm sure." Elizabeth munches on something. "Dad said he could find you a room to rent in Oxford until you get your old one back; you could go to all your classes as normal. He would even give you a living allowance."

"I'm sure he would."

"Don't say it like that." She sighs again. "He's just concerned. We all are. This isn't like you at all."

"And what is like me?" I ask, wary.

"You're responsible, focused." Elizabeth tries to make it sound like a good thing. "You wouldn't just take off and risk your grades, your chance at a good internship."

"I've already applied for the internships, and besides, why is everyone so sure they know what I'll do? I'm eighteen years old, not some middle-aged spinster!"

"Spinster?" Elizabeth perks up. "Emily, is this about Sebastian? Because—"

"It's not about him!"

"Fine." She sighs again. "Just think about it, OK? It wouldn't be like you were admitting defeat."

"I'm not coming home," I tell her determinedly, the memory of Sebastian giving me new resolve. "I . . . like it here."

"You do?"

"Yes," I say carefully. "My roommate is really nice, and there are lots of interesting courses I can take."

"Oh." She pauses. "Well, I guess you know what you're doing. . . ."

"I do." I finally let my legs drop, thirty repetitions later.

"Then look after yourself. And call Dad. He's worried."

"I will. Love you."

"You too."

I roll over and catch sight of the exchange information pack on the desk. I haven't yet brought myself to look at my class schedule, despite what I told Elizabeth. I can only imagine what Natasha — amateur lingerie model and table dancer (according to the photographs on the wall) — was signed up for. Intro to Early Education, probably, or Remedial English.

But flicking through the stapled pages, I see with horror that I'd overestimated her. Film Crit: The Modern Blockbuster? Teen Movies: Brat Pack and Beyond?

The girl is a bloody film major?

I catch a shuttle bus from our apartment and then practically power walk across campus to catch the international office before it closes. It's one thing to alienate my family, risk my chance of a top-five law firm internship, and voluntarily spend twelve weeks in a confined space with Morgan, but take that joke excuse for a class schedule? Even I have my limits.

All around me, tanned and happy students are sauntering in the sunshine, completely oblivious to my plight. It's a mass of activity I'm still adjusting to; there are four hundred undergraduates at Raleigh, but here they number closer to twenty thousand. I've gone from recognizing every face I pass to being completely lost in a sea of tanned strangers.

But to my surprise, I don't feel as alone as I expected. In fact, weaving my way through the crowds, the ocean sparkling in the distance, I find a strange sense of satisfaction begin to form. This anonymity, this freedom, is something new for me. I can't cross the Raleigh campus without somebody stopping me to talk about classes or events, but here nobody shows a flicker of interest as I speed by. I could be anyone, not just Emily Lewis, future lawyer and study fiend, the person I have been half my life. As far as anyone here knows, I could be somebody who usually does things like this: a girl who takes off to the other side of the world, a reckless adventurer.

Reckless . . . I have to give a hollow laugh at that. The first truly adventurous thing I do in my entire life, and it's because of a boy. Pausing in the afternoon sun, I remember my sister's comments and what Sebastian had said, just a week ago, the night he broke up with me. Because I was a control freak. Because I was afraid of intimacy. Because the conversation was taking place *on* my bed, instead of *in* it, wearing more clothing than he would have liked. Other girls would have gone out and spent too much money on a low-cut dress or cut their hair off to show how spontaneous they were, but not me. No, I had to pick up the phone the very next morning when that Global Exchange lady rang, and I had to tell her yes. Yes to the last-minute switch. Yes to California. Get me out of England.

As much as I—and my liberated, post-third-wave feminist self—hate to admit it, my sister was right. This is all because of Sebastian.

Ignoring the dull fear in my chest that comes whenever I think of what he said, I cut past a group of boys in too-low denim tossing a Frisbee around and push into the air-conditioned cool of the International Students building. It didn't matter how I ended up here: I'm stuck. Until April. I suppose I might as well make sure I get a proper education while I'm here, at the very least.

Tasha

So this is what studying is like.

Don't get me wrong, I've worked hard before. Exams, term papers, finals—just because I'm not an honor student or anything, it doesn't mean I haven't put the time in. But there's a huge difference between cramming stuff you kind of know (but just need to know better) and working flat out for three days trying to get your head around concepts you haven't even heard of. And even then, after all that work, knowing your paper still sucks.

I'm back in Professor Elliot's badly lit study, this time with only a couple of other students for company/camouflage. Sporty girl and blond boy, aka Carrie and Edwin. Yes, Edwin. They call their kids things like that here. Anyway, I'm bundled up in my warmest sweater because for some reason, English people are, like, morally opposed to heating, and it's still raining: gray and gloomy outside the slim windows. Carrie has just finished reading her essay aloud, which involved a lot of phrases like "basic ideological dichotomies" and "inherent value systems," and now Professor Elliot is looking at us expectantly.

"Any thoughts?" she asks as I try to avoid eye contact. This is becoming a routine for me, but maybe that's not so bad. Aren't routines supposed to give your life structure and purpose?

"Well, actually yes." Edwin speaks up right away, flicking back a few pages to the start of his notes and launching into an attack of everything Carrie just said. ". . . And finally, she's completely overstating the intrinsic value of democracy as an end."

"But of course it has value!" Carrie bursts out. "Are you saying we shouldn't have a say in our government?"

"Of course not." Edwin sighs. He's tall and aristocratic-looking like a lot of the boys here, with faintly blushed cheeks and a kind of delicate look about him, like he's a temperamental classical composer or something. "But by giving it a sort of lexical priority, you risk overlooking other important factors."

"What about you, Natasha?" Elliot interrupts them, staring straight at me with her sharp blue eyes. I haven't even heard of "lexical priority," but there's no escape. "What was your take on the essay question?"

If this were one of the romantic-comedy movies I've studied, this would be the point where I'd speak up with some insightful comment that would win everyone over and show how my hard work and pluck have paid off.

But it's not.

"Umm." I blink quickly at my own essay. "I kind of agreed with what the Davies book said. About the different faces of power?" I pause, looking quickly around for signs that I'm on totally the wrong track. I get nothing, so I stumble on. "Like, how real power is getting someone to do what you want without them even knowing it?"

Carrie sighs, her hair pulled back with a brightly patterned green scarf. "It's nothing but speculation whether any of the factors actually applied, or to what extent, or . . ."

She keeps going, rattling off a long list of the ways I'm wrong, while I sink lower in my seat and feel myself blush. I never minded being shown up in class before, but somehow this is different: the small room, the look on their faces. Carrie and Edwin seem exasperated, like they could be coming up with a Middle East peace plan if it weren't for me.

". . . Really, Lancing covers all of this in his first chapters." Carrie looks at me impatiently. "Didn't you get a chance to read him?"

"I . . . No," I admit. Covering just the main texts on the list had taken dawn-to-dusk effort. I'd barely left the library except for food and sleep. And yes, I was still on a Ramen diet. "Sorry," I add, hating myself even as the words leave my mouth.

Carrie exchanges a look with Edwin.

"No need to apologize, Natasha," Professor Elliot says calmly. "Davies's arguments are certainly relevant here. In fact, one might say that even considering Lancing's objections, he still offers the best way to approach the topic."

I cringe. The only thing worse than coming off as a total dumb-ass is having the teacher try and stick up for me.

"Now, Carrie, if we can just go back and talk about your first point . . ."

Luckily, I get to keep quiet for the rest of the class, throwing in the odd murmur of agreement or worried frown based on if the others seem to agree. They're too busy trying to score points off each other to notice. I swear, if I hadn't already pegged Carrie for a lesbian, I would put money on her and Edwin hooking up soon: the way they keep firing arguments back and forth practically screams "unresolved sexual tension." But anyway, at least they're too wrapped up in tearing each other to pieces to deal with me, and soon the hour is up and I can escape back to my room and the comforting fact that I have a whole four days until my next class torture session. That's one good thing about Oxford, I guess: their weird study system means I only have two of those brutal discussion groups a week. Lectures seem to be optional, so that just leaves me with reading. Tons of reading.

Kicking off my damp sneakers, I collapse onto my bed and look around the room, which is now way more livable since I started pinning up photos and tear sheets from *Cosmo* and *Elle*. It's only 5:00 PM and I'm getting restless. After all that time in the library, I want to go out, do something, party! But what? In California I had tons of stuff to do and loads of friends to do it all with, but here . . . I sigh. Here I'm treading dangerously close to social leper territory.

It's not like I haven't tried. I went down to the college bar the other night to meet people, but after hanging around on the edges of crowds while the preppy kids all ignored me, I gave up. The other Americans and international students must have the same problem, because they all seem to keep to their own cliques. They may seem to be total nerds, but I can't risk them recognizing me from Tubgate, so that leaves me back at square one: alone in my dorm room with nothing but the last season of *Heroes* on DVD for company.

If only I'd known this would happen. Maybe then I'd have thought harder before throwing on my candy-pink bikini and going back to Tyler's that night . . . OK, who am I kidding? I didn't give it any thought at all. But of course not. I mean, you don't stop and think, "Hmm, do I really want a video of this leaked all over the internet?" every time you hook up with a hot guy. Because, barring a few crazy exhibitionists, the answer will always be no. No, I don't want to be known as the slut who broke up America's Most-Beloved Couple (seriously, they won the *Seventeen* reader survey last year). No, I don't want to see my own tanned and not particularly toned body staring back at me from the supermarket tabloids for weeks. No, I don't want a half hour of drunken fun to be the single defining moment in my whole nineteen-year existence.

Sighing, I grab my shower caddy and head for the bathrooms. I've had weeks to mope about the whole thing, but even I have to admit that being alone and anonymous in England is way better than being a recognizable joke back in L.A. Lathering up my hair under the dribble of lukewarm water, I resolve to be more positive. I managed to get out of the States; now all I have to do is find some kind of social life. It'll just take some effort, right?

Wrapping myself in my huge, terry-cloth robe, I step back out into the communal bathroom. I thought the place was empty, but now that the shower is off, I can hear a kind of muffled sobbing coming from one of the stalls. I pause.

"Hey, are you OK?" I ask.

There's a sniffling sound, and then a thin voice emerges.

"I'm fine."

"You don't sound fine," I point out. "Can I get you anything?"

"No." Another sniffle. "I wish you could, but . . ." She starts sobbing again.

I gingerly push open the cubicle door and find a girl curled up on the toilet seat, legs tucked tightly against her chest. She's wearing striped pj's and has limp blond hair hanging in her face.

"Really, I'm fine," she protests, trying to wipe her face with a shirtsleeve. "I just . . ."

"Don't worry," I say softly, not wanting to scare her. She looks younger than a freshman, but maybe that's just the distress on her pale face. "Look, my room's just down the hall. I could make you a coffee. Or tea, if you want," I add, remembering how Brits are about their tea.

"Thanks, but . . ." She shakes her head and grabs another handful of tissue from the dispenser. "It won't help."

"Won't help what?" I ask again. "Look, I know you don't think I can help, but maybe I can."

She takes a deep breath and then looks me in the eye for the first time. Another sniffle, and then her voice comes, so soft I have to lean forward to hear.

"This morning . . . The condom split. I don't know . . . I don't know what to do."

Other people's problems may suck for them, but at least they give you some perspective. It takes me less than twenty minutes to Google the Oxford student services, wait for Holly to dress, and make our way down the twisted, cobbled streets to the offices behind the student union buildings. I've done this with Morgan so many times, I didn't even raise an eyebrow when Holly told me about the boyfriend (older), the sex (bad), and her feelings of general helplessness that were clouding whatever judgment got her into Oxford in the first place.

As it was, she only had to chat to the physician for a few minutes before emerging with her prescription and the glow of somebody who will never, ever have unnecessary sex again. Morgan usually lasts about a week before jumping the next guy, but I'm betting Holly waits longer.

"OK?" I ask, my ass already numb from the cheap Formica seats they have lining the small waiting area.

She nods happily. "Yes. Thank god!"

"Cool." I look around. The place is empty, littered

with flyers and health-awareness posters. "Want to stock up on freebies while we're here?"

Holly blushes, but she goes over to the jar of condoms all the same. I browse the notice board instead. There's no way I'm so much as going to *kiss* a guy while I'm over here. No dating, period.

"Yes, just let me check for you." A voice emerges from a back room, and then the familiar stocky body of my classmate walks out. I cringe.

"Oh. Hi. Natasha, right?" Carrie looks as uncomfortable as me, frozen by the front desk with an armful of paperwork.

"Yup. Hey." I give an awkward wave.

"What brings you . . . ?" Carrie glances from me, to the physician's door, to where Holly is helping herself to a liberal supply of condoms. "Oh, right." She gives me a knowing look. Of course the dumb Californian would be stocking up on birth control.

I control my flicker of irritation and try and make nice. "You work here? That's great."

Carrie looks surprised. "Yes, I volunteer. But not for long. They're closing the place down at the end of March."

"They are?" I look around again. "Why?"

"No funding." Carrie gives a bitter laugh. "The bene-factors leave thousands to the rowing clubs and libraries, but we get nothing. Typical, isn't it?" She takes a paper from the desk and hands it to me. SAVE WOMEN'S SERVICES, the Day-Glo orange flyer protests.

"Is there anywhere else in town to get this stuff?" I ask, worried. I may be planning to give nuns competition in the chastity stakes, but that doesn't mean I can't be concerned for everyone else.

"That's not the point." Carrie folds her arms, already defensive. "That's only half of what we do here. There's a support hotline and a night safety group and—"

"I get it," I cut her off quickly. She's got an angry gleam in her eye, and I don't want to be on the other end of it. "Well, good luck." I put the flyer down and pick up my bag. "I hope you pull it off."

She turns back to her paperwork, while Holly and I push through the smudged glass doors onto the street. Students stream by on bikes, long striped scarves around their necks, and a bunch of Japanese tourists hover by the gates of the college next door.

"So . . ." I start, turning to her kind of awkwardly. Now that she's OK, Holly probably has plans. "You're all set?"

"Yes." Holly smiles shyly. "I only have to go to the chemist's."

"Cool, I'll just—"

"Would you come with me?" Holly asks suddenly. "And then maybe, I know this great café nearby. We could get something to eat?" She looks at me hopefully. "I mean, you probably have things to do, but . . ."

"No! I mean, I don't. I'm free." I smile back, pulling my scarf tighter and thanking the god of coincidence for sending me a possible friend. "I'd like that."

Emily

Apparently the international office doesn't subscribe to my standards of what constitutes a proper education, because by the end of the week, I find myself sitting halfway back in a cavernous lecture hall while our professor addresses us on the challenging topic that is screenwriting for mainstream movies.

"By now, you'll all have had time to look over our next script." He's relaxed and charming, and far too tan. I'm immediately suspicious. Real professors should have spent their lives buried in dark, dusty libraries, researching papers and striving for expert status. They shouldn't have time to develop a healthy, outdoorsy glow, let alone advanced social skills. "So let's hear what you think."

I look around. The half of the room that is actually paying attention and not checking their mobiles, doodling notes, or chatting softly to the person nearby are looking through a sheaf of papers. I tentatively raise my hand.

"Ah, an eager critic." He bares his gleaming teeth at me.

"No, actually, I don't have the pages," I hurry to explain. "I just arrived on exchange."

"Well." He pauses to assess me before gesturing dramatically. "Can anyone help out our British friend here?"

The students nearby reluctantly make a show of shuffling their pages. It doesn't help that my neatly pressed skirt and short-sleeved shirt make me look like a tax auditor stranded among their beach-party ranks, but eventually a boy sitting a few empty seats away leans over and hands me the script.

"Thank you," I whisper, grateful for rescue.

"No problem, I had a spare set." He has dark eyes and cropped dark hair, slouching low in his seat wearing disheveled black jeans and a fitted navy T-shirt with a cartoon robot printed across the front. "You're from England, right? What brings you over here?"

I look distractedly back to the front of the class, torn. Professor Lowell is still talking, something about presentation and formatting, and I don't want to miss it. "England, yes," I say quickly. "I'm just here for the rest of the term."

"Cool." He grins a boyish half smile, and I'm reminded again that shining white teeth seem to be a basic constitutional right over here. "You picked a great class. Lowell really knows his stuff."

"He seems to." I try to follow what the great professor is jotting on the whiteboard.

"He worked at Fox for a while in the nineties, development," he continues enthusiastically. "Rumor has it he was the one who bought *Speed* and—"

"Look," I stop him apologetically, "I really appreciate your help, but this is all new to me, and I don't want to get behind . . ."

"Sure." He studies me for a moment and then leans away, leaving me to despair over my lack of social skills and quickly skim-read this script I'm supposed to be so well acquainted with.

Twenty minutes later, I've reread the script, made copious notes, and now I'm sitting, bemused at the outpouring of praise that's coming from the class. Surely we haven't been reading the same thing?

". . . And the characterization was great." A thin emo boy sweeps back his slice of fringe and finishes his critique, which turned out to be light on any actual criticism. I'm itching to add to the discussion, but something holds me back. After all, I only watch films for an escape, some entertainment. I don't know anything about this topic, and while Lowell may have asked for our instinctive reactions, I always think opinions need to be backed up with research and facts. Otherwise, what use are they?

"And I really liked the part where he confesses his feelings," a girl with funky, cropped red hair adds, her expression wistful. "It was so romantic."

I can't help but give a little snort of laughter. Quickly, I try to disguise it with a cough, but it's too late. Lowell swings around from his place at the front table and fixes his stare on me.

"Our Brit!" he exclaims. "Care to add anything?"

I pause, looking around cautiously.

"Come on, now, don't be scared," Lowell prompts. "We'll go easy on you."

"Well," I begin, flicking back to the beginning of my notes, "I don't really agree."

"With who?"

"With anyone." I give an awkward shrug, feeling curious eyes on me. "It just didn't work for me. Take the scene you were just talking about." I nod at the redhead. "It wasn't believable at all. His lines were far too polished."

Lowell gives a chuckle, and the dark-haired boy turns back to me.

"But you're totally missing the point," he objects, restlessly tapping his pen against the side of his seat. "If he's been waiting for years to tell her how he feels, then it would be polished, right? He's been rehearsing his words in his head forever."

"No, I don't think it would work like that," I say, my confidence building. "If anything, it would make them *more* scattered—I mean, nothing ever comes out the way we plan, does it? And if she's supposed to mean so much to him, then having the scene play so perfectly just sort of dilutes the emotional impact. We don't get to see any of his fear or anxiety."

I remember sitting dumbly on the bed as Sebastian told me it was over. There had been so much I wanted to tell him, but I hadn't been able to say a word. I just sat there, picking at the fraying edge of the bedspread as my relationship slowly unraveled.

"Interesting point." Lowell nods. "So—"

"And that scene shouldn't even be so early in the story," I continue, trying to banish all thoughts of Sebastian. "It's the emotional climax of the whole piece, but it comes so soon that we don't care enough about the characters yet."

"But it's not a love story." Emo boy sighs. "The romance isn't the main theme. And isn't it better that the script is being different, not having the weepy scene at the end like all those chick flicks?"

I might have left it at that, just let the class carry on now that I'd contributed my part, but there was just enough condescension in his tone to make me keep talking.

I happen to like "chick flicks."

"Perhaps, but this isn't innovative—it's bad," I exclaim. "The whole structure is a mess, there's no journey or tension. Things just happen!"

"What do you know about structure?" the boy next to me asks, his voice even.

I remember my layperson status and blush. "I might not have studied film, but narrative structure is universal. I mean, it goes all the way back to the Greeks and classic literature." I look to Lowell for confirmation. He inclines his head slightly in what could be a nod, so I press on. "There has to be something the characters want, and then obstacles in their way before they get it. This script has that, but in such a messy way, there's no real reason to care what happens." I send silent thanks for those years of dull Classics lessons I had to take in school. Memorizing Latin verbs was torture, but I always loved the great myths and legends. *The Odyssey*, Hercules, Theseus and the Minotaur. There's a strange kind of order to the tales: a world where everyone is doomed to tragedy and death. There are few happily-ever-afters, but I found the tales satisfying all the same.

"I'm afraid we're out of time, but it's been a great discussion." Lowell claps his hands together, and immediately a rustle of activity sweeps through the room. "Remember, I want a couple of pages about your script of choice by the end of the week. You can find all our guinea-pig projects on the class website."

I start to pack my things away, but a moment later, Lowell appears by my side. "Good points, ah . . ."

"Emily," I reply. "Emily Lewis."

"Well, Emily, it's a class requirement that you be part of a project group: making your own short feature." Tilting his head, Lowell regards me with an amused look. "Since you seem to have so many opinions about this script, how about you work on it?"

I move to speak, but someone beats me to it.

"What?" The boy who lent me his pages is frozen midstep, looking at us both in horror.

"Ryan, meet Emily." Lowell grins. "She'll be rewriting your script. I'm sure you'll make a great team."

"But—"

"Really, I couldn't—"

"No excuses." Lowell cuts off our protests and regards us both with satisfaction. "Consider yourself partners for the rest of the semester. I look forward to seeing what you come up with."

He saunters away, no doubt to the beach, while Ryan stands, glowering at me.

"Sorry," I offer, picking up my bag and moving down the steps toward the front exit.

"You could have just let it slide." He follows, scuffing battered black Converses on the floor.

"And what, pretended your script is some kind of masterpiece?" I pause in the doorway and look back at him curiously. "It was just a little constructive criticism."

"Constructive?" He raises his eyebrows rather sarcastically. "Sure. Anyway, don't think this means you can tear it apart. I spent all vacation writing, and I'm not having it wrecked by some . . ."

"Girl?"

Ryan folds his arms. "Someone who knows nothing about screenwriting."

"Not according to your professor," I remind him, annoyed by the way his friendly act dropped the moment I had something intelligent to say. Just like a boy to be threatened by a challenge.

"Look, just leave the thing alone. We'll put your name on the end, and everyone's happy, OK?" he proposes. "I get my script; you get the credit."

"Thank you, but no," I reply, baffled that he thinks I'll just agree.

"Come on." He sighs. "It's not like you even care."

"How do you figure that?"

Ryan smirks at me. "What's your favorite movie?"

"What?" I frown.

"Your favorite movie, tell me."

I shrug. "I don't know."

"Exactly!" He stares at me with satisfaction. "You don't even care enough to decide that. So, just leave my production alone and we'll be cool." He slings a grafittied messenger bag across his chest and begins to walk away, as if we're done now that he's had his say.

"I'll be cutting whatever I want," I call after him. Ryan spins back and glares at me, as if by sheer will he can make me disappear. "It was nice to meet you," I continue, taking at least a little pleasure from his annoyance. "I'll let you know when my first draft is done."

I go straight to the library after that to stock up on film textbooks. My father always drilled us to make the most of all opportunities: if we had to do something at all, we should do it well. Hence if I'm going to waste a term in film classes, I may as well emerge with an A. And if I'm going to be doing battle with Ryan's smug grin on a weekly basis over our final project, I can't afford to give him any ammunition. *Love Actually* to *Citizen Kane*: I plan to know them all.

Hoisting my stack of books up the stairs to the apartment, I begin to plan the next few days. Without the essays I had due at Oxford, my week is decidedly structure free, but I'm sure a quiet hour with my day planner will remedy that. Unlocking the door, I see a routine taking shape. I can work out a timetable of movie viewings, library time and research, and perhaps even . . .

"What are you doing here?"

The door swings open to reveal a familiar body stretched on the sofa, flicking through a magazine. Ryan sits bolt upright at the sight of me. "What are *you* doing here?"

"I live here," I inform him icily, crossing the room and stacking the books neatly on the table.

"You're . . ." He blinks. "Of course. The uptight British chick."

"The *what*?"

But before I have a chance to ask anything else, Morgan appears from her bedroom. She's wearing her hair loose and straight, with a white denim skirt and matching tank. She practically glows with tanning product and sunshine.

"Awesome, you've already met." Morgan beams at us, as I begin to get a very bad feeling. "Em, this is my boyfriend!"

Tasha

"No, I get it—it's cool."

Sighing, I kick off my heels and drop my purse back on the floor.

"I'm really sorry," Holly apologizes on the other end of the phone. "I tried to get all the reading done in time, but I've still got another six chapters left and labs to write up, and—"

"Really, it's cool!" I say again, trying to hide my disappointment. "We can party another time."

"Thanks, Natasha." Holly already sounds distracted, and I just know she's already got her textbook open. "Perhaps at the weekend? I've got practice on Saturday, but Sunday could work."

"OK." It's not like I have any other plans. "Sunday, then."

"See you soon."

I hang up and let out a long sigh. Holly can't help it, I know. She's pre-med, which means more lectures and labs than any normal person could handle. My two essays a week are nothing compared to her workload, but somehow she manages to take crew as well: waking up at five every morning to go train in the gym or row lengths on the icy river. I think she's insane.

Crazy or not, she's my one and only friend in Oxford— if hanging out a couple of times in the two weeks since we met counts as friendship, I mean. So when we made plans to go out to a bar tonight, then maybe on to one of the tiny clubs for some dancing, well, it was pretty much the social highlight of my stay so far. I even took time away from the library this evening to straighten my hair and give myself a manicure.

Some good perfect nails will do me now.

"Hey, wait up!"

"Come on, we'll miss kickoff."

"Give me a second. . . ."

A group of people clatter loudly past my room, and then they're gone and it's silent again. I hate the quiet around here; it makes it easier to hear all the fun everyone else is having. And when I say fun, I don't just mean the good, clean stuff; my walls are so thin I can hear every passionate grunt and moan from the room next door. Every night it's the same: murmured conversation, the sappy Robin Thicke starts up, and then showtime, while I press my headphones tighter and blast Kelly Clarkson so loudly I probably do lasting damage to my eardrums. I haven't seen the guy yet (and come on, it's got to be a guy. I mean, Robin Thicke?), but he's a player all right.

I check if Morgan's online to chat, but nobody's there. Now that I'm all dressed, I can't bear to just stay in and watch DVDs again, so I grab my coat—and scarf and gloves—pass the cluster of kids by the stairs, and head out, tripping down the uneven stone staircase and letting myself out the side gate. Inside the battlements, Raleigh is calm and ordered, but the moment I pass out onto the street, I'm almost hit by speeding cyclists and the rush of traffic and city life.

I plug in my iPod and set off into town. It's past 8:00 PM, but I've already spent six hours in the library today, gone for my gym workout, and written my next paper, which leaves me the one final choice in my now-regular routine: bookstores. I never got the appeal of hanging out in one before, but in a city where everything except the pubs and bars close by seven, Borders offers one last place to spend the evening. Warm, quiet, and full of armchairs and distraction, it can almost lull me into believing I'm not completely alone.

There are groups of students hanging around by the ATM outside, and I can't help but stare, the girls in bare legs and tiny jackets despite the fact my face is going numb just peeking out between my hat and scarf. I'm used to girls dressing trashy—I mean, I own skirts that would make Band-Aids look demure—but that's in seventy-degree weather! Oxford girls may look totally prim during the daytime, but after hours, it's like the search for the next Pussycat Doll came to town.

I push past the girls, and once I'm out of the damp winds, I make straight for the Starbucks at the back of the store. It's totally pathetic, I know, but after coming here every night for a week straight, I've settled into a routine. First, I stake my claim on one of the prize armchairs. They're arranged in a little nook, back from the café, and if you can believe it, winning one takes strategy and determination. Sometimes I have to hover, annoying the customers before they give them up, but tonight I spy a free one and only have to slip past an old guy before he can grab it. Stripping off my winter gear, I leave it draped over the seat to mark my territory and then wander back into the main bookstore area to gather my distraction.

Usually, I speed right past the magazine racks, but tonight some masochistic instinct makes me stop and look, and there they are on the cover of *US Weekly*. "Tyler and Shannon: Wedding Bells?" the cover screams, under a photo of them on the red carpet, grinning for everything they're worth. With a gulp, I take a copy, face-down, and browse the new fiction aisles for a good ten minutes before I can bring myself to settle in my armchair and look at the piece.

"Rumors . . . sources close to the couple . . . body-language expert claims . . ." It's nothing new, I realize. Just the same old breathless speculation, fueled this time by Shannon's confession to a "close friend" that she dreams of a spring wedding. But just as I think I'm free and clear, I turn the page and there it is.

You'd think by now I'd be used to the sight of my own pixilated body. You'd be wrong. I still taste metal in my mouth when I look at the picture: half naked for the (hidden) camera as I straddle Tyler in the hot tub, so clear you can see the harmony tattoo I got on my right hip with Morgan in freshman year. It doesn't matter that under the water, I've still got my bikini panties on, or that I didn't go all the way with him. No, that picture is all that matters—and the fifteen minutes of giggly, drunken footage that wound up online showing my face, and B cup, to the world.

See, this is the reason I couldn't stay in California, the reason that no matter how much time goes by, I can't escape that night. Because every time something happens in Planet Tyler and Shannon, they drag it up again.

And those two are total publicity whores.

Ever since the first season of the reality show *5th Avenue: The Real Gossip Girl,* when America's teens fell in love with the charming bad boy Tyler and sweet Shannon, who'd been crushing on him, like, forever, the two of them managed to build whole careers out of being themselves. Think the kids from *Laguna Beach* and *The Hills* did good? LC and Heidi have got nothing on these guys. Their on-off flirtation lasted Tyler's whole senior year, so when they finally got together (at an oh-so-spontaneous loft party in Williamsburg), the audience and press went crazy. Would Tyler reform for his high school sweetheart? Could their love last the distance to UC Santa Barbara for college? Tune in to Tyler's spin-off show next season to find out!

I know all this now, but before autumn, I only had a hazy recall of *5th Avenue*'s complicated plot—and the audience's fierce devotion to dear, sweet Shannon. So when I met Tyler hanging out with some friends at a college party and he hit on me hard, I figured they'd split. Anyway, he invited me back to his off-campus apartment for some hot-tub time, and through my alcoholic blur I figured what the hell? He was cute and seemed totally sweet, and there were no cameramen around. Wouldn't I have to sign some kind of release before they were allowed to put me on TV?

Yup. Naïve and wasted, what a great combination. There were hidden cameras on the deck, and refusing to sign the release only meant the producers blurred out my face when they broadcast the clips—but not when they leaked the footage online.

He may have been a great kisser, but trust me, I would have needed an orgasmic night with screen god Chris Carmel for it to be worth these kind of consequences.

I toss the magazine aside and go get a latte and a cupcake, trying to shake off my blast from the past. One day (soon I hope), the country will get bored of those talentless posers and move on to something way more important, like Brad and Angelina's rumored split or Jessica's new diet, but until then? I'm in exile. It seems so stupid when I lay it out like this. Some people can't go home because they offended the government or risked their lives for justice. I'm banished because of five Jell-O shots and a guy who was way more take than give when it came to . . .

Never mind.

I'm smothering my coffee with cinnamon and nutmeg

when an American voice behind makes me turn. "Hey." A blond guy is hovering near the condiment stand, kind of stocky in a NYU sweater. "Don't I know you?"

I freeze. No, no, not here. Not so soon. My heart is suddenly speeding as I prepare for the worst.

"Yes, it's you." He nods, features smoothing out again. "McKenna's economics lectures. You sit by the window, right?"

God, the relief that flows through me is nearly more than I can take. I manage to breathe and grip my coffee mug. "Sure," I force out, waiting for my heart to slow. "That's me."

"Cool." He nods. His eyes slowly drift down my body as he checks me out, and right away I wish I'd thrown on some sweats before I left. I'm still dressed to party, in tight dark jeans and a clinging black jersey top. I take a step back.

"So which college are you at?" Blond Boy's smile is wider now, showing plenty of teeth.

"Merton," I lie, deciding I don't want him knowing anything about me.

"I'm at Balliol." He edges closer. "Oxford's a trip, right?"

"Totally," I reply lightly. "Anyway, I've got a ton of reading to do." I force myself to flash him a grin before I grab my coffee and scoot back to my corner. I've been avoiding the Americans ever since I arrived. They seem to think sharing a place of birth gives us an automatic bond, but as much as I want friends, I can't risk them recognizing me.

"Tough reading assignment." I'm only a few pages into a new romance novel when another seat gets vacated and Blond Boy collapses next to me. He laughs at my book. "I've got eight chapters of UN procedures to get done tonight."

"Oh." I feel irritation flare. This is my place—my sanctuary.

"The professor's a complete ass." Kicking his feet onto the low table, Blond Boy starts to dominate the space: spreading out his notes, pulling his sweater off. I feel invaded. "I interned at the UN last summer, and this guy knows jack about the place, but what can I do? I mean . . ."

He keeps talking awhile as I sip my coffee and try to think of a way out. It's ironic, I know—I've been longing for company all week, then the moment someone actually talks to me, I can't shut them up fast enough. But he's not just anyone; barely a minute in, I can tell he's an obnoxious jock like all the others I left in California. So, with a flash of inspiration, I don't say a thing. I just reach for my headphones and plug back in, looking back down to my book as if he doesn't even exist.

And I'm alone again.

Emily

I've never had to share my space. There's my sister, of course, but we always had separate rooms, and by the time I reached the age where an inalienable right to bathroom time was necessary, she'd already left for her time at Oxford; the pink-tiled sink was mine alone. When it was my turn to go to university, I moved into my box of a room and refitted the lock on the door. I even managed to schedule myself around peak shower hours so I had the communal bathroom to myself.

Now solitude is a thing of the past.

"The blue or the green?" Morgan fishes a couple of skimpy vests from a shopping bag and dangles them in front of the two girls who are sprawled over my bed, flicking listlessly through fashion magazines. Apparently, Natasha had an open-door policy, so now her stereo is thundering with a rock song; the floor is littered with folders, shoes, and accessories, and there's nothing I can do to hold back the chaos. Despite all my best efforts, Morgan is undeniable—the only concession I've won is that she keeps Ryan out of the way while I'm around.

"I like the blue," says Lexi, a petite blond with arms no thicker than my wrist.

The other girl, equally skinny with big dark eyes, looks up. "Yeah, it matches that bangle you got last week."

Morgan lights up. "I didn't think of that. Brooke, you rock!"

I turn another page of my textbook. I've long since finished studying; the amount of time required to achieve a perfect score in every one of Natasha's classes is less than I would spend in the gym at Oxford, but I always recheck my notes, just in case.

"I love this song," Lexi declares, twisting onto her back and kicking her tanned legs in time with the heavy rap track that comes on. "Justin and me made out to it for the first time."

"Have you trained him yet?" Morgan asks, stripping off her T-shirt and wandering back to her room for another bra. That's another thing I miss about living alone: the absence of naked breasts at every turn.

"In progress," Lexi answers with a gleam. "Less drool now, thank god."

"Eww!" Brooke squeals. "Why do you even bother?"

"'Cause he's totally hot, that's why." Rolling her eyes, Lexi gets up and begins to browse my wardrobe. "It's my service to the world. His future girlfriends will thank me."

"What about this?" Morgan interrupts, pirouetting in the blue top. Her black bra is clearly visible underneath.

"Trashy." Lexi spares another glance from *Glamour*'s riveting spring editorial shoot.

"Well, yeah, but, like, sexy-trashy or slut-trashy?"

"Sexy-trashy," Brooke assures her. The distinction is lost on me.

"Awesome. Then we're good to go."

"You coming, Em?" Brooke asks, looking over. "They're having a beach volleyball tournament, and there'll be a bonfire later."

"Don't bother." Morgan sighs. "All she does is study."

I blink. Usually I wouldn't care what my roommate says, but something in her tone sparks me into gear. Two weeks since I arrived, and she thinks she knows me? "I'll come," I say, almost before I reach a decision.

Morgan spins around, surprise spilling across her face. "You will?"

"Sure," I agree, letting the textbook fall shut and reaching for my pack of aspirin to ease the low ache in my head. So far, I've only been down to the shore to assess a jogging route, but color-coding my screenwriting research can wait. And didn't "making the most of the exchange opportunity" extend to integrating with the local culture? "Let's go."

An hour later, I'm settled in the midst of a colony of blankets, towels, and tanning lotion. Despite it being late January, the afternoon is warm and sunny, the ocean is sparkling blue, and the beach is packed with perfect, tanned flesh. Global warming has its perks, I suppose. As I look around, it's clear that anyone who lectures about America's obesity epidemic has obviously not visited Santa Barbara during winter term. Stationed on prime territory next to the volleyball courts, I have a full-circle view of sweaty players, bronze-chested surfers, and the hoards of svelte, bikini-clad girls batting their fully made-up lashes at both.

"Can you believe what Susie did to AJ?" Lexi carefully rubs oil into her calves.

"I know, right?"

"In front of everyone—and with Patrick!"

Their conversation drifts around me as I stroke swirls into the sand. I feel like an anthropologist buried deep within an alien culture as I try to decipher the significance of each squeal and comment. Instead of lowering their voices for a particularly scandalous piece of gossip, Lexi's and Morgan's voices seem to carry, and a group of younger girls nearby look over with envy.

"I don't know, he was kind of annoying. Always hanging around, like a lost little puppy."

"Morgan!"

"What? I'm just saying, I'd get sick of it too." Morgan turns and looks down at me over the huge white rims of her sunglasses. For all the deliberation over her outfit, she's now stripped down to a tiny pink bikini, matched with an anklet and lip gloss. I wish I could say that her style was out of place, but from the look of the ranks of college girls spread out around us, she's underaccessorized. "What about you, Em?"

"Hmm?" I lift my head slightly.

"Any guys around?"

I pause, trickling grains through my fingertips, and feel the familiar pang at the thought of Sebastian. To my relief, it stings less than it used to. Maybe one day it won't sting at all.

"There was," I say at last, "but we broke up just before I came here."

"That sucks. What happened?"

"Nothing in particular," I answer quietly. Just the fact that I'm emotionally crippled. "It didn't work out."

"Come on, details." Brooke opens a bag of fat-free, sodium-free, and no doubt taste-free crisps and offers it around. "How did you meet? How long were you together? Spill."

Nibbling one, I try to keep my tone light. "He lives next door to me, we went out for three months, and can you pass me the water?"

Brooke tosses the bottle at me. "So did he have a cute accent, like Prince William?"

I smile with relief. Americans and royalty . . . "Yes, he's English."

"British men are so hot." She sighs. "They're way classier than guys here."

I stifle a laugh, thinking of crew drinking sessions. If Brooke could see a man facedown in his own vomit with his underpants on his head, she wouldn't think the Brits were so distinguished.

"So what are British guys like in bed?" Lexi flips over and fixes me with a mischievous look.

53

"You know . . ." I take a nonchalant sip of water. I wouldn't know. "What are American men like?"

She smirks. "The usual."

"We should fix Em up," Morgan decides, surveying the surrounding prospects with a predatory stare. "They'll go crazy for your accent." She pauses and tilts her head. "You know, I'm surprised you haven't dated anyone yet. These guys are usually pretty fast when it comes to fresh meat."

"Not with me." I manage a grin.

"And it's not like you're ugly," she adds, bluntly assessing me. "Although you could use a tan and a suit that isn't so, you know, functional." I purse my lips a little. My navy two-piece isn't up to Morgan's dental-floss standards, but I'm not really in the mood to let the whole beach see my buttocks. "Chill," she says, seeing my reaction. "I was just saying . . ."

"No, it's fine."

"Anyway, you want to go get a soda?" She nods in the direction of a beachfront snack stand.

"OK." I pull on my khaki shorts and start to button my shirt, but stop when I see Morgan's look. Apparently you're supposed to wander onto the street with your body in plain sight over here. I compromise to local culture and leave my navy shirt undone, while Morgan and Lexi reapply lip gloss, smooth down their hair, and pull on embellished flip-flops.

"Get me a Coke, please." Brooke lies back and yawns. "Diet."

"And you'll keep an eye on our stuff?" I ask. Lexi and Morgan exchange another look.

"It'll be fine."

We head up the beach, Morgan and Lexi sauntering along as if this is a catwalk. I can feel everyone looking over as we pass: the girls giving quick judgmental glances, and the boys all staring for longer. I shiver. Something about how blatant it all is makes me nervous, like I really am nothing more than a block of meat. Suddenly I'm painfully aware of my pale, pale skin and "functional" bathing suit.

"How about Christian?"

I tune back in to the girls' banter.

"Hell no! Remember what happened at Christmas?"

"Right. Ali? Lulu gave him a good rep."

"Maybe but, like, she's not exactly an expert."

"Ha, so true."

"Ooh, there's Sam." Morgan looks toward the snack stand. "Cute."

"And single," Lexi notes.

"And no psycho exes."

"Or STDs."

"Perfect," Morgan decides. She takes my arm and propels me forward. "You can get him to take you to the new Jennifer Aniston movie."

"I what?" I don't have time to ask what she means because I suddenly find myself in front of a tall boy with spiky, wet blond hair. He's wearing nothing but a pair of fluorescent surf shorts and a shark's tooth necklace.

"Hi, Sam," Lexi and Morgan chorus.

"Hey." Sam's face widens into a broad grin. "What's up?"

"Nothing much," Morgan chirps. "Just showing Em here around. She's from England," she adds helpfully.

Sam looks at me with new interest. "England, cool."

I nod. Morgan nudges me.

"Hi," I say, attempting not to stare at his chest. Surely he has to be on steroids to have that sort of definition?

"So how do you like it here?"

"Oh, it's lovely." I realize that my accent has become more defined and arched. Another few weeks and I'll sound like I'm aristocracy.

"We'll catch you later, at the bonfire, right?" Lexi interrupts, flicking her hair back.

"Absolutely." Sam nods.

"Awesome." Lexi beams, and then Morgan drags me away.

"Perfect," she decides. "Now he's had a look at you, he has time to ask around. And tonight you can make a move."

"Look, guys, really—"

"Come on, Em!" Lexi scolds me. "What are you going to do, just mope around after your ex? Have some fun."

"It's not like he won't be out getting whatever he can," Morgan adds, pulling a couple of cans from the drinks cooler.

"And you could do worse than Sam. He's a sweetie."

I stand mute against the onslaught and stare at a rack of sweets. Their world of casual hookups is a galaxy away from the awkward friends-but-maybe-more scene I know. To just start flirting with a random stranger? You might as well ask me to solve nuclear fusion. Even with

Sebastian, we only got together romantically after six months of fraught friendship and silent pining. There are plenty of girls who can go pull a guy on the dance floor or in a dark corner of a bar, but no matter what continent I'm on, I am certainly not one of them.

When dusk settles, we pack up and drive over to a more secluded stretch of shoreline where a crowd of people are already clustered around a bonfire. I tail silently as the girls greet their friends, recognizing faces from around our block of flats and names from Morgan's gossip.

The night is warm, and people are sprawled on the sand in college sweatshirts and skirts; some couples already intertwined, while the party girls shriek and flit between groups.

"Glad you came, right?" Brooke passes me a red paper cup of Coke. I nod, deciding that was more a statement than a question.

"It was kind of weird for me adjusting when I was a freshman." Brooke's face glows in the reflection from the fire as she watches the crowd. "I'm from this supertiny town in Idaho," she adds in a whisper. "But I always wanted to go to college in California, so I figured everything out pretty quickly. You'll have fun if you just, you know, go with it."

"Hey, England." Sam comes up behind us and drapes an arm over my shoulder. I stiffen.

"Ooh, Chandra!" Brooke does a bad job of pretending to spy somebody across the group. "I've got to catch up with her. You'll be OK?"

"I'll look after her," Sam promises.

"Cool, I'll catch you later." She speeds away, leaving me alone with the surf god. I turn and try to look relaxed. He's wearing a pale-blue polo shirt, the same shade as his eyes, and objectively I have to agree with Lexi. He's cute.

"Having a good time?" Sam asks, moving his arm away to brush back his fringe. "I was going to bring you a drink, but . . ." He gestures to my full cup.

"Oh, right. Thanks anyway." I busy myself taking a sip.

"You must feel a long way from home."

I pause. His tone is warm, sincere, and he's looking down like he's actually interested in my response. My nerves unravel a little.

"A little," I admit. "Everything here is very . . . relaxed."

"What?" He grins. "Don't tell me that whole stereotype of uptight English people is actually true!"

I laugh, warming to him. "I'm afraid so. I'm still sort of adjusting."

"You're doing great so far," Sam assures me. "Bonfire on the beach, some beers — you'll be a real Californian in no time."

"Thanks, I think."

"You want to sit down?"

I nod, and he leads me to a free space on one of the logs. Sam sits close, the side of our bodies pressed together as he tells me about growing up in a small beach town.

"It sounds great," I say, distracted by the heat of his

torso. "We lived in the middle of the countryside, nothing but rolling hills all around. I'm not exactly a beach girl."

Sam laughs. "I don't know." He slides his arm back around me and leans closer to whisper in my ear. "You looked pretty cute out there."

I glance up. He's looking at me with a flirtatious smile, moving his other hand to brush back some of my hair. We're surrounded by people, but that doesn't seem to matter as he slowly tilts down again, this time so that his lips graze the edge of my mouth.

And then I panic.

"I need to find Morgan," I exclaim, leaping up. "I'll be right back!"

I catch a glimpse of his confusion before I dash away, weaving through the crowd until he's out of sight.

What on earth was that?

I gulp. Shoving my hands deep in my pockets, I drift away from the group. Their noise fades slightly as I near the ocean, settling cross-legged on a stretch of warm sand and watching the inky water.

Why didn't I just kiss him? Morgan was right—I do need to get over Sebastian, so why did I freeze up the moment Sam made a move? Sam is nice, smart enough, and far more attractive than any boy I could find back in England, but no, I had to bolt like a petrified schoolgirl.

I sigh, kicking sand into tiny heaps. Nothing has changed. Sebastian would always complain about how I held back, how I would get so disconnected from being together. The voice in my head never takes a break: it's always analyzing, assessing, pulling me back from the brink of just letting go. And now, thousands of miles away, it's still there. I shiver, suddenly afraid it won't ever go away. Is this just the way I am—doomed to be on the outside of myself forever?

I blink back tears. Some recovery trip this is turning out to be. My family are so busy that they quickly gave up on making me come home; now my father just sends me news items ("because we know what insular attitudes to world affairs they have over there"), my mother makes me email twice a week to check I haven't been shot, and Elizabeth reminds me about skin-cancer statistics. I assure them all that I'm having fun, but . . .

. . . Is this really it?

Tasha

Professor Elliot wants to see me before class. I emailed my new essay over last night, and now there's an ominous note in my mailbox asking me over for "a little chat." Like I can turn her down.

I meant to read through the summary chapters again to be totally prepped for the meeting, but by the time I'm finished cramming the latest econ chapters and have worked through a nightmare of a worksheet, it's twelve already. So, instead of arriving cool and confident, I turn up five minutes late: red faced from racing across campus, stomach growling in protest at missing breakfast and lunch, and not exactly dressed to impress in my grayest fading sweatpants.

"Natasha." Greeting me with a raised eyebrow, Professor Elliot ushers me into her cluttered room. She's wearing a mismatched green cardigan over a pair of old tweed trousers, but somehow I still feel like the slob. "Sit down, please. Would you like some tea?"

"Umm, no. Thank you," I add, looking nervously around as she begins to fill a small kettle and set out a mug. I know Oxford likes to make a big deal about the informal students-staff vibe, but if I'm in trouble, I'd rather she just give it to me straight. Elliot fusses with her drink for a couple of agonizingly long minutes as I wait. I can see my essay on her table, covered in red marks. My stomach gets tight.

"Now . . ." Settling in an armchair, Elliot finally turns to me. "How are you finding it here?"

"Fine," I answer. "Good, I mean."

I don't mention that it's been the longest, loneliest three weeks of my life.

"Good." Elliot nods. "And you're managing the workload all right?"

"Well"—I hesitate—"I'm trying. It's a pretty different system from the one back home."

"I can imagine."

"But I'm working really hard and doing everything I can to keep up," I find myself explaining anxiously. Buried in the Global Exchange small print had been a clause saying that both colleges could kick us out if we didn't meet their "minimal academic criteria." There's no way I'm letting that happen.

"And I can tell," Elliot reassures me. "But I think perhaps we should look at doing something different with you."

I blink. "What?"

"From now on, I'll be setting you different work from Carrie and Edwin." She continues, "You'll still be a part of the tutorial group, and you're more than welcome to tackle their reading lists, but for your own essays, I think we'll set you something more suitable. A little less . . . challenging." She shoots me a smile that's supposed to be comforting, but I'm still stuck on her words. Different. More suitable. Less challenging.

I'm being demoted.

"Does that sound good to you?"

"Sure," I manage. "But . . ." I swallow, suddenly feeling tears well up. "Were they really that bad? My essays, I mean." I think of the hours I've been slaving over her reading lists: battling to find sense in modern themes of feminism or crazy theoretical constructions of the perfect society. I know I'm not anywhere near my classmates, but I didn't think I was doing so bad.

Elliot laughs lightly. "We don't think about things in those terms here. But if you really must know, your work has been . . . fine."

A rush of relief floods through me: she can't send me home on "fine." But then I think about what she's saying.

"So why change things?" I try to keep my voice steady, embarrassed to feel so emotional over a dumb reading list.

Elliot looks surprised. "I thought you'd be happy to take the pressure off. This way, you get to have some more fun, really enjoy this exchange the way you want."

The way I want.

63

I fold my hands carefully. "It's been fine," I lie. "I can manage."

Elliot doesn't look convinced. "It's all right to admit it, Natasha." She gives another little laugh. "I know this isn't your usual style, so why not take the new assignments and have fun? I'm trying to do you a favor here. My other students would kill for an opportunity like this."

"So why not give it to them?" I ask before thinking.

She glances away, and then it hits me. To her, I'm just the dumb Californian, the party girl who doesn't need to be here. She knows it doesn't matter if I flunk, because I'll just go back home to my film classes. The other kids actually need to work hard, to be smart, to succeed. But not me.

The truth stings me hard behind my rib cage. My work is "fine," but she's still writing me off just because I wear cute skirts and keep my hair blown out. It's clear she's never seen *Legally Blonde*. Aren't smart people supposed to be above this kind of blatant discrimination?

"I can manage," I finally repeat in an icy voice, before she can confirm my worst suspicions. "I'd rather do the same as the others."

Elliot studies me for a minute. "Fine," she agrees, obviously bemused. "But you might want to spend some time reading MacKinnon and Dworkin, in addition to next week's books. There were some rather gaping holes in your argument."

"Right," I answer quietly.

"And maybe you should get copies of Edwin's essay, to have a better idea of structure and summary."

"OK." I nod, wondering how to ask the boy for a favor when he's never said a word to me, except to attack my opinions.

"Right." Elliot's forehead crinkles slightly. "I suppose that's everything, then."

"Good." I reach for my folder. "I've got to get a drink before the tutorial. I'll be right back."

I flee before she can see me cry.

"That's terrible!" Holly exclaims. We're sitting in the corner of the crowded Raleigh bar that evening—her with a white wine, me with a Diet Coke (my teetotal pledge still working)—and, at last, I can vent. "What did you say?"

"What could I say?" I shrug off my sweater and raise my voice to be heard over the loud rock song on the jukebox. The bare stone walls of the bar are adorned with old oars and sports photos, and it's full with students crammed around small wooden tables. "She already thinks I'm a moron. I should have just taken the easy option; now I'm stuck with her hard-core assignments and I can't take it back."

"You'll be fine," Holly assures me, and even though she has no idea about my scholastic inaptitude, I let myself believe her. "It's always hard at first. It took me a whole year to get my head around the format for my organic chemistry essays. I had to retake my exams."

I don't have a year, but I figure I've been moaning long enough. The last thing I want is to be a drag and risk boring my only friend. "What about you?" I have a drink and try to make my voice happy. "What's up?"

"Nothing new," Holly muses, biting her bottom lip. "Aaron is still calling me. He doesn't know about . . ."

I pat her shoulder. "And you don't have to tell him."

She nods. "I know, but I still feel bad."

"Don't. He was the jerk who got you into this in the first place." Not that I'm bitter and jaded when it comes to guys.

Holly seems to pick up on my tone. "Have you ever had a scare like that?"

"No," I admit thankfully. "But even if I needed to get Plan B or whatever, I wouldn't feel guilty. That's just screwed up, like you should be sorry for having sex."

Holly grins. "See, now I know you've been taking Professor Elliot's classes."

"No way, really?" I laugh. "Tell me if I get as bad as Carrie—she's impossible. Everything's a freaking male conspiracy to, like, keep us in the bonds of submission or something."

"Umm, I know!" Holly exclaims. "Last year she kept the JCR meeting running three hours talking about how the college shouldn't subscribe to the *Sun*." I look blank. "This newspaper," she explains, "they run topless models on page three."

"Weird."

"The paper or Carrie?"

"Both! Seriously," I say, "what's with her? I mean, she gets so angry over everything."

"I don't know." Holly sighs, taking a sip of her wine. "But there are tons of people like that here, campaigning over everything. It's a breeding ground for future politicians."

"Egalitarian," I quip. Morgan or Brooke would have teased me, but Holly takes it for granted that we both know what I mean.

Holly brightens. "I nearly forgot, there's a European Affairs Society ball this weekend—you should come!"

"A ball?" I see visions of chandeliers and string quartets.

"They're so much fun," she promises, eyes wide and eager. "It's a great excuse to dress up, and there's a dinner. We could go shopping."

"Will it be stuck-up?" I hedge. Dealing with the preppy brats around Raleigh is enough for me.

"No more than usual." Holly shrugs. "Anyway, balls are part of the Oxford experience. You can't come here and not go to one."

She sounds so bossy, I grin.

"OK." I'm already thinking of the perfect dress I have, the one I wore to my senior prom. I never usually do formal gowns twice, but this one is Gucci and gorgeous and took three weeks of begging the stepfather before he buckled. "I'm in."

"Great!" Holly beams, before a group of students in scarves and coats bundle around our table and loudly greet her.

"You know we've got practice at six tomorrow?" A guy with pink cheeks and floppy brown hair throws his coat on top of mine.

67

"And Milton says we're doing weight-training all next week," adds a petite redhead, almost spilling her beer.

"He'll kill us all!" Holly groans. She turns to me. "Everyone, this is Natasha. Ellen, Alex, James." She nods at each person in turn. I wave, and they offer assorted hellos.

"So where are you from?" asks the guy crammed next to me. Alex, I think it is.

"L.A. originally." I smile, glad to be buried in the middle of a crowd for the first time in what seems like forever. "But I go to school just up the coast."

"California!" The redhead sighs longingly. "Beaches, sunshine . . ."

"Surfing," Alex adds. "What on earth are you doing here?"

I giggle. "It's cool to have a change."

"Bloody freezing, you mean."

"Yup, the weather does suck," I admit. "But Oxford is amazing—all the old buildings, the history . . ."

". . . the sadistic rowing instructors." Another guy arrives at our table in time to finish my sentence. "Did you hear what Milton wants us to do next week?"

And with that, I'm buried in the middle of a raging debate on rival crew teams and Raleigh's chances of success. As their enthusiastic conversation surrounds me, I feel a glow of warmth that has nothing to do with the overheated room. Professor Elliot is wrong—I'm not here for the easy way out. I can do this. I know I can.

Emily

After my mini-breakdown at the beach, I don't accept any more of Morgan's invitations. As much as I want to get along here, I can't bear the thought of that panic or uncertainty again, so by the end of my third week, I'm back in a perfectly structured routine, every hour from eight until five neatly accounted for—thanks to my wall-chart organizer. Morning runs, library sessions, classic film watching, and, of course, classes; if I ever get lonely or start to question what I'm doing here, all it takes is a quick glance above my desk at the daily schedule to calm myself down again.

In addition to Professor Lowell's screenwriting session, Natasha is also signed up for a range of core curriculum and film modules. The core material is a breeze: the sort of basic education requirements I could complete in my sleep, but to my surprise, the film work is actually interesting—full of ideas and concepts I've never come across before, everything from the business side of the industry to sociological readings of performance and script. Throwing myself completely into the work, I can almost see why someone would voluntarily choose to study it.

As the rush of students around me stampedes toward the door of my only morning lecture, I take a moment to check I have all the photocopied notes and reading suggestions. I'm finally adjusting to the size of this place, with cavernous lecture halls full of earnest film geeks and slacker students. My days of personal debate with my tutor are on hold for now, but the anonymity is refreshing. I see the same faces from some of my other classes: emo boy, perky girl, and Ryan, but nobody expects anything more than a smile or nod from me. I used to have to always be the one with the superior argument or insightful comment, but here I only have to show up.

It's the first time people have ever expected so little from me.

I finally finish double-checking my books and slip into the aisle, bumping straight into somebody else. "Excuse me," I apologize, still fastening my bag.

"No problem," a familiar voice drawls, edged with the slightest hint of sarcasm.

My head snaps up and I find Ryan in front of me, slouched in a maroon print hoodie and regarding me with extreme impatience.

"Oh, it's you."

"Could you sound any more thrilled?" His face twists into a half smile. "You're giving my ego a bruising."

"I don't think your ego needs any more help from me," I mutter, and then wish I could take it back. Ever since I found out Ryan was Morgan's other half, I've fought to keep things civil between us. I may never have had a roommate before, but I presume not fighting with her boyfriend is part of the basic requirements.

Ryan looks amused at my comment but lets it pass. "We're meeting at four, right?"

"Right," I agree. I've been working extra-hard to get my rewrites finished; we start filming next weekend, after all. "I booked us a study room at the library."

His face wrinkles. "Want to just get a coffee instead? The library's dead."

"Exactly. It'll be easier to concentrate there."

"Whatever. See you then." He saunters away, and I just wonder how much more reluctant his expression will get when he hears my proposals.

When I get back to the apartment, there's a hair tie on the door handle and not-too-subtle moans emerging from inside. Again. Apparently Morgan has a penchant for lunchtime sex, preferring to burn off calories rather than consume them. She also prefers not to limit herself to her room. I hoist my bag up again and walk slowly back down to the street. It's bad enough that Ryan is a fixture in all my classes, but does he really have to take over my personal life too? I mean, I don't know what—

Wait a minute.

I pause, frozen on the sidewalk outside. Ryan had just been in class with me at the main campus. I power walked to the transit stop and caught a shuttle bus straightaway, so even if he drove himself, he still wouldn't have had time to get through traffic and get naked with Morgan by the time I got back.

She wasn't with him.

It probably makes me a terrible person, but a small smile spreads across my face at the thought. Ryan acts as if he knows everything, but Mr. Know-It-All doesn't know this. And I'm not about to tell him.

"So, what's the verdict?" Ryan collapses in the seat opposite me and shoots me a wary look. Unlike the creaking old bookcases and dark wood back at Raleigh, the library study room here is small and bright. I've set out the table with copies of my changed script, as well as plain notepads, pens, and bottled water. Everything is planned for this to be as quick and painless as possible.

"Why don't you take a read through it and then we'll talk?" I pass him a stack of pages I've had bound in a blue folder. He gingerly takes one between his thumb and forefinger as if it's toxic. I pretend to scan through a textbook while he reads, but I can't help sneaking looks across the table to try to gauge his reaction. He's pulled another seat next to him and kicked off his Converses, resting the pages on his brown cords. I thought he was one of the hipster boys, with those black skinny jeans and plaid shirts, but today he's looking more nerdy in a stripy knit vest.

I wonder who Morgan was with.

Time stretches on. He clears his throat and I glance up, but his face is entirely free from emotion, giving me no hint at all what he thinks. Despite myself, I'm nervous. Ryan's original script was the story of a boy who finds some of his grandfather's old letters and is inspired to make changes in his life: admitting how he feels to his long-term crush, finally breaking away from an old friend who's become a bad influence. It's a sweet concept, but Ryan tried so hard to be unconventional that he forgot that conventions exist to give the story structure and conflict.

"You killed the grandfather?" Finally finishing, Ryan looks over at me, his expression still hard to read.

I nod. "This way, he's got a reason to follow the advice. It's emotional blackmail."

Ryan narrows his eyes thoughtfully. "And you moved the scenes with his crush around."

"We went through that in class." I try to keep my voice gentle. I can tell he's liable to get defensive. "I know you don't want the romance to be the main focus, but they're the best scenes. You want them to be the dramatic high point."

There's a long pause. Ryan looks back down at the script and flicks his pencil against the edge of the table. *Tap-tap-taptap*. It echoes in the tiny space. *Tap-tap-taptap*.

"Can you not do that?"

Tap-tap-taptap.

I glare at him. He smirks back.

"Relax," he tells me. I sigh, pulling my hair back into a tighter plait.

"The changes?" I remind him.

"Sure, whatever." His voice is so nonchalant, I can't believe it.

"'Whatever'?" I repeat. "I thought this was the most important thing in your life."

"Lowell's always telling us to get distance from our work." Ryan begins to smile now that he knows he's annoying me. And just for good measure, he begins with the pencil again. *Tap-tap-taptap*. I have to fold my hands together to stop myself reaching out and snatching it from him.

"We start shooting on Saturday," he says, as if I don't already have a schedule mapped out, complete with time for delays and weather problems. Not that there's any weather in California. "The first few days will probably be working out the kinks, getting light and sound figured."

"Fine." I run my eyes down the long, long list of pre-filming tasks I've been making. Another boy from class, Mike, is supposed to be producing, but I only needed one look at his red-rimmed eyes and bagful of snacks to decide I'd better run this myself if I want anything done. "Here." I tear off the bottom of the page—the least necessary things—and pass it to him. "You'll need to get these sorted before we start."

Ryan folds the paper carelessly and throws it in his bag.

"It's important," I remind him. "You won't get anyone working without clear schedules and a shot-by-shot plan."

"Already covered," he drawls, surprising me. "Don't

look at me like me that. I've been planning this longer than you."

"Well, all right." I frown. "I think that's it." I'd set aside another hour for this meeting, expecting tantrums and ultimatums at the very least.

"Cool, I'll see you by the equipment room on Saturday." Ryan pulls his shoes back on and slings his bag over his shoulder. "Nice work on the rewrites."

He's gone before I recover from the parting compliment.

With time to spare before a graduate screening of short films, I linger in the library and browse the social science sections for a little pleasure reading. I organized for my Oxford professors to email me the assignments so I can be certain that I don't miss too much, but sometimes it's nice just to wander the stacks and see what catches my eye. Picking out a couple of books on democracy, I find a quiet area with some desks and couches and settle in.

But I can't concentrate. Usually I can put a book in my hands and be oblivious to the world. It's a great skill for studying, but for some reason my superpowers aren't working today. Every movement, every sound: they all catch my attention, and soon I'm watching the people around me closer than my work. Back in Oxford, libraries are silent and sacrosanct, but here people don't seem to care about keeping quiet. Two boys in sports shirts are complaining over their notes, a blond girl bobs her head in time to her iPod, and two girls are giggling together behind a stack of books. Their desk is spread with candy wrappers, magazines, and colored pens, and studying looks like the last thing on their minds as they hiss at each other.

"Shhh, she'll hear."

"No way."

I glance around and find the object of their gossiping. A girl is curled up in the corner, her dark hair cut short and choppy with pink streaks. She's utterly absorbed in her book, so much so that she hasn't noticed the strip of toilet tissue stuck on the bottom of one chunky boot, fluttering in the air-conditioned breeze. The gossips giggle again, louder this time, and the girl looks up. She shoots a defiant look at them but doesn't see what they're laughing about and tries to turn back to her book.

"Excuse me." I lean over and catch her attention. She stares at me with a hint of suspicion. I smile apologetically and gesture to her foot. "You've got . . ."

"Oh!" She plucks it off. "Thanks."

"No problem." I give her a weak grin and nearly turn back to my book, but something about her lack of concern for the whispering makes me pause. "I like your hair," I say shyly. I could never have the nerve to do something so bold—or permanent.

"And I"—she surveys my shirt and plain jeans— "don't like anything about your outfit. Except your earrings, they're kind of cool," she adds with a grin.

I should be insulted, but her comment seems more sincere than anything I've heard all week from Morgan or Lexi. She's wearing black jeans and a shirt in purple and green, a leather cuff on her wrist, and silver bullets in her ears.

"Nobody gets them," I say, toying with the tiny metal symbols. I'm about to launch into an explanation, but the girl nods, her eyes thickly lined with purple ink.

"A thunderbolt and an owl—that's from the Greeks, right? Zeus and his daughter Athena."

I grin, surprised. "Right!"

"What classes are you taking?" She nods at my books.

"Film," I admit. "These are just for fun."

"Huh." Studying me, she pauses, then holds out her hand. "I'm Carla. Carla Reyes."

"Emily Lewis." I shake, feeling strange at the formality.

"Good to meet you." She grins. "Now, I better get back to this." She glares at the thick textbook. "Parliamentary democracies won't learn themselves."

I deflate a little. My brief chat with Carla is the sum total of my social interaction that week. "Wait, is that Tsebelis?" I ask, turning over the textbook.

"You know it?"

"Intimately." I grimace at the memory. "It killed me last term."

"So you know what the hell they're going on about with comparative factors and all that?"

"It took a while, but yes." I nod. "I could lend you my notes, if you want."

Carla bounces up. "Seriously?"

"I've got them all on my computer." I shrug. "I could print you off a copy. And if you're studying that, you'll probably need the material on Lijphart and Sartori as well."

77

"Girl, you'd be saving my butt." Talking at full volume now, Carla grins at me and sweeps her notebooks into a purple patent bag. "Let's go."

I decide that even Morgan doesn't have enough stamina to still be naked back in our room, so I follow Carla out of the building.

"You know, you're the first person who hasn't asked me about my accent," I realize, hurrying to keep up as she strides ahead down the busy pavement.

She shrugs. "I figure everyone came here from someplace else."

"Did you?"

Carla snorts. "Do I look like one of those girls?" She shakes her head, hair shimmering in the sun. "L.A.," she explains. "Inglewood. I wanted to stay and go to UCLA, but this place offered more scholarship money."

"So you're a first-year? I mean, freshman," I correct myself.

"Yup." Carla comes to a halt by a crowded coffee stand. "Hey, Rico, what's up?"

"Nothin' much, girl." The boy on duty wipes his hands on his apron and gives Carla an adoring smile. "You want your usual?"

"Sure, and . . ." She turns to me expectantly.

"Oh, a latte would be great. Decaf," I add, remembering my sister's lectures about caffeine being one step away from crack when it comes to addiction.

"Doesn't that negate the whole point of coffee?" Carla laughs before turning back to Rico. "But you heard her."

"Coming up." He sets to work, the machine spluttering away as Carla surveys me.

"So, do you just hang out in libraries taking pity on us poli sci kids?"

I smile self-consciously. "I suppose so. The guardian angel of democracy essays, that's me."

"And there's no catch?" Carla is still looking like she's testing me.

"Why would there be?"

She smirks. "You're new to town, I can tell." I must look puzzled, because she adds, "In Southern Cali, there's always a catch. Don't worry." She takes our coffees and pays the boy. "You'll learn."

"Oh." I sip my drink carefully. "So what's the catch to this?"

"The coffee?" Carla raises an eyebrow. "Straight swap: your notes for the drink."

"I can live with that," I agree, warming to her boldness.

"Cool." She strides off again at double speed, leaving me rushing to catch up. "Now tell me about Oxford— full of entitled jackasses, am I right?"

Tasha

I can tell my dress is all wrong before we even get inside. We're waiting in the street by the hotel for the rest of Holly's friends, and snaking down the block are groups of guys in tuxedos and girls tripping along in heels and long gowns; only thin wraps protecting against the cold night air. At first, I was feeling smug because these outfits are seriously Miss Teen Ohio, covered in sparkles and asymmetrical necklines, but after watching a parade of identigirls slip by, my gorgeous Gucci doesn't feel so special anymore. The skirt is short, for a start, and although the fabric is draped black silk and totally classy, it doesn't seem to make up for the amount of leg I have on show. At least, not judging by the smirks that other girls are shooting in my direction.

"You look wonderful." Holly catches my nervous look, but her comment just makes me feel more self-conscious. If she thinks I need reassuring at all, then it must be clear I'm totally out of place.

"So do you," I'm quick to add. And she does—even if her turquoise gown could have used fewer sequins along the bustline. Holly's hair is pinned up in tiny curls, and her eyes have a sweep of shimmer. It took us an hour getting ready with curling irons and eyelash curlers, but I always love that part.

It strikes me that the preparation may be the most fun I'll have all night, but I push the thought away and turn to the guy next to me in line to try and make conversation. "It's James, right?" He's the one with rusty red hair, now slicked back and neat to match the crisp lines of his tuxedo. I swear, put any guy in the black-and-white combo and they get cute.

"Yes." He shoves his hands into his jacket pockets, and I wait for something more, but there's nothing.

OK, the silent type. I can work with that.

"This is my first Oxford ball." I make sure to smile, despite the fact I'm shivering violently in my thin gold shrug. "Do you go to many?"

"At least one a term." James looks at me with what I'm afraid is amusement.

"That must be cool, having so many big parties. Back home we don't really do the formal thing, but there were way more smaller events." He nods politely. "Like, you guys only seem to have those bops every month." I name the weird costume parties they have in the Raleigh bar.

"But we have dorm parties and beach things and ..." I can see his eyes flickering around for someone to save him, so I give up and wait in silence as the line inches forward until finally we make it inside to the joy of heating.

"Come on!" Holly drags me through the main lobby and down a hallway draped with heavy fabric flags. The rooms are standard Oxford decor, paneled in dark wood and hung with stern oil paintings, but they've gone all out for the ball. There are huge vases of red and purple fresh flowers everywhere, silver platters of canapés, and a bunch of silent wait staff circulating. I can hear classical music playing and think what Morgan would say if she could see me now. We've been emailing and IM-ing since I got here, but the time difference makes me feel even farther away. All she does is ask about guys and then boast about how much she's hooking up. Sometimes it feels like there's way more than just an ocean between us.

"I think you're over here, next to James, and I'm across with Ellen ..." Holly reaches the long dining room and takes a quick look at the seating chart before ushering me over to my place. "I'm so glad we picked the first dinner session. Last year we signed up for later, but they ran over and we were completely famished." She's glowing, utterly at ease in the stiff, starched surroundings. "This way we get drunk on complimentary wine before the dancing." I laugh along, still weirded out by being offered drinks instead of sneaking them with fake IDs. Not that I'll be drinking tonight. My post-Tubgate rules are still set in stone: no drinking, no dating, no R-rated YouTube clips.

An older man hits the ceremonial gong with a small metal hammer, and we all take our seats. A trio of stiff-looking boys gives a speech welcoming us, then there's a smattering of polite applause and the room is full of buzzing conversation. I look around eagerly as the first course is brought out. It's so different from any event I've been to, the sense of history and privilege as thick as the scent of hyacinths in the air. Holly is out of talking range, seated on the other side of the table and three places down; Mr. Talkative himself, James, is next to me, and on my other side is a super-skinny blond girl in an ice-pink dress.

"Hi," I greet her with a grin. "I'm Natasha, from Raleigh."

She offers a limp hand for me to shake. "Portia," she replies, "Christ Church." She doesn't seem to be wearing any makeup (but I know how much time and effort that takes), and her gown is a plain sheath, simple and totally sophisticated. "Pleased to meet you."

"Pleased to meet you too," I echo. A waiter leans over me to pour a glass of wine. "Not for me," I say quickly, "but thanks anyway." He ignores me, and when it comes to Portia's turn, she simply places one elegant hand over the top of her glass and he moves on. Minus one point for me and my babbling.

"I love your dress," I say. James is leaning down the table to another group, laughing loudly, so it's Ice Queen or nothing.

Portia smiles faintly, as if a real expression would be too much hassle. "Thank you. Yours is . . . cute."

I blush, suddenly self-conscious. It's crazy—I used to

be comfortable whatever I was wearing, wherever I was, but now this feels like somebody else's skin. Like I'm not good enough to be sitting at the starched white linen table, sneaking sideways looks at the other diners to check that I'm using the right gleaming silver fork.

"Where did you . . . ?" My words fade on my lips. Ice Queen has turned away from me with a sigh, picking daintily through the salad on her gilt-edged dish.

Whatever.

As my opponents for Psi Delta Princess crown will tell you, Natasha Collins is no quitter. I muster strength for one last try and flash my brightest beam right across the table to the red-faced guy with glasses and a yellow bow tie.

"Hi." I grin. "What's up?"

He reddens even more. "Umm, nothing. I mean, there is . . . you know, the ball."

"Right!" I laugh. "It's a blast. Are you part of the society?"

"Actually, I'm the secretary."

"Really?" Since there's nothing else around, I try my best to sound interested. "What do you guys do?"

"Well"—he clears his throat—"the society was established to offer a forum for debate about European policy and culture." I smile and nod encouragingly as our appetizers are cleared away and replaced with perfect round medallions of beef in a rich cream sauce. ". . . is so crucial, don't you think?"

"Sorry." I quickly swallow a mouthful of gratin and look up to find him staring at me expectantly. "What did you say?"

"The power balance in the Bundestag; have you been following the latest developments?"

He's not kidding—I check.

"Well." I slowly take a sip of water, running through the entire contents of my mind just in case I have some awesome German political knowledge lurking there. Surprisingly, I don't. "I must have missed that," I finally admit.

"The coalition collapse?" Portia leans in, candlelight gleaming off the delicate gold cuff on her toothpick wrist. "Isn't it a nightmare, Anthony?"

"And the economic ramifications if those socialists get back in." Anthony is apparently so distressed he has to take a moment to polish his glasses.

"Exactly." Portia nods. She shoots a sideways glance at me. "You're so lucky you're not a politics student; I wish I could just ignore all world events too."

I pause. As veiled insults go, it's pretty good.

"What is it you're studying?" she inquires.

"Politics," I answer, just to see if she'll look embarrassed. She doesn't, instead just giving me another one of those pale smiles and flicking her attention back to Anthony.

"How are Milly and Tom?" she coos. He must be seriously loaded for someone like Portia to give him so much attention.

"Just dandy," he says with a straight face, and then launches into a long story about country-house weekends and something to do with a sheepdog. I manage to catch Holly's eye down the table; she grins and shakes her head.

"Be strong," she mouths, and I figure that even a

fairy-tale evening is bound to have some downtime. This just means I can enjoy my food without interruption, right?

By ten, things have picked up. Once dinner is finished (with enough calories to make me pledge to double my gym time), I can escape back to Holly's group—far away from Anthony, Portia, and their never-ending list of old friends. I swear, between them they seemed to know half the country, and all of them stuck with names like Bunny, Blakey, and (I kid you not) Shotter.

"You should have seen your face." Holly laughs, dragging me down the hall into a back room where they've picked a DJ over Mozart. "You looked so bored!"

"I was!" The heavy bass reminds me of clubs back home, and I start to relax. With the music so loud, nobody's going to ask me my opinion of western European political reform, or the mortgage markets, or any of the million other topics I know jack about.

"I have to take a break," I finally yell in Holly's ear as the beat switches to another crazy jam. I gesture toward the door. "Be right back!"

The hallway is blissfully silent after such loud beats, and I quickly duck through the elegant crowds until I reach the pale marble haven of the women's restroom. Everything is soft blue and cream—from the tiny, thick towels to the hand lotion—and just breathing in the faint smell of jasmine calms me down. I've managed to avoid the rush and slip into a stall right away, but just as I close the door, I hear a group of girls come in.

"God, you've got to save me, Venetia." Arch, plummy vowels drift over to me, and I think I can recognize

Portia's voice. Although half the girls here talk like they've got marbles stuffed in their mouths. I always thought *My Fair Lady* was totally exaggerating. I was wrong.

"Anthony is sending me comatose."

Yup, it's Portia. Instead of flushing and walking out, I wait.

"But he's social secretary," another voice adds. "If you're running for committee, you need him."

"You don't have to tell me," Portia complains. "Why do you think I've been listening to all his dull stories? Between him and that stupid American, dinner was a complete bore."

There are giggles and the rustle of fabric and cosmetics. I stand quietly, feeling that tightness back in my chest.

"Can you believe her dress? It's not as if . . ." The door swings shut behind them, but some masochistic instinct makes me rush out of the stall and hurry into the hallway after them. I know I won't hear anything good, but I can't help wanting to know what they really think.

I follow Portia's pink silk at a safe distance until they linger by a dessert table. The main hall is full: the dance floor packed with couples slowly waltzing to the string quartet, while others stand chatting in tight knots. A complicated champagne fountain is set up in the center of the refreshment tables, so I maneuver closer, using the tall arrangement of glasses as cover as I strain to listen in.

"You'd think they'd have standards about who they let in, especially somewhere like Raleigh."

"Maybe it's an outreach program." There's the sound of bitchy laughter.

"God, do you remember that other American, Rhiannon? She fucked practically half the JCR in just one term."

"What is it with them all being so . . ."

"Slutty?"

"I was going to be more tactful." More laughter.

I shrink back. This was a mistake, I know. I already feel like the trashy outsider without hearing it spelled out by a group of snotty girls.

"I would understand if she was trying to land a rich husband," Portia continues, her haughty voice cutting through the background noise like a missile, sent to wound me. "But surely she realizes, men don't marry *those* kinds of girls!"

I'm still backing away, but suddenly I hit something solid. There's a crash, and I spin around to find one of the tuxedoed waiters, his silver tray empty and broken glass shards on the ground between us.

"Omigod, I'm so sorry!" I breathe, champagne pooling around my toes.

"It's quite all right," he insists, but when I glance up, Portia and her friends are staring right at me, smirks of delight on their pale faces.

"Did you see that?" One of the other girls laughs, a loud braying sound that attracts way more attention than my tiny mishap. Other people start to look over, and right away I get a flashback to what it was like around campus after Tyler. The whispers. The sneers. That awful black hole in my stomach. Then and now mix in my head until all I know is I'm done. It's over.

Through the mess of memories, I finally remember how to walk and slowly edge away from the crowd. I didn't bring a coat, thank god, so there's no line for me to wait in: just me and my tiny beaded clutch hightailing it toward the exit. I pass a couple more uniformed door staff, and then I'm out in the freezing night.

So much for my fairy-tale evening.

Emily

"Yes, Dad, I'm getting plenty of sleep." I try not to kick my heels against the back of my chair as he runs down the obligatory welfare checklist. "No, I'm not drinking. Or neglecting my work. Yes, I'm eating fine too."

Late on Friday night, it's getting dark out, my desk lamp bathing the room in a soft glow. Morgan is off at a frat party with the rest of her clique, so I decided to take advantage of the peace and get some reading done. My father, already up tomorrow morning, decided to take advantage of the time difference to lecture me a little more.

"I ran into Kirk Morgan at the tennis club yesterday," he says in that tone I've now come to recognize as trouble. "His boy is a Fulbright scholar, at Princeton."

I sigh. "Good for him."

"You know, providing you keep your regular results up, there's really no reason to put this on your résumé." Dad is trying to be helpful, I know, but I still feel the burn as if he's scolding me. "And when you've done the summer internship . . ."

"I haven't heard back about those yet."

His laughter booms down the line. "Don't worry, you'll be fine. With your stellar record at Oxford, this is just a hiccup. Who wouldn't want you?"

"Thanks, Dad."

"In fact, I was thinking of giving Giles Bentley a call — remember him? We took our pupilages together back in the day. I haven't seen him in a while, but I think now would be a good time for a drink. He's senior partner at Sterns, Cahill, and Coutts. Weren't they one of your picks?"

"Yes, but really, you don't—"

"I'll give him a call." Dad speaks straight over me. "I don't know why I didn't think of it sooner."

"Right."

"In fact, why don't I check if there are any alumni in California? There are a lot of big firms down in L.A. — not that you'll be doing entertainment law, of course — but it could be good to shake some hands." I can hear Dad warming to the idea. "If you were on the East Coast . . ." He sighs. "But we should make the most of what we have at the moment. Keep our plan moving forward."

I nod on cue, forgetting that he can't see me. It doesn't make any difference.

"Elizabeth has been invited to present at a cardio-vascular symposium next month, did she tell you?" His pride is obvious.

"No, that's great."

"And your mother sends her love, of course. She's busy with another project—something to do with low-energy lightbulbs in all the village buildings." I laugh along. "I better leave you to your rest now; it's getting late. Take care now."

"I will. Good night, Dad."

"And remember what I said about your résumé—"

I carefully hang up the phone. Late? On campus, everything is just getting started. I'm the only one left sitting quietly in her room. Alone.

As I look at my neat belongings and the pajamas already laid out on my pillow, I feel it again: the itch under my skin. The novelty of being away wore off once my first month was over; now every night feels the same. I look over my notes for next week's classes, make myself a nutritionally balanced meal, watch a classic film on DVD, and make sure I'm tucked up in bed by ten thirty. A few chapters of my novel and then it's lights-out, and hopefully I'll be so deep into REM cycle by the time Morgan stumbles back at 2:00 AM that she won't even wake me.

I'm so bored I could scream.

With a burst of energy, I leap up and go to my dresser. Dad's talk of plans and preparation is suddenly too much. All I seem to do is prepare for a future that is just ahead of me, always out of reach. In school I was getting ready for Oxford: the committees, the student government campaigns, the sport, and the extra projects that would tip me over into the privileged few applicants. Then, as soon as I got to Oxford, it became about life after university. Internships, networking, career strategies.

Isn't anything I do for me, right now?

Quickly, I pull my hair up, exchange my T-shirt for a black vest top, and even swipe on a dab of tinted lip gloss. The desire to be normal is overwhelming, just for one night at least. A party, music, some friends. Not the overachiever—alone again—but a teenage girl out having fun.

Do I even know how?

Morgan forwarded me the invite, so I have all the details. I'm out of the building before I have a chance to take it back.

There are half a dozen noisy parties spilling out along Del Ray Drive by the time I arrive, so I double-check the address Morgan left just to be certain I'm in the right place. It's a warm night, and students are clustered on the front lawn of a three-story red-brick house, all conversation drowned out by the insistent thump of the "Come git it, git it" track playing over the stereo system. Not that they're looking for conversation. In tiny skirts, polo shirts, and lashings of eyeliner, the girls are dressed for battle, and the boys—shoving each other around in a raucous mating ritual—seem to know it.

I slip past a couple exploring each other's esophagi and into the din, already feeling out of place. I'm not good in crowds, preferring small groups to the mass of bodies here tonight, but I remind myself why I came in the first place. Normal. Teenage. Fun.

All right.

"Morgan?" After a loop through the house, I spot a familiar mane of blond hair in the lounge. I greet her with relief. "Hi, how are you?"

"Em?" Morgan squints at me from the couch. She's wearing a draped, glittery top and sitting on a muscular blond boy who is most definitely not Ryan. "You came?"

"Yup." I remind myself to smile. "What have I missed?"

"Nothing much." She giggles. "Right, Ben?" He nods, jiggling her on his lap so she squeals and pretends to bat his hands away.

"Stop it!"

"You stop it."

"I'm serious!"

I wait awkwardly while they flirt until I spy Brooke by the loudspeakers, swaying rhythmically in the middle of a group of guys.

"I'll see you later." Leaving Morgan to her hunk, I watch the makeshift dance floor for a moment before approaching. A couple of girls are grinding away like they're in MTV videos, but the rest look casual enough, nothing but bobbing in time with the loud beat. I can do this.

"Emmy!" Brooke squeals immediately, hugging me tight and pulling me into the group. "I'm so glad you're here!"

Dancing is a good move. Nobody tries to talk over

the shaking bass, and soon I'm breathless and having something close to fun.

"I need a break," Brooke calls, miming a drink. I nod, following her out of the tangle of people and through to the crowded kitchen. "Wow," Brooke gasps, grabbing a red plastic cup from the table by the keg and pushing a space for me beside her. "Cool crowd, right?"

"Right," I agree, taking my own cup. It is a party, I suppose, and after all that dancing, the beer is cool and refreshing. "Do you go to these often?"

"Every week, sometimes more." Brooke scans the room quickly. "It's what college is for." She grins. "That and fifty grand of student loans."

I gasp. "That's terrible!"

"Tell me about it." She shrugs, her loose red top shimmering with the movement. "So I may as well have as much fun as I can before I'm doomed to earn it all back."

"Good plan." I tip my cup to hers in a toast. She quickly downs the rest of hers.

"Screw this, how about some shots?"

I hesitate.

"C'mon, just the one. Trust me, it'll be fun."

There it is again, the F-word, dangling just out of reach.

"Sure," I decide, linking my arm through hers. "Why not?"

"Yay!" she cries, tugging me out onto the back porch. It's slightly quieter there, and some boys are playing a strange game involving beer cups and Ping-Pong balls. "Sam, you still got that Cuervo?"

I stop with a jolt. I haven't seen him since the scene at the beach, but I've definitely thought of him—and my complete ineptitude. I wonder if he considers me an utter idiot. Thankfully, Sam doesn't seem to notice any awkwardness. He hugs Brooke and then turns to me.

"Emily." He grins, blue eyes gleaming. "How've you been?"

"Great," I answer as he pulls me into a long embrace. His jeans actually fit instead of falling around his crotch, and his black shirt makes those ice-blue eyes stand out even more.

"Get a room," another male voice exclaims, and I draw back to see an athletic-looking guy with close-cropped black hair. He's tossing a Ping-Pong ball from hand to hand. "Are you in this game or not?"

"Lay off," Sam calms him. "Let's give these girls what they came for, OK?"

Brooke blushes. "Hey, Louis." She grins, broadcasting her crush for everyone to see. His eyes graze her body, and evidently she passes his test because soon he's chatting and flirting with her.

"So, you ever done tequila shots before?" Sam looks down at me intently.

"Of course." I laugh, deciding I've seen enough films to fake it. "Lime and salt?"

"The lady's demanding." He laughs. "I like it. OK, everyone, it's on!"

He produces a row of shot glasses and lines them up on the edge of the table. Louis fetches the accessories, and soon I'm staring at the glass of innocuous-looking amber liquid.

"One." The three of them lick salt from the back of their hands. I follow, half a beat behind. "Two!" Sam yells, downing his shot. I do the same and almost choke from the oily, bitter taste. "Three!" I stuff the lime slice in my mouth, shuddering, and suck hard to rid myself of that awful tequila taste.

"Ugh!" Brooke's face is screwed up. "Why doesn't that get any easier?"

"No pain, no gain." Louis slips an arm around her. "Now what do you say we whip these pussies at beer pong?"

"Emily?" Sam raises his eyebrows. I nod, feeling the strange warmth in my chest as the tequila burns its way down the inside of my body.

"You'll have to teach me, though."

"My pleasure." Sam grins, and I think that perhaps I haven't ruined it with him after all.

A victorious beer pong game leads to more dancing, and soon the night is a blur of laughter and Sam's body is pressed warm against me. "I'll be right back," I promise, levering myself up from the porch seat when the need for a toilet break can no longer be denied.

"You better." Sam keeps his fingers intertwined with mine as I back away. "Otherwise I'll send out a search-and-rescue team."

With a glow that has nothing to do with alcohol, I go

in search of a free bathroom. It's a futile task, I know, and eventually I'm resigned to crossing my legs at the back of a long line. Nonetheless, I'm grinning.

He likes me.

"Hey, Ryan!" I call out, seeing a familiar Thermals T-shirt wind its way through the crowd.

"Emily." He stops, confused. "Having fun?"

"Tons!" I exclaim before I register that his tone is sarcastic. "What about you?"

He shrugs, scruffy in skinny black jeans. "Have you seen Morgan? I kind of need to talk to her."

"Umm." I lean back against the wall and try to think. "She was in the lounge last time I saw her, but that was hours ago."

"Thanks." He's gone before I remember what Morgan was doing the last time I saw her — and who she was doing it with. Evidently she's still at it, because my bathroom line has barely inched forward before Ryan storms back down the hallway, his face set and furious.

"Did you know?" He stops in front of me, glaring, but even behind the anger, I can tell he's shaken. I shrug uselessly.

"Thanks a lot," he hisses, disappearing toward the exit. I feel a pang of guilt, but what was I supposed to do? Morgan is my roommate. Besides, it's none of my business.

What is my business, however, is Sam. I scoot back to his side as soon as I can, sending silent thanks to Morgan and her friends for pushing us together. They're right: the best way to get over Sebastian is to start seeing somebody else. As I snuggle closer to Sam, my ex-boyfriend and supposed intimacy issues seem very far away.

"What's on your mind?" Sam touches my nose lightly.

"Nothing at all." I smile up at him, determined not to repeat my last mistake.

"You look kind of sleepy." Pulling me closer, Sam starts to trace light circles on my back. I practically sigh with pleasure. "It's getting late. You know, you could crash here in my room. We closed off everything upstairs, and it should be quieter up there."

"I don't know . . ." Even in my pleasantly tipsy state, I still think of college rape statistics and "safety first" lectures.

"Nothing shady, I promise." Sam mimes crossing his heart. "Well, unless you count making out." He grins. I melt. "You'll be safe, I promise."

His expression is so sincere that I find myself wavering. The other girls do this all the time and come home with nothing worse than a hangover. Isn't it my night to cut loose a little?

"OK." I smile. Sam takes my hand and maneuvers us through the party stragglers up to the top floor.

"See? Quieter," he says, closing the door of a room that just screams "college student." I collapse onto the bed and look around. Posters of cars and surf girls in bikinis, stacks of CDs—nothing but typical, average teenage-boy possessions.

I relax, kicking off my shoes. "No bong? Or porn collection?"

"I hid those," Sam quips, suddenly looking a little nervous. I feel a rush of affection. Maybe he isn't so smooth after all.

Bold, I reach up and take a handful of his shirt. "What was that you said about making out?"

He laughs, leaning down to meet my lips. "I thought you were tired."

"Not that tired." I exhale against him and then kiss, tasting beer and something different from Sebastian.

Normal. Teenage. Fun.

Tasha

I walk back to Raleigh in a total daze. The streets are dark but full of kids on their way to clubs or coming home from the bars, and though I get my usual round of whistles and catcalls, I can't be bothered to glare back.

The scene keeps replaying in my head. Maybe it's because I've sat through so many movies for class or maybe it's just shock, but right now I see the whole thing at a distance, like I'm sprawled out in my dorm room with popcorn and this is just the latest mishap of some adorable romantic-comedy cutie. You know, the ditzy leading girl who keeps falling over herself until the hero picks her up again. Only nobody thinks I'm adorable, and I sure as hell know no hero's going to come along to save me.

What can I do?

The question bounces around all the way home. Nothing I seem to try makes a difference to these people—I just don't blend in. If I was back home with my friends, I wouldn't give a damn what those stuck-up bitches thought, but after a long month of loneliness, I just want a break. The silence, the cold shoulders: they've worn me down, and I'm so freaking sick of feeling low, I could scream.

I don't. Instead, I stop at one of the fast-food carts and fill my mouth with greasy fries, smothered with chili and cheese and enough calories to make a girl faint.

Maybe my mom was right: all those times she said I'd have to face the consequences of my actions. Maybe this is it, my karma, my payback for playing around and bringing shame on my family. God, I remember all those screaming matches we had after the video broke. She couldn't believe that she'd brought me up so badly to turn out a cheap slut, a whore. That's what she says, but whatever. I tried to defend myself at first. I mean, I'm not pregnant or on drugs, and if the video hadn't got out, she wouldn't think any different of me. But I guess having everyone you know email you with shots of your half-naked daughter makes you lose all perspective, because anything I said only made her madder, until we couldn't even stay in the same room without screaming.

And now I get the silent treatment. Money goes into my account every two weeks, but aside from that, I haven't heard a single word from her since I left California. I don't miss her; I just miss what it was like between us, before.

Sighing, I use my late key on the back gate and wander across the quad. It's silent and still, and usually I find that the neat lawns and pretty stone archways calm me down, but tonight I wish it were humming with activity, anything I could be a part of. Cold staircase, empty hall. Emily's room is as depressing as ever, and I collapse in front of my computer and reach for another fry, now soggy and gross. I check email, but as usual there's nothing except junk and the handful of Tyler-related Google alerts, so I boot up my instant-messenger program and send out a silent prayer that somebody's on.

AJ369, magikman, rudeyrude—only boys I used to flirt with. And then I catch sight of the schedule still pinned above the desk and figure there might just be someone who feels as much of an outcast as me. I've got her email and screen-name details somewhere in the exchange paperwork, so I only have to spend ten minutes rooting through every freaking pamphlet they sent before I find it.

Send chat request to user EMLewis.

Emily

When I wake up the next morning, Sam has disappeared and there's nothing but wrinkled navy sheets tangled around me where his body used to be. My jeans are digging into my hip, and the underwire from my bra is squashed against my ribs, but nothing can stop the satisfied grin that spreads across my face when I remember last night. Just as he promised, Sam proved himself to be a complete gentleman, happy to keep things decent.

But oh, can that boy kiss.

Squinting, I catch sight of the digital clock display. Eleven? I never sleep that late! With a start, I sit up.

Ouch.

Falling back onto the bed, I wait for the thump in my head to subside. So this is what a hangover feels like. After a few more minutes, I sit up—far more cautiously this time—and try to ease the tension from my neck. Searching for my shoes, I wonder if I should leave a note for Sam. He's probably at the gym, and it seems rather rude to just go without a word, but post-kissing protocol is completely beyond me.

Eventually, I find a scrap of paper and a pen, and then spend another ten minutes deliberating over the contents.

Hi — last night was fun. E.

After half a dozen tries, I finally strike the right carefree tone and let myself out. His room is on the third floor of the frat house, and as I make my way down the back stairs, I can see party debris spread throughout every room. Beer cans, empty convenience-food wrappers, and even a few boys, still passed out in doorways and on couches. It looks as if I made my exit just at the right time.

As I cut through the littered front lounge, something catches my eye. A computer is open on a coffee table, the screen showing photographs in some sort of grid. I move forward to take a closer look.

PSI DELT DOABLES, the page heading reads. The photographs are of girls—some in a state of undress, mugging for the camera, others obviously asleep—and next to them is written a name and score.

MANDY LEE, owned by OWEN MICHAELS.
> 6/10.
> She scratches!

CASSIE WILCOX, owned by BRETT ALLSTON.

> 9/10.

> Kinky bitch!

I realize what the grid means and take a step back. They're keeping score. I wrinkle my face in disdain. Typical frat-boy exploits, I suppose, but still, I don't know why Sam lives with them. He's far more . . .

And then I see it, halfway down the page. A photograph of me, eyes closed, hair spread on familiar navy sheets.

EMILY LEWIS, owned by SAM RICH.

> 4/10.

> English—enough said.

I can't believe it.

Backing away from the screen, I slam the front door behind me and practically race down the street. How could he? I break into a jog, not caring about the thunder in my head or what a madwoman I must look like in last night's clothes. What is it with these boys, acting as if sex is the single greatest achievement in all humanity? First Sebastian, pushing me with his hints and nudging until I nearly gave in just to get it out of the way. And now Sam, treating me as if I'm just another notch on his bedpost— when technically I wasn't even *in* his bed!

Am I a particularly bad judge of character, or are they all like this?

I finally slow down, out of breath. Four out of ten. *Four out of ten.* It's not as if I'd feel any better had he given me a more complimentary score for my imaginary sexual performance, but the low mark is salt in my now-gaping wound. Do I seem like somebody who would be bad in bed? Shaking my head, I stop myself before I get pulled down that line of reasoning and instead return to the important matter of Sam. All those sweet comments and nice-guy lines were just a lie; he must have been laughing at me the entire time. And I fell for it.

I'm supposed to meet Ryan and the film-class crew after lunch for our first meeting, but there's no chance at all I can manage that, even after picking up a grande extra-shot latte en route to my room. I refuse to use my meager energy reserves to dwell on bastards and their bastardly stunts, so after a shower and some food, I throw myself into "research": passing the day in a blur of Ben & Jerry's Phish Food and all the bad romantic-comedy movies I've been saving. Reese. Kate. Julia. They never have to put up with this.

Four out of ten. The website. His grading. Everything about it makes me feel cheap, but more than that—naïve. Did he pick me out because I seem so clueless? Was the fact I'm so clearly out of place part of my appeal? I can't help thinking that Morgan or Brooke would never get fooled like this. Even in their drunken states, those girls are ten times more streetwise than me. I may be able to evaluate an emerging democracy's chances of political consolidation, but they know how to handle guys, to joke around and have fun.

Another movie finishes, and I slouch over to my computer, my envy of the breezy California girls growing.

They're at ease here, among the tans and teeth. This is their territory, not mine. I've been keeping it together with schedules and study plans, but the moment I try to venture out into the world, my careful control falls apart. At the beach, at the party—I end up bumbling around, making an idiot of myself. I'm so used to finding order in the midst of chaos, but this time I just can't seem to work it out. I have no rule book to help me fit in, no study guide for the finer points of being an early twenty-first-century California teen . . .

A beeping from my instant-messenger program catches my attention. There's a box flashing on my screen.

Request to chat from totes_tasha.
Accept/decline?

I frown, running through the list of classmates or Oxford contacts it could be. And then it strikes me. Tasha. Natasha Collins—the girl whose bed I'm sleeping in, whose life I inherited.

Accept.

EMLewis: Hello? Is this Tasha?

totes_tasha: yup hey

EMLewis: How are you?

totes_tasha: i'm cool. just saw your screen name and
        thought I'd say hey.

totes_tasha: how's school?

totes_tasha: is morgan driving u crazy??

EMLewis: She's . . . fine. She's been very friendly.

totes_tasha: ha. u hate her i can tell.

EMLewis: No, really, she's been great.

EMLewis: Are you settling in over there? Your tutorials
        are going well?

totes_tasha: umm . . .

totes_tasha: not exactly

EMLewis: ?

totes_tasha: that prof elliot is on my case. i just can't seem to get things right for her.

totes_tasha: and what's with all the stuck-up bitces here?

EMLewis: bitces? Oh, right, bitches. Are you having problems then?

totes_tasha: kinda

EMLewis: Thank God!

totes_tasha: ??

EMLewis: No, I mean, that's not a good thing, but I was worried I was the only one.

EMLewis: I'm having problems too.

totes_tasha: what kinda stuff?

EMLewis: I just can't seem to fit in. My film partner is being difficult, and last night was awful.

EMLewis: I spent the night with this boy . . .

totes_tasha: !!!!

EMLewis: No, not like that!

totes_tasha: o

EMLewis: And I thought he really liked me, but this morning I found out he put me on this horrible conquest website.

totes_tasha: wait a mo. you got owned by a psi delt?

EMLewis: :-(

totes_tasha: aww hon, don't worry. easy mistake.

EMLewis: But I just feel so stupid!

totes_tasha: u feel stupid? everyone here thinks i'm a dumbass. i made a fool of myself at a ball tonight & there's no way i'll ever live it down.

EMLewis: I'm sorry.

EMLewis: Sigh. Some cultural experience this is turning out to be.

totes_tasha: so what's ur secret? to blending in i mean.

EMLewis: In Oxford? It's easy. You just act superior and fake as if you know all of their intellectual crap. Everybody's pretending, in the end.

totes_tasha: sounds too easy.

EMLewis: No really, it's that simple. If you look like them and read the books they do, it's easy to blend in.

totes_tasha: so is that what you're doing over there?

EMLewis: . . . Not exactly.

totes_tasha: :-)

EMLewis: I just like to have things sorted out, you know? But the people here are just so RELAXED. I've trying to work on a script with this guy, Ryan, but he's being difficult and

totes_tasha: morgan's ryan?

EMLewis: They broke up last night, I think.

totes_tasha: lemme guess—he found her cheating.

EMLewis: How did you know?

totes_tasha: everyone knows. that's what morgan does.

EMLewis: Oh. Well, now he's angry at me because I didn't tell him. What do I do?

totes_tasha: same thing u told me—go along with his bullshit and pretend.

EMLewis: That's too vague! I need specifics.

totes_tasha: like what? there aren't any rules.

EMLewis: God, I wish there were!

totes_tasha: ha seriously. that would so make life easier. like a guidebook for life.

EMLewis: You know . . .

EMLewis: That's not a bad idea.

totes_tasha: ???

EMLewis: We should do that for each other.

EMLewis: Things to say, what to wear. A complete switch survival guide.

totes_tasha: haha should have guessed.

EMLewis: What do you mean?

totes_tasha: nothing. just, well, i figured you were . . .
    organized.

EMLewis: :shrugs:

totes_tasha: u know, it's not a bad idea . . .

EMLewis: Being organized?

totes_tasha: the switch guide. think about it—i can tell
    you how to be me, and you can make me someone
    who fits in here.

EMLewis: But could we really do that?

totes_tasha: why not?

EMLewis: You don't know me—I could never be like
    these girls, not even if I tried.

totes_tasha: hello, remember me? the hot-tub girl?!

EMLewis: Oh, right. That. Yes . . . Morgan mentioned
    something. . . .

totes_tasha: exactly. so about this switch guide . . .

totes_tasha: where would I start? hypothetically. if we were doing it.

EMLewis: Hmmm . . .

EMLewis: I'm not sure.

EMLewis: Maybe with the way you dress? If you look like the girls here, then you'd be really out of place in Oxford.

totes_tasha: totes.

totes_tasha: so what do i change?

EMLewis: I'll send you some links to photographs. You'll need a Raleigh jumper, for a start. And some shirts and jeans. But not those low-rise or skinny jeans. These need to be

totes_tasha: boring?

EMLewis: No, **normal.** And if you wear makeup like Morgan, you'll need to tone it down. Very natural.

totes_tasha: right: boring.

EMLewis: Do you want my help or not?

totes_tasha: sorry. :-(it's been a bad day. go on.

EMLewis: Sigh. That's OK. I know how you feel.

totes_tasha: sucks, doesn't it? i thought this switch would make everything better.

EMLewis: I know! But instead, it complicates everything even more.

totes_tasha: u want my advice?

EMLewis: Please.

totes_tasha: get morgan to take u shopping. you've got some cash, right?

EMLewis: Yes.

totes_tasha: cool, then have her & lexi take you out. get your hair & nails done, buy the outfits she says. if anyone can make you look like a UCSB girl, it's morgan.

EMLewis: And then what?

totes_tasha: let go a lil.

totes_tasha: or at least pretend. if u walk around like everything's serious and dull, then people will get bummed out.

EMLewis: So I should have a personality transplant?

totes_tasha: haha, no it's cool. just smile and act like you don't care. go with the flow. party. have fun.

EMLewis: I've been trying!

totes_tasha: so what went wrong??

EMLewis: I don't know. No matter what I try, it doesn't make a difference. And just when I thought things were working out with Sam, he betrayed me to his frat buddies.

totes_tasha: sam? aww, he's a player.

EMLewis: Morgan said he was nice.

totes_tasha: morgan thinks any guy with a 6-pack is nice.

EMLewis: Yes, I'm realizing that.

totes_tasha: look, we're both in the same place right now. we want to fit in and have fun, but nothing so far has worked out.

EMLewis: Right.

totes_tasha: so why don't we try something different? it's just for the semester.

totes_tasha: don't know about you, but i can't stand being so frakking lonely.

EMLewis: :hugs: It'll be OK.

totes_tasha: i know, because i'm going to figure how to blend in. if you help me.

EMLewis: All right. I'm in.

EMLewis: After all, how much worse can this get?

totes_tasha: haha, good point.

EMLewis: I'll email you some material tonight.

totes_tasha: and tomorrow u go shopping w/ morgan?

EMLewis: Sigh. If I have to.

totes_tasha: awesome.

totes_tasha: this'll work, i can tell.

totes_tasha: laters!!

EMLewis: x

Tasha

When I find Emily's first switch survival guide in my inbox the next morning, I decide to start with Natasha version 2.0 right away. She's linked to items in some preppy stores here and the instruction *Watch everyone carefully!* Also, I've been ordered to join a group of some kind as a way of becoming part of a crowd. Let me think, do I want to be a stuck-up hack running for student government or a stuck-up sports girl running for real?

Chill, I remind myself. Just because Portia and her crew are complete jackasses, it doesn't mean everyone else here is. I'd found Holly, right? So there must be *some* sane people hanging out in the library or dorms. I get up and out of the Raleigh campus with new determination, reading lists taking a backseat for the first time since I arrived. The day is crisp and clear, with a blue sky that reminds me of home—if it weren't for the mittens and scarf I'm wearing—and as I walk down the main street into the center of the city, I make sure to look around and make mental notes of the girls here.

Like in any town, they don't look all the same, but by the time I reach the first store on my list, I can notice a definite trend for messy pinned ponytails, sculpted jackets, and blond hair. Only, instead of the serious California blond I'm used to, this is kind of honey-toned and fake-natural looking. In fact, fake-natural seems to be the theme: from the way their hair seems to be falling out of a style (like they're saying, "Oh, yes, I've been too busy reading Sartre in the original French to bother with such superficial things") to the neutral makeup in caramel and pale flushed tones that's still flawless.

Looks like I'll need some work. I've held off the blond thing for ten years now, so there's no way I'm ruining my brown hair with bleach, but I figure I can master the styles with some pins and practice. And although my makeup routine is like second nature, I can switch foundation for tinted moisturizer, cut the eyeliner, and get some crème blush. So that's everything above the neck. . . .

For the next couple of hours, I do what I do best. I shop. Bargains, new styles, and cool looks are in my blood, only this is like a reverse experience for me: I look around the store, and if something cute catches my eye, I put it down and find the total opposite. That sparkly black low-draped top? I ditch it for a high-necked Victoriana-style white blouse. A denim skirt with torn edges and a studded belt? I leave it on the rack and go pick out a knee-length plaid pencil skirt.

By the time I've got an armful of bags, I'm totally into my new task. It's not like I'm selling out, I figure, just . . . presenting a different side to me. Everyone always goes on about first impressions counting, and here at Oxford, they seem to matter more than anything. If I can just get people to stop thinking of me as the dumb Californian, then they'd see I'm a pretty cool girl. I mean, I like me!

Besides, every preppy sweater and pair of ballet flats is taking me further from the girl in that hot tub, until soon I can't see her in my reflection at all. And if I don't recognize her, chances are nobody else will either.

When I figure I've worn out my emergency credit card, I decide to take a coffee break. But walking into my haven of Borders, I pause. In the month of hanging out there, I've only ever met that other American. This is so not the place for the new me to start friend-hunting. Turning, I walk right out again and down a paved side street to the other bookstore in town, Blackwell's. This one is British, based in an old building that probably pre-dates everything in California. There's a coffee shop on the second floor that is full of dark wood furniture and serious-looking Oxford types. Perfect.

I slip up to the restrooms and quickly change into my first new outfit: a plaid skirt and a pale pink crewneck. I add thick gray tights and a delicate gold charm necklace like the one Portia wore, and I'm good to go. Instant prep. On my way back to get coffee, I even pick up a couple of textbooks to look over for this week's essay: the ultimate Raleigh girl.

I read in silence for a while, helped along by a slice of cheesecake and an extra-large latte. The room is full of people, and to my relief, I blend right in. Older men pore over stacks of printed pages, younger boys stare intently at their battered novels, but everyone looks stuffy and, well, British. It's a kick knowing that nobody would guess from looking at me where I was from or what I'd done, but all the crewnecks in the world don't make a difference to my reading list. After staring at the same page for ten minutes, I put my pen down with a loud sigh.

"Are you, ah, are you having difficulties with that?" The boy at the next table speaks up, and I look over in surprise. He's got longish brown hair falling in his eyes and an angular kind of face, but his interested expression seems for real.

"Yup," I admit. "I can't figure it out. At this rate I'll need a tutor just to get to the end of the chapter!"

He smiles, kind of nervous. "Well, in that case . . . I, I do some tutoring."

"You do?" I brighten.

"Uh-huh." He clears his throat. "Political philosophy?"

"Right." I beam, taking in his cord pants and navy pullover. The outfit is kind of nerdy, but I guess nerdy is good in a potential tutor. "I've got this feminist professor who's really laying it on."

"Elliot?"

"How did you know?"

He shrugs. "I had lectures with her last year, plus she's the only feminist tutor around."

"So you're in your third year?" I ask, taking another bite of cheesecake.

"Yes, I'm a finalist."

"Oh." My face falls. "Then you probably won't have time for anything extra."

"No," he quickly replies. "I've got some time. It would be a nice break."

"Tutoring counts as a break?" I laugh. "Sad."

He gives me a wry smile. "I suppose it is. I'm Will, by the way." He reaches across to shake my hand.

"Oh right, I'm Natasha." His hand is soft and kind of delicate: another one of those composer-type guys. "So, do you have any time now, or do I book you, or . . ." I trail off, hoping he's available right away. This paper is turning out to be a nightmare, and since I threw Elliot's offer right back at her, there's no way I can turn up to class with my usual mess.

"I can do a little now, if you want."

"Awesome!" I beam. "I'll pay whatever, I just need to get my head around this."

Will smiles at me. "I'm not that expensive, don't worry."

"How about I get us some more coffee," I offer, reaching for my purse. "And then you can do your thing and make me a genius."

An hour later, I'm sending silent prayers of thanks to whatever god is listening. Will is a total angel.

"I can't believe it's this simple." I stare at the pages of notes I've made, all of them neat, ordered, and making actual sense. "Why didn't I get this before?"

Will sends me a supportive grin. "Don't be so hard on

yourself. All the books make things seem far more complicated than they really are. If you just break it down
into the main arguments, you'll be fine."

"Come on." I roll my eyes. "Just admit you're a
superbrain and I'd be screwed without you."

"Natasha, that's not true! You almost had it on your
own, and . . ." He's flustered and almost blushing.

"Relax, I was kidding," I reassure him. "But seriously,
how do you do it—make sense of everything so easily?"

He plays with his coffee cup. "I don't know.
Remember, I do have an extra year of experience."

"Right." I pause. "The finals system here is pretty
weird, isn't it? Back home, we take them at the end of
every semester, but you've got them all in one go."

Will nods slowly, like the thought of it is wearing him
out. "In the summer, I'll take eight papers that last three
hours each. They're spaced over a few weeks, but that's it,
my entire university grade."

I gape. "So if you screw up on the day . . . ?"

"Then I'm done for." He looks so forlorn, I feel like
giving him a hug.

"But you'll be fine." I try and lighten the mood. "It's
only dumb-asses like me who would have to worry."

"You're not dumb," he scolds me. "You're just new
to this style of thinking."

"I wish it was that simple, but with Elliot . . ." I shake
my head. "I can't figure her out."

Will pauses. "You've read her book, haven't you?"
I shake my head. "You should." He gives this wry grin.
"It's a long rant about the new generation's betrayal of

feminism. How every girl in a short skirt undermines decades of activism — stuff like that."

"And you believe that?" I shift in my seat, totally uncomfortable. If we'd met two hours ago . . .

But luckily Will just laughs. "Elliot oversimplifies everything. But she's rather uncompromising. All or nothing, I suppose."

I sigh. "Anyway, enough about work. I think I've got enough notes to manage my essay now. Tell me about you — what do you do for fun here?"

"Fun?" He gives a snort. "As I said, I'm a finalist. This is as close to fun as I'll get until after my exams."

"There's got to be something you do to relax," I prod, trying to move the conversation on. "You're not a robot."

"Well." He hesitates. "You'll probably think I'm a loser . . ."

"I won't! C'mon."

"I play Scrabble," Will admits. He looks so sweet, I have to try not to laugh.

"Scrabble?" I repeat dubiously.

"See, I told you." He sighs.

"No! It's . . . interesting. I've never met somebody who likes it. My friends don't really go for that kind of thing." Understatement. If Morgan was here, she'd be cracking up, but there's something so endearing about Will's confession. The guys I know back home would never tell me something like that in case it ruined their chances with me, but Will couldn't be less of a player.

"So why do you like it?" I look at him carefully. He's

pushed up his sleeves to reveal pale forearms and is sitting on the edge of his seat.

He pauses for a long time. "I suppose . . . I suppose I find it relaxing. There's an order, a pattern to it. I don't have to think about anything except letters on the board." He shoots me an embarrassed half smile. "Pathetic, I know."

"It's not!" I insist. "At least you're doing something. If I want to relax, I just veg out in front of the TV." It strikes me that Will would have a whole lot in common with Emily, Queen of Order. Then I notice the time.

"Frak!"

Will lights up. "You watch *Battlestar Galactica*?"

"Hell yes." I grin. "It's a total guilty pleasure, but I caught an episode a while back, and ever since, I've been hooked." I think I spy some new admiration in his eyes and wonder why I didn't drop that into the conversation earlier. Sci-fi shows are prime nerd-bonding material. "Anyway, I have to go. I've got to get to the library before it closes."

"Of course." Will gets up. "Well, it was nice meeting you."

I grin at his formality. "You too. And I'll set up another session next week. You're on Facebook, right?"

He nods but reaches to scrawl his number on my notebook all the same. "Or even just call, you know, if you have any random questions, or . . . anything."

"I will." Packing up my notes, I see he's still hovering out of his seat. "Umm, bye?" I don't know if I should hug him good-bye like I'm used to, or what.

"Good-bye." He looks as awkward as me. Finally, he sticks his hand out again. I shake it.

"Later." I turn away and quickly bounce down the stairs and out onto the street. Finally, some luck! He's awkward but an angel for sure, sent to save me from academic oblivion. I grin, thinking of his blushes and cute politeness. Any other guy would have hit on me, but not Will. And in my new outfit, he didn't think I was one of those short-skirted underminers of feminism. The switch survival is working out just great.

So great that when I pass a couple of students with flyers outside the library, I pause. They're signing people up for a protest group against the closing of the women's health center — that thing Carrie was going on about the other week. Didn't Emily say that getting involved with a group would be good for me?

"It's a vital cause for all Oxford women." A short girl with cropped hair thrusts a leaflet at me. "We're meeting Thursday lunchtime, in conference room B."

I add my name to the chart.

"Wonderful," she exclaims. "Bring all your friends."

"Sure," I agree, taking the slip of paper and heading into the library. I might not have any friends to bring, but I may as well show up.

Hell, it's not like I have any other plans.

From: totes_tasha
To: EMLewis
Subject: switch survival 1.0

· ·

ok, the first secret is that "california casual" totes isn't casual at all. before you leave the room in the morning, you'll need to blow-dry your hair and put your makeup on—even if you're just going to the gym. like, it doesn't matter if you're just wearing a sweat suit (cute and fitted, obvs), you've got to be shiny and sleek, that's just the way things work. maybe cut out some study or get up earlier?

xoxo

p.s. do I really have to stop wearing my uggs? i know the girls over here don't go for them, but they're sooooo comfortable and it's "bloody freezing" as u brits would say.

. . . .

And I swore I'd never be one of those girls who spends half an hour on her makeup every day . . .

Now for your guide: agree with people. I don't just mean smiling and nodding along with whatever they're saying, I mean fake enthusiasm a little more. The thing about the students at Oxford is that a lot of them are self-important and egotistical — they've spent most of their lives being told how wonderful they are, and they like to keep that going. So if somebody's off on a long rant or lecture, actively agree. Make murmurs of assent, say "Right" and "Exactly what I was thinking" a few times, and they'll think you really do know what they're talking about. Also, start reading the news headlines online and scanning the main arguments: the people you're around are very into current affairs and politics, so you'll need to be able to bluff your way through discussions.

I hope everything's working out. I told my father that I needed new textbooks and screenwriting programs, so he's letting me use the credit card. I'm going shopping with Morgan whenever she's done in the shower: wish me luck!

Hugs,
Em

P.S. Unfortunately, Uggs aren't really Oxford. Stick to low-heeled leather boots, and if you're getting cold, try layering two pairs of tights: one patterned over one opaque. You've got earmuffs, right?

Emily

Natasha was right: Morgan is the undoubted queen of local shopping. All it takes is a morning on State Street with her, Lexi, and that emergency credit card for me to be transformed. I draw the line at anything uber-slutty, of course, but even taking into account my "must cover my crotch" rule of taste and decency, the pair of them still manage to outfit me in a complete range of skintight jeans, little polo shirts, miniskirts, and sneakers.

"I still say you need some time in the tanning salon." Morgan assesses me again from her seat at the nail parlor.

I shake my head. "No, thank you. The dye and nails are more than enough." My thin strawberry-blond hair is now definitely more blond than strawberry; blow-dried out in a full, straight mass. All I need is a pair of Ugg boots and a small, yappy dog, and Emily Lewis could, "like, totally" pass for a native. If I don't open my mouth, that is.

"Sure, if you want to look freakishly pale . . ." Lexi pipes up from my other side. She's getting blood-red varnish painted on her toenails, to match the new lipstick she bought.

"I'm fine," I insist.

"Maybe just go for some tinted moisturizer?" Morgan bargains. " 'Cause you really do look like you haven't been outside in, like, forever. No offense."

"None taken."

"But those Pumas were a cool find." Her gaze travels over me, and I get the distinct impression that she's seeing me as a collection of parts rather than a whole person. "We made a great start."

Start? I pretend to study my one finished hand, wondering what on earth else is in store for me. Despite the fact that my reflection is now shiny and very blond, I still don't feel any different from the old, non-trendy me. In fact, I have to force myself not to stare anxiously at my watch as the meeting time for our film group draws ominously near.

Which reminds me that in addition to the dubious honor of being a newly owned Psi Delt Doable, I'm also not exactly riding high in my study partner's good books.

"So," I begin hesitantly, wondering how much warning I need, "what happened at the party the other night—with Ryan, I mean. He looked rather upset."

Morgan pauses. "Omigod, you didn't hear? He freaked out. It was crazy."

"So crazy," Lexi echoes.

"I can't believe you missed it." Morgan brightens, wriggling her toes in the small bowl of warm water. "It was so scandalous."

"Because he saw you with . . . Ben, was it?"

"Right. But it's not like we were even *doing* anything!" she exclaims. "Just hanging out. I mean, did he expect me to be a total nun?"

I think of her lunch-hour "workouts" and stay quiet.

"And technically you never said you were exclusive," Lexi points out, her lip-gloss wand wavering midway to her mouth.

"I know!" Morgan flips back her hair dramatically. "So anyway, I was just chilling out with Ben—and there were tons more people there too; it wasn't like we were on our *own*—and Ryan comes storming in, totally mad." I get the sense she's taking some dramatic license here, but she's in full narrative flow, so never mind. "And he's all, 'What are you doing with him?' So I'm like, 'Is it any of your business?' And he goes, 'Uh, yes, I'm your boyfriend.' And I just laugh like, 'Whatever.'" Morgan finally pauses for breath. "And then he starts going on about honesty and trust, and I'm like, 'Enough.' Right?"

"Right." Lexi nods.

"You were there?" I ask as the silent Chinese woman finishes my nails and retreats. I say a "thank-you" to her back.

"No, but she called me, like, minutes later."

"It was so terrible!" Morgan demands our attention again. "I was a wreck."

"Total wreck," Lexi confirms, head bobbing.

"I mean, how could he be so mean?"

I blink.

"And yelling at me in front of everyone." She pouts. "Where does he get off thinking like he owns me? I mean, that's not how we *do* things here."

"How do you do things?" I spy the opportunity for some inside information. "With dating and boys, I mean."

"Oh, everything's totally casual," Morgan pronounces. "Like, unless you've been dating forever and you've both said you're exclusive, then you can hook up with whoever you want."

"But you wouldn't, like, sleep with other guys," Lexi adds. "That would just be skanky." I swear I see her shoot a sideways glance at Morgan, but she seems unconcerned.

"So if I'd hooked up with Ben—*if*—then it would have been totally legit," Morgan insists. "If I'm exclusive, I don't cheat, but we weren't, so it's not cheating."

"That makes sense." I'm surprised at just how straightforward Morgan's dating logic actually is. I feel a short pang of guilt for thinking she was a heartless bitch.

"I know." She looks at me as if to say, "Keep up." "Ryan was just mad I blew him off to go to the party in the first place. And he loves the drama. Like, I swear he's just playing out this big script in his head, and I was around at the right time to be the main part."

"He is rather . . . devoted to film," I agree.

"Try totally obsessed!" Morgan says. "Like, I figured it was cute to begin with. He was totally sweet and treated me so good, and after what happened with Casey—"

"Oh god, Casey!" Lexi squeals.

"Right!" Morgan catches my confused expression. "You don't even want to know. Psycho."

"Oh."

"So I just wanted someone nice, you know? But not *serious*. And we've only been dating since, what, Christmas?"

"About then." Lexi pulls her shoes back on.

"So you see, it's no time at all."

As we gather our things, I make mental notes of these new rules. Casual. Dating. Non-exclusive.

"So you want to get a frappe?" Morgan pushes her oversize sunglasses on.

"I could totally go for a mocha." Lexi does the same.

"I can't, I've got . . ." I catch sight of the time again. "Oh no, I'm late! I was supposed to meet my film group half an hour ago!"

"Chill, it's only a project." Morgan shakes her head at me. "Seriously, you need to lose this stress. It's not good for you."

I take a breath. "I know." I knew so much that I was willing to make myself over as Beach Barbie in order to hopefully gain some perspective.

"So a frappe, then." Linking her arm through mine, Morgan steers me onto the bright sunlit pavement. "And then you can go to your project and report back how Ryan's doing. I bet he's a mess."

"What the hell happened to you?" Ryan regards me with narrowed dark eyes when I finally turn up, two hours late.

136

"What do you mean?" I twist a piece of my newly blond hair around a perfect nail and wait for some reaction to the change of style. But Ryan just hoists the camera case onto his shoulder and begins walking toward the car park.

"You ditched our first meeting yesterday."

"Sorry." I look around, wondering how much I've missed. "I thought you could handle it." Plus the little fact I was deep in rom-com wallowing after the party.

"Yeah, well, you were the one who insisted on it in the first place." Ryan picks up speed so I have to hurry after him. "It was a total waste of time."

I ignore his tone. "How far along are we today?"

"Nowhere. People only just started showing up."

I brace myself. All right, two hours behind schedule isn't terrible. And at least they haven't done anything wrong in my absence that would require repeating. "So what are we doing outside? The car-park shots weren't down until next week."

"I changed the timetable."

"You what?" I can't help myself screeching. That schedule was a work of art: logical, neat, and with plenty of space for contingencies. It took me five drafts before I had it perfect.

Ryan shrugs. "These things happen. I figured we'd be better starting with the establishing shots—let the actors have some time with the script. This way, the camera guys get to grips with the tech side. And since you were late . . ."

I take a breath. Remember: you are a calm, go-with-the-flow kind of girl now.

"OK," I agree slowly.

Ryan raises an eyebrow. "That's it?"

His confusion is reward enough. "That's it," I say sweetly. "Good idea. Do you need help carrying anything?"

"No, I've got it." Frowning, Ryan comes to a halt in front of a small gaggle of students from our class. "You know everyone, right? Lulu, AJ, Keith, Maura. The other actors are starting tomorrow."

"Hello." I try a casual nod and make sure to smile at them all, as if I haven't already Googled each person and assessed their strengths and weaknesses from various class contributions.

We start to set up: the tech guys, AJ and Keith, taking obvious pride in the shiny new equipment while Lulu and Maura faff around doing absolutely nothing. I edge over to them.

"I don't know," Maura is musing, sitting cross-legged on the low wall. "The L'Oréal always dries my ends out."

Lulu nods, playing with the frayed edge on her jeans. "I have to put the serum on before conditioning; it totally locks the moisture in."

I stop myself from rolling my eyes. "Hi, Lulu, how are you?"

Lulu blinks at me, her blue eyes wide. "I'm good. What's up?"

"Nothing much. Have you run lines yet?"

"But we're not shooting till tomorrow."

"Right. But we won't have much time, because

of classes, so we need it to be perfect straightaway," I explain. "And since you're already here . . ."

"OK." She shrugs. "But Peter is busy."

"Well, I'm sure Maura could help you out." I wonder just how incompetent these people are.

"But I didn't bring my script."

"Then it's a good thing I have spares!" I pass them each a folder.

"Oh. OK." She begins flicking listlessly through the pages.

"Why don't you start with tomorrow's scene?"

"Sure." Lulu turns to Maura and begins reciting while I find a spot to sit nearby. From this vantage point, I can keep an eye on everyone, so I pull out my black binder of all knowledge and wait for somebody to do something wrong.

By the time we're finished with the shots, I've learned a vital new fact that may well save my sanity. Either that or it will drive me utterly insane—I haven't decided yet. Ryan is a perfectionist.

"Can we please go?" Maura whines while our director sets up for another sweeping panorama of the asphalt. "We're not even in these scenes, and it's been hours!"

"OK," I agree, but can't help reverting to my old self. "Just meet us on time tomorrow. And check your schedules for props and costume, everyone!" I add as the other crew members take my cue to quickly disappear. I walk over to Ryan. "Have you got it yet?"

He keeps his head down, glued to the display. "Just a couple more."

"You know, these were only supposed to take an hour." I begin to gather the folders they've all abandoned nearby.

"It takes as long as it takes."

Fifteen minutes later, my patience is wearing a little thinner. Usually I can admire anal attention to detail, and it's not that I have anywhere else to be, but I can't help thinking that this is setting a dangerous precedent: my precious schedule is under threat.

"That's enough," I say in a pleasant voice, moving so I block the shot. Ryan looks up, glaring, but I refuse to be swayed. I carefully make sure everything has been saved and stored, and reach over to turn off the camera.

"But—"

"You got the shot," I assure him. "You got the shot five times over, at the very least."

Ryan lets out an irritated breath, eyes clouding over. "You can't just—"

"Is this what it's going to be like?" I stand my ground. "Because we've only got a few weeks for filming, not forever."

Scowling, Ryan turns away and begins to pack up.

"I'm sorry." The words are out of my mouth before I take a chance to consider them, but when they linger between us, I know I've made the right decision. I can't take another few weeks of this: we need to clear the air. I take another breath and continue. "About what happened with Morgan. I knew, well, I knew she wasn't being completely honest with you. I understand if you hate me for that."

Ryan doesn't look at me for a minute, but I stand my ground and wait. At last, he stands up straight and meets my eyes. "It's not your fault," he says quietly. "I mean, it's not like we're friends." His expression is tired, as if he doesn't want the reminder of what's happened. I can understand. I wanted to get away from Sebastian so much that I crossed the Atlantic.

"Yes, but . . ." I don't want to say anything bad about Morgan, so I just shrug. "I would want to know. If it was me, I'd want to know everything."

He nods slowly, the sun shining like a halo behind his closely cropped hair. Finally, a little tension seems to ease out of his posture. "OK." He nods at the trolley we've loaded with equipment, and I realize that the moment is over. "Help me take everything back to the equipment room?"

I follow him, arms full, across the campus. It's always full of people, but today was another hot, sunny day, so the girls are still out in force: sprawled in packs on the quads and benches in their tiny skirts and even the odd bikini, while boys pretend to play soccer and basketball nearby. I think of Oxford, the neat lawns adorned with KEEP OFF THE GRASS placards until well into summer so we have to scurry down the long, tiled pathways. I begin to smile.

"What's up?" Ryan says, seeing my expression.

I shrug, embarrassed. "Nothing. It's just . . . I never realized what a difference the weather could make."

"Seriously? I thought you Brits were always going on about it."

I laugh. "Yes, about the difference between rain and sleet, or drizzle. But here you've got all this sunshine . . . It just seems like people are actually happier, that's all."

Ryan shoots me a look as we enter the arts building. "Too much good weather is a dangerous thing. Stay in California and you'll see what I mean—some people are so laid-back, it's hard to get anything done."

"You mean worse than your lot?" I tease.

"You have no idea." He grins. "Hang on." He fumbles with the keys to the equipment room. "Now, have you got everything?"

"All accounted for." I brandish the list, ticked off and double-checked.

He shakes his head with a grin. "OK, so maybe you *should* go lie out in the sun some more."

"Maybe I will," I say, considering the possibility. After all, I can get my class reading done just as well on the front lawn as in a library.

"But don't be late tomorrow," he calls in my direction as I leave. "And don't ever touch my camera again!"

Tasha

When I arrive at the protest meeting on Thursday, there's already a group of people chatting at the front of the room. Most of them are activist types, with dreadlocks or painfully unfashionable hempy clothes, but they all seem totally relaxed and friendly with each other. I sidle in and take a seat near the back, pulling out some reading so I don't look awkward and alone.

"Hello, everyone." Carrie arrives in ratty denim and some serious boots and calls for attention. So she's the boss here; I should have guessed. I mean, she acts like the defender of all feminism in our classes—all she's missing is the cape and mask. "Thanks for making it today; we've got a lot to talk about."

People settle down, and I can see that aside from a couple of angel-faced boys in skinny jeans, the room is full of girls. Strident, political-looking girls who probably boycott lipstick and heels on principle. I send silent thanks that I picked the dullest, most functional outfit possible: a plain navy corduroy skirt (that actually covers my knees) and a crisp shirt and sweater.

"First of all, I'm Carrie, and this is Uma." She points to the petite girl in an Amnesty pullover. "As you all know, the Oxford board has decided, in all their wisdom, to shut down the most vital resource we have: the women's health center." Carrie nods at her companion.

"This isn't just about the center itself," Uma continues, her voice lilting with a faint Indian accent. "But the fact that women's services are the first thing to get cut: before sports funding, before entertainment budgets. Oxford is breaking its commitment to the welfare of its female students, and we can't just stand idly by and let them."

There's a rumble of agreement, and even I see it's pretty lame to cut our services before, like, the cable subscription.

"We want to put together a group to make women's voices heard, any way we can." Carrie folds her arms. "That means emails and letters, postering, handing out leaflets, and even demonstrating."

A girl farther down my row waves her hand in the air, rattling with an armful of beads and bangles.

"Yes?"

"What about fund-raising?" she asks. "Wouldn't it be a better use of time to actually raise the funds to keep the center open?"

Carrie exchanges a look with Uma. "It would, if we had time to raise half a million pounds."

"Oh." Her faces falls.

Carrie shrugs. "I'm not going to lie, people. This is a last resort. They slipped it in the last budget meeting and gave Judy and Sue only one month's notice. We don't have the time or resources to make up the shortfall ourselves, but you know what? We're not going down without a fight."

Another rumble.

"The board thinks they can just sweep this under the rug, like our welfare doesn't matter. Well, not on my watch." Carrie's voice rings with determination. "We're going to make our voices heard. We're going to make a difference!"

"Yes!" It's an easy crowd, but I'm impressed with the way she's riling them up.

"So, let's all split into groups and come up with some ideas. Ten minutes of brainstorming, people, then let's share!"

The room clatters with the sound of chairs getting dragged around. I turn hesitantly to the girls beside me.

"Hey." I lift my hand in a wave. We pull ourselves into a circle and quickly run through the introductions. Mary is one of the dreadlocked girls, in ripped tights and a chunky sweater. Louise glares out from behind thick black-rimmed glasses, and DeeDee has a super-bossy look to her thin face, like she's always in charge.

"So, ideas."

I was right—nobody has a chance to speak before DeeDee opens her notebook and begins to underline a heading, already acting like our leader.

"We could have a march," Mary suggests, "or a rally, with speakers."

DeeDee notes it down.

"I still think Jo was right—we need to look at fundraising," Louise complains. "Even if it's just to cover demonstration costs. Remember when we did the campaign against Nestlé? I spent a fortune on photocopies."

"Plus, it could work with the board," I speak up. "Like, show them we respect their budgeting and everything. When we wanted to throw a spring break concert at school back home, they totally said no until we matched their costs."

The three girls look at me.

"But we've got no way of raising that amount of money," DeeDee eventually informs me. "Bake sales and car washes don't really work over here."

"You could do a college calendar," I suggest, with a flash of inspiration. "They sell out right away. Just pick the hottest Oxford girls and have them pose in, say, college scarves and bikinis all over the city. Low cost, high return!" I sit back, happy. The UC Honeys calendar was always one of the biggest fund-raisers back home: I came *this* close to making March until Cammi Sanders got enlarged from C to double-D and beat me at the last minute.

"Bikinis?" Louise repeats, rolling the word around like it's a dirty word. "You want us to save the women's health center by whoring out our bodies?"

I pause. "Whoring? What? This'll be fun."

"You think the sacrifice of your integrity and sexual identity is a price worth paying?"

I can't believe them. "No, I just—"

"Really, Natasha." Mary shakes her head. "If that was a joke, it's not funny."

"But—"

"Objectification of women is part of the reason we need the center to begin with." DeeDee completes the circle of disapproval. "To create a safe, nonjudgmental space away from patriarchy."

The trio sits back, staring at me with disgust like I'm one of those big, bad patriarchs.

"Sorry." I find myself blushing, even though I have no idea what the hell they're getting so wound up about. "I, umm, I didn't think."

Note to self: in this crowd, bikinis equal, like, *napalm*.

"So do we have any other real suggestions?" DeeDee asks, ignoring me completely. Louise and Mary start talking about information packs and write-in campaigns, while I sit quietly and wait it out until Carrie claps her hands and calls us all back together.

"OK, what have we got?"

"Well, I think we should go with the personal angle," a girl with dangling gold earrings starts to speak. I realize with a shock that she's the first black person I've seen in any of my college meetings or classes. Way to go on the diversity front, Oxford. "We need to prevent them from thinking of the center as an abstract body and start relating it to women's lives."

"You mean like personal testimonies?" Uma asks.

"Right. Our literature needs to have the stories of the girls who've used the center, so people can see everyone benefits from it."

"I like that." Carrie nods. "How many people here would be willing to share their experiences?"

Almost everybody raises their hand.

"I use the safety bus to get home."

"Me too. And I use the center for, you know, contraception."

"My friend used the rape hotline when she got attacked last year."

"And it's easier to get the morning-after pill there — my college doctor couldn't get me in for an appointment until the next day, and by then . . . it's too late."

Soon we're flooded with everyone's stories.

"OK, I think we've got enough!" Carrie tries to get control back, but they keep talking until DeeDee pierces through the noise with a sharp whistle. She turns to Carrie with a smug grin.

"Anything else?" They spend ten minutes running through other plans and then bickering over the color of paper to use for their flyers. I begin to lose interest as the orange-versus-green debate stretches out, until another voice pipes up from the back.

"But isn't this all redundant, rearranging deck chairs on the *Titanic*? We need to make a statement, something bold."

"Like what?" Carrie doesn't seem thrilled at the threat to her authority.

"Like a sit-in."

I turn. The girl is heavy in an all-black outfit that totally washes out her complexion. "We can occupy the lecture halls," she announces. "Then they'll have to take notice."

Carrie is unimpressed. "It's too risky. These things have a way of leaking out."

"Not if we do it right now," the girl insists. "That famous astronomer is visiting today, so there will be lots of people around. Media, even. It's the perfect opportunity."

"Come on," DeeDee butts in. "You heard her, we need to get noticed."

"OK, OK, everyone, settle down." Carrie sighs. "Let's take a vote. Everyone in favor of possibly alienating direct action . . . ?"

There's a loud chorus of "ayes." Maybe everyone else was as bored of the debate as I was: they all seem eager to get out and just do something.

Carrie purses her lips. "Then I suppose it's settled."

"Let's go!" the goth girl cries.

People grab their things and make for the exit, but I linger behind. Getting all hyped up to chant slogans and march around in circles isn't really my style; this seems like a good moment to just slip away. I came, I participated, I checked the box; now it's time for real work.

I follow them as far as the library lobby and then cut a left, but before I make it to the doors, Carrie plants herself in front of me.

"Natasha, I thought that was you." She looks at me, confused. "What are you doing here?"

"You know, I figured I'd check out your campaign." I wave a bunch of flyers as evidence.

"That's great!" Her face kind of relaxes. "I didn't think this was your sort of thing."

I bet she didn't.

"Well, it's kind of an important cause, so . . ." I'm not lying—the angry feminists may have sucked all the life out of the thing, but I do actually see their point.

"Good for you." Carrie seems to be looking at me with a new expression. "And it's really admirable for you to give up your time, when you won't even be around in a couple of months."

I shift uncomfortably. "Well, I guess it's like you said: it's the principle of the thing."

Carrie's face shifts into a full-on smile. "Brilliant! Come on, we're losing the others." She pulls me down the hallway and out onto the street after the group, talking all the time about campaigns and patriarchy. My plan to ditch is totally screwed.

The lecture halls are based in a huge old building with marble floors and statues carved into the walls. There's only one main entrance, a towering lobby with big wooden doors, so Carrie decides that's our best bet for maximum exposure and ushers us to the ornate railings that stretch across the back wall.

"Here." The washed-out girl pops up beside us and pulls an armful of chains from her bag.

"You came prepared?" I ask, hoping she doesn't just carry them around for everyday use.

"Maybe." The girl winks. "Here, drape these around you. Don't worry," she adds, catching my expression as she laces some handcuffs through the grille and fixes me into them. "They don't lock; they're just for effect."

By now a curious crowd has gathered around us, and I can see staff talking on the phone. Carrie grabs her megaphone and begins to yell.

"Save the women's health center! Women of Oxford, say no!"

The other girls join in, chanting along until the room is a chorus of loud shouts and stamped feet. I have to admit, it's kind of exciting to be in the middle of all the drama, although I make sure to shrink back, out of sight behind a pillar. The last thing I need is to get ID'd as part of this.

After about ten minutes of demonstrating, a stern woman approaches from the front desk. She pauses a moment, watching us, then cuts through to reach Carrie. They murmur off to the side, the woman showing her several pages of printed type.

"OK, people, time to clear out." Carrie returns. The protestors moan. "We're breaking city bylaws doing this. They've called the police, and we've made our point now. Come on." People sigh, but they begin to pack up.

I tug against my handcuffs. They don't move.

"I can't," I whisper, my stomach sinking at warp speed.

"What?" Carrie turns back to me.

"I said, I can't!" I'm rattling the chains like crazy now, trying to figure out when they locked. They weren't supposed to lock! "I can't leave!"

I panic. The rest of the girls are looking over at me, and campus security is heading toward us. But the freaking handcuffs stay clamped around my wrists.

"She's right!" Carrie suddenly declares with a cry, pumping her fist in the air. "We can't leave! Not until the board agrees to hear our case!"

"Yeah!" The other girls begin to whoop and holler.

"Not until the female students of Oxford get the welfare services they deserve!"

Oh boy. Carrie's in full flow beside me, but I just want the ground to open up.

"Not until we're respected as equals, until the outdated patriarchy in charge of our futures understands that we will not be ignored!"

Security pushes their way through the crowd and takes hold of us.

"Let go of the railing," a burly guard demands.

"I can't." I shrug apologetically. "Seriously." I rattle the handcuffs for effect as Carrie is hoisted over another guard's shoulder and carted away.

"Natasha is right," she screams to the crowd. "We cannot leave!"

They all turn and look at me.

"Natasha! Natasha!" DeeDee begins to chant. The other girls join in. I sink to the floor.

"Natasha! Natasha!"

Invisible. Right.

From: totes_tasha
To: EMLewis
Subject: About that blending-in thing . . .
Attached: studentdemo.jpg

. . . .

A lecture by renowned astrophysicist Brian Lupen was post-
poned yesterday after a group seized control of the lecture halls
for a sit-in, protesting the forthcoming closure of the women's
health centre. . . .

hey, em.

see that brunette blob half hidden behind the pillar? that's me:
the one chained to the building. long story, but i guess i'll have
to work harder at this invisible thing!

what's up in cali?

-t-

From: EMLewis
To: totes_tasha
Subject: Well done!

. . . .

You got involved in the demonstration? Good for you! I can imagine how wound up Carrie and her crew must be, but it's definitely a worthy cause. Things with me seem to be good — I'm definitely making progress on becoming a true California girl. You probably wouldn't recognize me, if you'd seen me to begin with, I suppose! Blond hair, new clothes . . . Now I suppose I have to start being more laid-back about things. It's not easy when my study partner is a temperamental artiste, but what can I do?

Keep me up to date.

X Em

Emily

Carla appears at my door at nine thirty on Friday night with an expression of extreme determination fixed on her face. She pauses for a moment to raise her eyebrow at the sight of me in a bubblegum-pink velour tracksuit, then stalks into the room, snapping gum.

"Get dressed. We're heading out." Looking over at the episode of *America's Next Top Model* that I have playing, she passes me a small envelope. "And then you can tell me how they brainwashed you, but, first, clothing."

I peer into the envelope and pull out a ticket. "Jared Jameson!" I squeal. "He's amazing!"

Carla rolls her eyes. "Yeah, whatever. The opening act is already on, so move it."

I quickly go to my closet and pull down a pair of jeans, my initial excitement—as always—overtaken by rational analysis.

"Your first choice canceled on you, didn't they?" I ask, shimmying into an outfit. "I mean, I haven't seen you in ages and then . . ."

Carla sits down on the edge of my bed and shrugs. "Sure, he bailed. So lucky for you, you're the only one I know tame enough to be into this frat-surf-acoustic-rock stuff. And I was right."

"Fair enough," I decide, adjusting my selection from my newly revamped wardrobe. It may cover most of my torso, but the fabric is, well, a little sheer. "How have you been, anyway—did the parliamentary paper turn out all right?"

"It was awesome." Carla grins. "I got the highest score in class, whipped that stuck-up Lindsay Mayhew's gold-plated ass."

"Congratulations." My makeup is still in place from earlier, so all it takes is for me to locate a jacket and bag, and I'm set to go.

"You won't need this." Carla takes the jacket from me, throwing it back on the bed. "It's, like, seventy degrees out."

"Old habits." I smile wistfully, thinking of the crisp February air back in Oxford and the way the tips of my ears would always turn red.

"So, what's with all of this?" Carla asks as I lock up behind me. "When I saw you last week, you were—" She's interrupted by Morgan emerging from the stairs, laden down with shopping bags and her oversize slouch bag.

"You're going out?" Morgan's eyes light up at the sight of me. "How long will you be?"

"A few hours, perhaps." I can see her running through her list of potential "workout" partners even as we speak. "The place is all yours."

"Cool." She grins. "Oh, hey, you up for some spa time tomorrow? My mom sent a gift card, and I could totally use the de-stress time."

"Of course, that sounds like fun," I agree. "I've got a lecture scheduled for noon . . ." I pause, the next words emerging from my lips with no small effort. "But I could always skip it." Breathe, Emily. "This is Carla, by the way."

"Hey!" Morgan exclaims sunnily, the thought of imminent privacy filling her with joy. "Cool, well, we'll totes spa." She starts walking again toward our room before turning back with another important thought. "Em, like, call me when you're on your way back, OK?"

"OK," I agree with a smile. At least she's being vaguely considerate, rather than just inviting him over the moment I step out to get dinner.

"Hmmm." Carla watches me as we step into the lift. "Spa time, salon, fancy sweats . . . I'm guessing there's a good reason for all this?"

"There is." I feel a faint sense of elation, just happy to be leaving my work behind and going out. Small victories, I know, but they matter. I haven't had a headache in a week.

"Figured. You would have to offer me a ton of money to get me playing nicely with that roommate of yours."

"She's not so bad," I find myself protesting as Carla leads me across the parking lot to a battered red car. "She's just . . . different."

"That's what they say about serial killers." Carla heaves the driver's door open and reaches across to open my side, sweeping stacks of CDs and junk-food wrappers off the seat.

"Right." I laugh, climbing in. "One of these days, she'll snap and stab me with a nail file."

There's a queue snaking down the street when we arrive, but Carla just flashes a grin at the doorman and strides straight past them all.

"Have fun, C." He winks at her as we pass through the main doors. I realize that he hasn't even checked our IDs.

"You know everyone," I observe with a little awe. "The boy at the coffee cart, the security at the dorm . . ."

Carla shrugs. "I've done enough shitty jobs in my time to appreciate them: waitressing, retail, you name it. We're invisible to the kids in this town." She peels off her purple cardigan to reveal a short black shirtdress with a chunky belt. "C'mon, you can buy me a beer."

The club is dark and full of students, the floor sticky underfoot, and the scent of beer and sweat in the air. Even though it's sort of ridiculous to be sneaking into a club when I'm legally allowed to drink back at home, I still feel a thrill of rebellion for getting away with it. Score another point for the new, spontaneous Emily Lewis.

Carla charges through the crowd toward the bar, so I don't have time to take in the scene; I need only follow in the wake created by her thick boots and lethal elbows.

"Sorry, sorry," I mutter, trying to keep up. Emerging from the pack, I gasp for air and attempt to catch the barman's attention, but he's already heading straight toward Carla as if he's her long-lost friend.

"Girl, where've you been?" he exclaims, skin reflecting blue under the stage lights.

"Around." She grins nonchalantly and proceeds to catch up, while I turn back to the crowd for some vital observations.

Carla was right—whereas in England, Jared Jameson has a reputation as being sensitive acoustic music, over here he seems to be the preserve of frat boys in team jumpers and, of course, their denim-miniskirted girlfriends. Groups of guys are well on their way to being drunk, the room filled with noise despite the fact that a fragile folksinger is currently trying to hum her way through a set up onstage.

"Poor girl." I sigh, watching her fumble a chord in front of the wholly unconcerned crowd.

"You kidding?" Carla passes me a bottle of beer. "She should be grateful it's not a game night. They usually keep the TVs on right through the opening act."

"Charming." I sip my drink carefully.

"So c'mon." Carla nudges me. "Spill. What's up with the new look?"

I give a rueful grin. And there I was thinking I'd evaded questioning. "Call it an experiment."

"In . . . ?"

"In being a little less . . ." I search for the perfect word. That's it. "Perfect. And organized and good."

Carla takes a swig and leans back against the bar. "I can't say I get the hair and makeup thing, but good luck to you."

"Thank you." I smile, relieved that she doesn't think I'm completely mad to want to change. My thigh suddenly starts to vibrate, so I flick up the display on my phone. Daddy. I waver.

"Who is it?"

"My father." I sigh. Lectures and career planning are the last things I want right now.

"So don't take it."

My thumb traces the "accept call" button. "I can't just not pick up."

Carla snorts. "You mean you've never blown off your parents?" She shakes her head in disbelief. "Forget everything I said: hair, makeup, do whatever it takes. You need to try *something* different." In one swift movement, she takes my phone and hits the "reject" button. "There." She hands it back. "Problem solved."

I gulp, wondering what Dad will think. Would he be worried, or just assume I'd fallen asleep studying again?

"Stop that," Carla warns me, as if she can hear my worrying. "This is a stress-free zone. 'K?"

" 'K," I echo meekly, as the crowd begins to chant and cheer. The poor folksinger has departed, heralding Jared's imminent arrival.

"Let's get to the front," Carla decides, grabbing my hand, "and see if we can't find a cute boy to amuse you for a few hours."

I decide not to disagree.

"The trick is not to expect anything."

An hour later, Jared has finished playing his set, I'm

breathless and sweaty, and Carla and I are fighting for sink space in the bathroom. Eager to round out my education beyond Morgan and Co.'s simple hookup philosophy of dating, I ask her for advice.

"Expect nothing," I say, endorphins from the show still lingering in my bloodstream.

"I mean, absolutely *nada*." Carla reapplies a layer of bold pink lipstick. " 'Cause if you have zero expectations, they won't disappoint. Although usually they find a way to do that too," she admits.

"What do you mean by expectations, exactly?" I push damp strands of hair off my forehead and wish, yet again, that my limp style had a little more volume.

"Like, everything," Carla explains. "Don't expect him to call, don't expect that he likes you. Don't expect anything besides the fact he wants to get in your pants."

"But surely he would like me a little if he was flirting with me or kissing—"

"Jesus, you really are clueless." Carla looks at me with sympathy. "They're college guys—they want to get laid, that's all. And sure, once in a million you'll find a guy who *maybe* cares about getting to know you before he gets laid, but the end goal is still the same."

"Oh."

"It's not all bad." She sees my disappointment. "As long as you remember that, you can get what you want too." She blots her lips one final time. "Like, I'm a total make-out slut, and sometimes I feel bad 'cause that's all I want from them. But then I remember they only want one thing too, so, you know, their problem."

I watch my reflection and wonder if it's really that simple. I assumed that Sam liked me because he spent time talking and flirting, but in the end sex was all that mattered. And as for Sebastian . . . I sigh.

"Depressing, right?" Carla shoots me a twisted smile in the mirror. "I'm hoping they grow out of it. It's cool for now, but one of these days I'm going to want a guy for more than rolling around in the backseat of my car, and then I'll be bitching nonstop."

"But perhaps it's better to be honest," I muse before we go back out into the noise of the club. "Rather than having these big fantasies about love and relationships."

"Right." Carla quickly scans the room until she spots the cute blond boy she'd been flirting with all through the show. "You good on your own for twenty or so?"

"Go ahead."

"Cool." She walks toward him, slow and measured, until she's close enough to lean up and whisper in his ear. Even in the dim light, I can see his eyes widen as she takes his hand and leads him toward the exit and, no doubt, the backseat of her car.

I should be more like Carla, I decide, going back to the bar for some water. And Morgan and Lexi too. No illusions, no big drama, just a simple, clear-cut understanding of the male-female dynamic. I was raised on fairy tales, with noble knights and virtuous princesses, but nothing could be further from the truth.

In short, I need to stop making such a big deal over it.

Without Carla to charm him, the barman ignores me,

serving the men on both sides of me until I feel like climbing over the bar and getting the drink myself.

". . . and whatever she's having."

"Huh?" I look up. A boy is staring at me expectantly. "Oh, just some water, thank you."

"No problem." He grins, dark hair cut neat and conservative. "Can't have you keeling over with thirst."

I grin. "Well, it's very chivalrous of you." He's wearing a band T-shirt and jeans: preppy but not too preppy.

"It's not a dying art." He flashes me a smile, and I feel my stomach skip again and—

Wait, I check myself, Carla's voice is in my head as if she's some kind of guardian angel. He's not being chivalrous; he just wants to get me into bed. But that doesn't mean I can't have some (normal, teenage) fun . . .

"What's your name?" I ask, heart suddenly beating double quick as I contemplate what I might just do.

"Brent," he says. "Sophomore, econ major, hometown in Oregon."

"That's quite a résumé." I laugh at his strange introduction.

He grins again. "You've got to get the basics out of the way."

"Well, in that case . . ." I pause. I was about to launch into my own list of vital information, but something stops me. I'm still anonymous to him: no name, no history. I sort of like it. "Just think of me as a woman of mystery," I finally say, wondering if that sounds completely cheesy.

But Brent is still smiling. "Intrigue, I like it."

"So"—I start to speak before I can overthink this— "do you want to go somewhere quieter?"

He looks surprised, and I would bet good money that surprise turns to shock when I don't wait for an answer; I just take his hand and lead him down a back corridor. Don't chicken out, I order myself. You need to do this.

"Where do you—"

"I have to go in a second," I interrupt him with my heart racing faster than I've ever felt it. And then I kiss him. Just like that. I reach up, pull his face down to mine, and kiss him, with people streaming past us in a dirty grafittied corridor in a club five thousand miles away from home. His hands move to my waist, and he steps forward until I'm pressed between his body and the wall, my mouth glued to his. My blood is singing and I cling tighter, caught up in the sheer recklessness of the moment. I don't do this. I'm not that kind of girl. But right now, I *am*—taking greedy handfuls of his shirt, levering my body closer, arching my hips so I can feel his gasp for breath against my tongue.

I break away, giddy. "Cheers," I tell him with a triumphant grin.

And then I walk away.

Tasha

When I get to my class with Professor Elliot, I can tell something's changed. It took the maintenance crew a while to find cutters strong enough to get through the handcuffs, so I'm twenty minutes late, but when I hurry into the room, Elliot greets me with a big grin instead of her usual frown of disapproval.

"Ah, Natasha," she says, getting up from her armchair and grabbing both my arms in a kind of celebratory hug. "Our agent provocateur!"

"Uh, hi." I retreat suspiciously. "Sorry I'm late."

"Don't worry about that!" Elliot exclaims. "Carrie has been telling us all about your noble stand."

I blink. "She has?"

"Don't be modest, Natasha," Carrie pipes up. She's smiling at me too, and even the usually bored Edwin has a kind of warm look in his eyes. I swallow self-consciously. After over a month of scowls, this is just creepy.

"Did you get into a lot of trouble?" Carrie asks, eyes wide. "I tried to wait for you, but they cleared us all out of the building."

"N . . . no." I carefully take my seat. They've even saved the prize armchair for me: the one with padding left and no rogue springs. "It all worked out OK. In the end." After an extreme charm offensive, that was, the kind I haven't had to use since I totaled my birthday Beemer two days out of the showroom. Compared to my stepdad, the security guys were a breeze: they hadn't had years to get immune to my tears. And when I weep, I *weep*.

"Well." Elliot passes tea in a mug that's not even chipped. "Officially, I obviously can't condone illegal activity . . ." She smiles again. "But off the record, I must say, I'm proud of you for taking such a bold move. Standing up for something you believe in."

"Mhhmm." I hide behind the mug, feeling like a total fraud.

"As you've been reading, direct protest is a key element of many political philosophies," Elliot keeps rhapsodizing. "Rousseau's tenets of civil disobedience, for example, have been hugely influential to the modern protest movement." This seems like it's directed at me, so I nod. "But I'm getting ahead of myself. Let's return to this week's topic."

She passes us back our essays. I try not to look too eager as I snatch mine and flick through in search of my grade: this one's got to be good; it's just got to be. After

Will's tutoring and all my planning, I don't know what I'll do if it doesn't . . .

Seventy-one.

Omigod. Seventy-one? I gasp. In Oxford that's, like, a first-class grade!

"Well done, Natasha." Elliot catches my elation and gives me another one of those supportive smiles. What am I, teacher's pet today? "You've made some real improvement. In fact, I know Edwin was due to present, but why don't you read yours aloud so we can discuss it? Your points were excellent."

I pause nervously before beginning, wondering if my work really cuts it, but then I replay her words. Excellent. Real improvement. It's what I've been fighting for ever since I arrived: for them to take me seriously, like I've got a right to be here too. Sure, their smiles may be freaking me out, but they're sure as hell better than all those disdainful frowns.

With a warm glow of pride, I start to read.

The tutorial goes like a dream. It's probably just another normal class for Carrie and Edwin, but for the first time, I'm holding my own. Explaining arguments, defending my ideas—with Will's expert tuition, I actually understand what they're going on about. I'm used to getting compliments on my cute outfit or amazing new lipstick, but I think this is really the first time in my whole entire life people are paying attention to what I'm saying.

"So are you coming to the next meeting?" As we leave Elliot's study, Carrie falls into step beside me. "We're assembling for a follow-up on Friday."

"I don't know," I say, hoisting up my bag full of books. "Are you sure? I didn't exactly do great the last time out."

"Don't be ridiculous!" Carrie exclaims, following me through a low stone archway toward the library. "You were wonderful. And everyone was very impressed."

"Oh, well, I guess . . ." Those magic words bring on another warm glow, and I find myself agreeing. If Carrie's reaction is anything to go by, maybe it won't suck as much as the last one did.

"Let me take your number," she says in that organized tone, so I happily exchange contact details on the stone front steps. "Uma and I are having a gathering tonight in Jericho," she adds, naming a pretty area on the other side of the city. "We'd love for you to come."

"Maybe. I'll check what I've got planned." I try to sound nonchalant, even though I already know what's happening tonight. Laundry.

"Wonderful." Carrie's face has none of the suspicion and eye-rolling impatience it used to. "After all, you're one of the team now."

As she walks away, I wonder if it could really be so simple. Is all it takes to win them over a new wardrobe? Or was it the couple of hours I spent literally tied up with campus security that got me my free pass? Either way, Emily was right. Being a part of a club or team is totally the shortcut to an instant social life.

I figured that the party would be a Portia clone-free zone, and when I edge through the doorway into the small ground-floor apartment later that night, I'm right. The place is packed with students, but I can't hear a single braying accent. Thank god.

"You came!" Carrie pulls me into a hug. She's wearing a "My God Hates You Too" shirt over a longer blue sweater, and with the contrasting red scarf in her cropped hair, I'd say she almost looks put together. "This is great. I've been telling everyone about you."

"You have?" My dubious reply is lost as she drags me back to the kitchen, where DeeDee, Uma, and Louise are picking at chips and dip.

"Natasha!" DeeDee pushes right through the others to greet me. "That was so amazing what you did at the lecture halls."

"Umm, thanks."

"It's like I've been saying." Flicking back her limp ash-blond hair, DeeDee puts a hand on my shoulder, like I'm part of her argument. "We have no alternative but to make a stand . . ."

And she's off, babbling bossily about protest and South Africa and civil rights. I duck out from under her arm and get a drink and some chips, all the time smiling along like I'm totally with them on whatever they're saying.

"I'm just going to . . ." I gesture back out to the party, but Uma and DeeDee are now talking in way heated voices about majority oppression, so I take the chance to slip out unnoticed. These girls seem nice enough, but, boy, do they get wound up over things they can't control.

I wander awhile through the party, getting a feel for

this scene. It couldn't be further from Raleigh, that's for sure. Instead of posh kids in carefully distressed designer gear standing around talking about Miffy and Butters, everyone here is in jeans and seems totally relaxed: chilled out chatting on couches or sitting in circles on the floor. Uma and Carrie have decorated the place with big maps and foreign objects like carvings, and there are ethnic cushions and fabrics everywhere. Upstairs I even find a group sitting around a hookah pipe smoking shisha in the small terra-cotta-painted bedroom. One of them offers me a smoke, but I politely decline and back out of the room, pretty sure my teetotal pledge should extend to unidentified substances.

"Will?" I suddenly catch sight of a familiar floppy hairstyle down the hallway and bound toward him. "What are you doing here?"

Will's got the same semi-nerdy style going on as the last time I saw him: worn cords and an Oxford shirt, but I can't help thinking he looks kind of good under all that awkwardness. "Natasha?" He gives me a hesitant wave, which I smother with a hug as soon as I reach him. "I have a class with Uma and—"

"You're amazing!" I declare, pulling away. But not before I've had time to clock the taut body he has beneath that loose shirt.

"Well, I, ah . . ." Will looks super-embarrassed at the compliment. I think he actually blushes.

I laugh. "Your tutoring! I got a seventy-one on that essay, can you believe it?"

He lets out a breath and relaxes. "Congratulations! You deserve it."

"Couldn't have done it without you."

"Of course you could have." Will frowns, pushing back his dark hair in what I can tell by now is a nervous gesture. "You knew that material even before I—"

"Enough!" I decide. "Not that I don't want to hear how amazing I am, but this is a party, right? Besides, I've had kind of a killer week."

"I heard about your brush with the law." Will's eyes wrinkle into the cutest grin.

"You did?" I groan. "Oh man, I was hoping it wouldn't get out!"

"Are you joking? That sort of stunt has front-page news written all over it."

I gulp. "You haven't said anything to anyone, have you? Because I really don't want it getting out, and—" My panic must have shown, because Will puts a hand on my arm and reassures me.

"Don't worry, it should be fine." He looks at me for a long moment. "I'm surprised. I would have thought you'd want the publicity—for the campaign."

I pause. "I guess I don't like the spotlight, that's all."

That and the fact my anonymity is the most precious thing I have in the world.

"Well, I can understand that." Will pushes both hands deep in his pant pockets. "I'm not particularly good with attention either."

"You, shy?" I joke. "No way!"

"So . . ." He sways from one foot to the other and looks at me again from under that smooth, dark hair. I have to admit, he's looking way adorable tonight. So adorable, that half of me starts picturing us together, walking hand in hand through Oxford's cute cobbled streets and—

Then the other half hits me over the head with a clue. I made myself a promise. No. Dating. Period.

I force myself back into friend mode. "Oh, hey, I think I saw some board games downstairs. Want to see if they've got Scrabble?"

Will rewards me with a smile. "Absolutely."

I follow him downstairs, half of me congratulating myself on being strong in the face of adorable cuteness, and the other half chanting, "Stupid! Stupid!" over again. This split personality thing sure is tiring.

We stay tucked in a corner of the lounge for the rest of the evening. He beats me at Scrabble three times, but that's only because he's using crazy fake words like *xi* and *qi* instead of, you know, *real* words. But even though it's the kind of night all my old friends would think is totally lame, I don't think I've had this much fun in forever. The angry feminists mellow after a couple glasses of wine, and soon they keep dropping by to give me game suggestions to try and beat Will (because apparently language acquisition is totally gendered), and we're all falling about laughing when the only words I can make from my letters turn out to be dirty ones, so the board gets covered with *nipple* and *phallus*.

And Will . . . Oh boy, am I in trouble. The more we talk, the more his awkwardness melts away, and soon all I can think about is how cute he looks when that chunk of hair falls in his eyes and those lush eyelashes and—

Bad Tasha. Down, girl.

See, I made that "no dating" pledge for a good reason, but as the hours drift by, I can't help wondering if it's *really* so important. I mean, sure, fooling around was what got me into this mess in the first place. And yes, I'm so used to bouncing from guy to guy that I don't think I've gone more than, like, a week without hooking up since I was fifteen and started filling out my tank tops. And OK, it's been kind of great not worrying about guys while I've been here, and rushing out without checking my makeup, and not obsessing over every tiny look and flirtation and—

Yeah, I know. Sigh. It doesn't matter how great Will is. I've got to stick to my pledge.

No. Dating. Period.

Emily

Now that I've committed to the switch survival guide, my list of accomplishments is growing. Of course, I haven't undergone a complete personality transplant, so those accomplishments are neatly recorded in my journal, but technicalities aside, I have plenty to be proud of. What started as a way to blend into the California crowds has somehow become much more important—a way to transform my life into something less rigid, more carefree. The more I try to break my control-freak habits, the more I realize just how ordered I need everything to be, and that's not a good thing. I'm eighteen years old; surely I shouldn't be so set in my ways?

Balancing my PowerBook on my knees, I block out Ryan's monologue about dramatic climax and write another quick email to Natasha running down the small victories that make up my new self.

- Lectures skipped: 5

- Grades I've dropped as a result of missing said lectures: 0

- Shopping trips: 3

- Fitted polo shirts purchased: 4—in pale blue, yellow, pink, and white

- New average time I arrive for events: 5 minutes late

- Amount of guilt I feel at turning up late: Minimal

- Parties attended: 3

- Parties enjoyed: 1

- Number of times I've missed my father's calls: 2

- Number of times I've read a magazine or the internet during his call: 4

- *Boys kissed: 2*

I emphasize that last statistic with mixed pride. In addition to the boy at the Jared Jameson show, I also hooked up (to use native parlance) with somebody else at a frat party over the weekend. Although it was fun, my initial reckless thrill is fading. I can see what Carla and Morgan like about this type of casual dating culture, but I'm not sure it's for me. Without the buzz of risk, there's nothing but a strange boy's tongue in my mouth and a faint sense of unease, as if my heart knows I shouldn't be kissing just random strangers.

I hit *Send* as Ryan yells "Action!" and the actors come to life. Peter wanders carefully over to the park bench where Lulu waits.

"I was looking everywhere for you." Peter tilts his head just right, looking at Lulu as if she's the center of his universe.

"So?" Lulu sighs, heavy and tired. "Haven't you said enough?"

They play the scene just perfectly, the exact mix of jaded hope I was aiming to get across. I've rewritten my first draft of the script a dozen times by now. Professor Lowell warned us that a script is never finished until the final edit is over; until then, it's a work in progress. I didn't believe him at first, determined to get it perfect straight-away, but the words end up sounding so different when they're spoken out loud. I've been constantly making tiny alterations to fit as we go on, but instead of getting tired of all the changes, I relish them: falling deeper into the characters and story with every correction.

"You're not listening." Lulu stares fiercely at her clenched hands, and I feel a shiver of pride. This was supposed to be a fight scene—full of rage and shouting—but two nights ago, I woke up at 3:00 AM with the words dancing around my head, and I realized it didn't need to be so loud at all. The emotion, the intensity, it would all be more dramatic if they played it quiet and tense. I was right.

"And . . . cut! Let's run that again, this time from the second angle." Ryan doesn't look up from his screen the entire time, preferring to watch the digital version to the flesh and blood in front of him. I've learned by now that it doesn't matter to him what real life looks like, only what comes across on the display.

We don't have time scheduled to capture the scene from a different angle, but I let him take it, just the same. I may have put my foot down in the beginning, but I know now that there's no point standing in his way. Yes, he's stubborn and argumentative, but more than that, he's got *vision*. Ryan sees this film in a way I never could. To me, it's linear, the narrative weaving smoothly through shots and scenes. Beginning, middle, end. But to him, it's a multidimensional entity. His dark eyes see angles and panoramas, subtext and symbolism.

"Got it." With a curt nod, Ryan reviews the scene again and finally stands back from the monitor. Taking a deep breath, he runs his hands over his head and blinks.

"Take a break," I urge him, walking over while the cast members unwind. In rumpled jeans and a faded gray shirt, he looks as if he hasn't slept for days.

"We've got tons left to do."

"And there's time," I assure him. "You really think I'd let you run over?"

Ryan musters a weak smile. "Maybe not."

"Exactly. Besides," I add, in case he thinks I'm getting soft, "if you have a nervous breakdown now, we'll never get the editing done."

"Good point."

I push him gently over to the bench and retrieve the Mountain Dew/Twinkie combination that seems to be his only fuel. "Eat. Drink. Breathe."

Ryan nods listlessly, and I can tell he's still analyzing the previous scene from a dozen angles.

"It's never going to be perfect," I remind him, perching on the edge of the seat. "We just don't have the time for that—or the resources."

"I know." He munches the snack slowly. "I just want it to be . . . as near to perfect as possible."

It strikes me as something of a role reversal: me preaching "good enough" while he strives for flawless. "There are just too many variables," I agree, watching the cast and crew kick back. "If we were able to handpick the team . . ."

"So I didn't have to direct *and* be cameraman." Ryan sighs.

"And I didn't have to produce, as well as write. Although," I add, "I think I'd probably produce regardless. You know I couldn't stand around and watch someone else in charge." Ryan laughs, and for a moment we're united: us against the forces trying to hold our baby film back. I sneak a look over at him, shoulders hunched, and wish I could say something to set his mind at ease—to reassure him that the film will work out wonderfully, that Morgan was an utter fool to cheat on him, that he's worth so much more than—

I gulp. What on earth am I thinking?

"Well, we don't—have the time and equipment, I mean." Forcing my voice to stay even, I finish upbeat and positive. "So it'll just have to be what it is."

Turning to me, Ryan pauses. "Do you, do you think it'll be good?"

The uncertainty in his voice surprises me. "Good? It's going to be amazing!" He lets out a breath. "Can't you see it?" I ask.

A shrug. "I guess, I just . . . I get so wrapped up in a project from the inside, I can't get an objective look."

"Trust me," I say forcefully. "I'm more than objective, and I know it's going to be great."

I know that you're great, I add silently, despite my brain flashing a vivid red warning sign.

He smiles at me again, this time with a little more spark in his eyes, and I can't help but feel a swell of pride. I managed to make him feel better.

"OK. You're the boss."

"Damn right, I am." I shift under his gaze and leap up. "Now back to work, you lazy boy."

"Yes sir!" With a mock salute, Ryan lopes back to the camera, and I wonder if he's still hurt over what happened with Morgan. He hasn't said a word about it since my demi-apology, but for all I know, his exhaustion is from pining after her.

It's pointless of me to even care, but I hope not.

Morgan, unfortunately, hasn't forgotten about her ex. We're at the beach later that afternoon, ostensibly to relax and do some reading, but I soon discover that Morgan is anything but relaxed.

"What's up?"

I barely have time to close my eyes and feel the late-afternoon sun seep into my bones before she nudges me.

"Nothing much." I trace idle circles in the sand. "It was a rather hectic day."

"Oh yeah?" Morgan flicks another textbook page over. Lexi and Brooke are in class for a change, so it's just the two of us. "Isn't that supposed to be done already?"

"Two days ago," I agree. But all my other advances must be having some effect, because instead of getting stressed about missed deadlines and contingency plans, I feel relatively calm. As far as study is concerned.

"So how is he?" Morgan regards me over her shades.

"Ryan? Fine, I suppose." I try to keep my voice even. I really don't want to be talking about him with her.

"C'mon, you must know something. Is he seeing anyone?" Morgan's voice is far too interested for somebody who claims to be so unconcerned. "Lulu said she saw him getting coffee with Maura."

"I don't know anything about that." I feel a sharp dig at the thought of them together.

"But has he said anything about me?"

"Not that I heard."

"You must have seen them together, on the movie." Morgan keeps pushing. "Did it look like there's something going on? Were they touching a lot or making eye contact, 'cause—"

"Morgan!" For somebody who has slept with at least four different boys since her breakup, she's awfully curious about "the loser ex." "I don't know anything. I'm the last person he'd talk to about that sort of thing."

"Whatever." She rolls over. "It's not like I care."

"Right."

After another hour on the sand, we get back into Morgan's car and go to meet Brooke and Lexi at the Psi Delt house. After what happened the last time I set foot on their property, I'm none too keen to return, but Morgan insists.

"No choice, Em." Turning into the driveway, she checks her hair in the mirror and reapplies lip gloss. "Brooke says Louis has been, like, pulling away from her. She totes needs our support."

"Fine." I sigh, pulling myself out of the car. "But I can't stay long."

"Awesome." She shoots me a smile and skips up the front steps. "In and out, I promise."

We find them on the back porch with a group of the frat brothers and a stack of empty beer cans. Lexi is perched on the swing seat looking supremely bored, while Brooke watches intently as Louis plays a game of pool.

"Hey, girl!" Morgan sashays over and loudly kisses Brooke on both cheeks. She's glowing from the sun and dressed in a swinging short white skirt under her UC sweatshirt, so I'm not surprised to see all the boys look over. I am, however, surprised to see Louis drag his attention away from the game and give Morgan a long, lingering hug. I edge over to Lexi.

"Did you see that?" she asks in a hushed tone. "This is gonna get *in-ter-est-ing.*"

I settle beside her, unnerved by the glee in her tone. I hope she's wrong. Out of all the girls, Brooke seems to be the most genuinely sweet; watching her heart get ripped apart is not my idea of a spectator sport.

"So, what's happening, guys?" Morgan drapes herself across the pool table. Even as I watch, Brooke seems to fade into the background. Alone, she's pretty, but Morgan just has a way of effortlessly dazzling that makes all other girls seem washed out and ordinary. It's no wonder Louis is showing off for her, trying to make a difficult shot.

"Way to go!" Squealing, Morgan presses herself against him in a celebratory hug, and I wonder for the first time if her show is quite so effortless. If it were anybody else, I'd say they were out to steal Louis. But this is Morgan—she wouldn't try that with her best friend's boy.

Would she?

Half an hour later, I'm amazed at my own naïveté. Morgan isn't just trying to take Louis; she's succeeding. Easily. Cheerleading every point of the game, Morgan ingratiates herself with Louis, until soon he's showing her how to take shots herself: leaning over with his hands on her waist and whispered jokes in her ear. Brooke has long since given up trying to hold her ground; she now slumps on a spare seat by the doorway, watching them with a resigned expression that makes me think perhaps she's seen this all before.

"Couldn't have done it without you, babe!" Ultimately victorious in the superhuman match of wit and skill, Louis picks Morgan up and swings her in a wide circle, her skirt flaring up to reveal bright pink knickers. Brooke slips inside, invisible. I follow.

"Having fun?" Her voice is edged with bitterness. She stands by the kitchen sink and runs cold water.

"I . . . I'm sorry." I don't know what to say to her. It seems like we're both stuck with Morgan, whether we like it or not.

Brooke shrugs, pulling her sweatshirt cuff down. "Not your fault."

"Yes, but . . . it's not right."

She laughs. "I don't know why I expected it to be different this time. Morgan's just . . . Morgan. This is what she does."

"Why do you put up with it?" I hop onto a counter and drum my heels against the cabinet. "Can't you say something?"

"And then what? It would make no difference." Brooke looks out of the back window. "I'd just feel worse for bringing it up."

"So she's done it before?" Morgan's account of her hookup code certainly didn't include boy stealing and betraying her friends.

"Oh, yeah, tons of times." She sighs. "It's just how it is with her. Like, always a competition." Brooke's face twists slightly. "She and Tasha were always up against each other, before . . . You know about Tyler, right?" I nod. "Anyway, sometimes she doesn't like them all that much — she just wants to be the one to win them. Prove she's the best."

"That's terrible," I say honestly.

Brooke just shrugs again. "It's like with Ryan, she wanted him because he usually dates smart girls, you know?" I raise my eyebrows. "She wanted to show she could get anyone. And sure, she liked him, but not enough to, you know . . ."

"Be faithful," I finish for her.

"Right." Brooke gives me a weak smile. "You learn to live with it. She just can't help herself."

It seems to me that keeping your hands off somebody else's boyfriend is a rather simple thing to manage, but for whatever reason, Brooke is standing by her. "If you say so."

Finally placing her water glass down, Brooke sends one last look to the backyard. "Want to get out of here?"

I nod. The whole afternoon has been nothing but tension, small betrayals, and inevitable awkwardness. I'm more than ready to leave. "You just lead the way."

Tasha

"I'm done with this stack." Licking the final envelope, I seal it shut and pass them down the table to Carrie. The whole group has taken over the warm back room at Blackwell's, stuffing campaign packets in preparation for our big showdown with the board in a couple of weeks.

"Great." She checks off a box. "Why don't you take a break before the next batch?"

"No, I'm good." I shrug, taking another stack of letters and relaxing back into the battered brown leather couch. "I'm in a groove now, and, anyway, I kind of like the taste of mail glue."

We fall back into companionable silence: Carrie, Uma, and me with the envelopes while Mary and Louise do some reading for class. We have a kind of rotating schedule now, some girls showing up just to drink coffee and talk if there's no work to be done right away, or just hanging out to work in a crowd when the library gets too much. I love it. The room is lit by cozy lamps, and as well as friendly faces, I have a constant supply of caffeine to get me through the afternoon. It's way better than those cold library carrels, plus I find I actually get more work done when I don't have to go take breaks at the vending machine or blast my iPod just to wake myself up.

"Has anyone done the Okin reading?" It's starting to get dark outside the paned windows by the time Louise takes off her glasses and rubs her eyes. She's almost hidden from view behind a table stacked high with books. "The material on justice and the family? I need a summary, but I just don't have the time."

"Sorry." Uma sticks another address label on and adds the envelope to our already-impressive pile. "Law, remember?"

"Right. And DeeDee is in a tute." Louise sighs. Out of all of us, only a couple are taking the same classes. "What about you, Natasha—have you covered it yet?"

"Hmm?" I look up. "Okin. Who was he again?" I'm hopeless with names, and the dead theorists all blur together for me. In the end, Will had to come up with a color code for me to keep them apart: red for right wing, blue for libertarian, pink for feminist-friendly.

"She," Louise corrects. "Susan Moller Okin. She critiqued Rawls from a feminist perspective."

"Oh, right!" I exclaim. "We did her a couple of weeks ago. Basically, her work forced Rawls to incorporate the idea of family as, like, integral to social justice." I quickly run down the main points.

"So Rawls responded?" Louise scribbles furiously.

"Yup. He caved—clarified that the family isn't exempt, it's the first school of justice, all things must be equal. Wait, there's a good quote . . ." I think hard. "OK, 'Unless there is justice in the family, women will not be able to gain equality in any other sphere.'" Ha. Tell that to my mom: still organizing Frank's laundry for the maid and throwing those way over-the-top dinner parties for him to woo new clients. She hasn't earned a dime her entire life, but she works more than most people just to keep the household going and my stepdad happy.

"You're the best," Louise swears, shooting me a grateful smile. I glow.

"Anyone want more coffee?" I ask, getting up and stretching out my shoulders. A chorus of "No thanks" and "I'm fine" follows, so I take my time wandering the bookshelves and picking out some interesting titles before re-caffeinating and buying a couple of slices of cake with five forks.

"*Lost Girls.*" Carrie spots the title of Elliot's book when I get back. "Have you read that yet?"

"No, I figured I should take a look." Especially since my professor used to think I was one of those lost girls, wandering helplessly around and, like, blinded by my mascara.

"It's quite good," Mary adds, looking up from her thick chemistry textbook. "Quite an old-school perspective, but then when I see those girls in Playboy T-shirts . . ." She gives this kind of long, disapproving sigh. The other girls all nod along. "It all makes so much sense."

"What do you mean?" I ask carefully, thinking of my own Playboy logo shirt. It's a cute shade of baby blue and perfect for working out.

"You know, that some women are as much an enemy of feminism as the misogynists." Mary looks at me quizzically. "I mean, think of raunch culture—all those stripper workouts and full bikini waxes—"

"As if women really should be emulating porn stars," Louise mutters. I shift uncomfortably. Morgan and me did cardio striptease a couple of times at the gym. It didn't herald the end of the world. As far as I know.

"You must have seen far more of this than us," Carrie interrupts. "California's the home of the bleached-blond-babe standard of beauty, isn't it?" They all look at me expectantly, like the fact I'm a brunette totally makes up for my hometown.

"I don't know." I try and stay casual, suddenly aware that I'm on pretty dangerous ground. I remember Emily's order to agree with them. "It's not a big deal, right? I mean, if we—if those girls enjoy that kind of thing, where's the harm?"

Carrie snorts. "They don't enjoy it. They've just been brainwashed into thinking they need to be sexual objects."

"That *Girls Gone Wild* thing, for instance," Louise adds through a mouthful of cake. "Writhing around half naked on-screen for somebody else's amusement. You can't tell me that they've made a genuine, intelligent informed choice to act that way. It's ridiculous."

I tense up. "You don't know that."

"Oh, come on, Natasha!" She laughs. "Have you seen them — drunk and squealing? They're pathetic."

"Girls would never act that way if they could just stop and think about it." Carrie rolls her eyes. "I'd like to think we're all together in this, but they're part of the problem. You know, sometimes I swear I just want to weep for my gender."

I keep quiet and eat more cake, trying to hide my unease. They're talking like anyone who gets drunk and has a good time is just some mindless doll, totally in the thrall of the evil misogynistic mass media, or whatever Uma keeps going on about. Well, I'm one of those girls, and I'm not brainwashed!

I scowl some more at my coffee cup. All those times I've gone out with Morgan and our girls — to clubs, bars, parties — they weren't just about men. They were about dancing, having a good time.

Right?

"It's a good book," Carrie continues. "You should get it."

"Maybe." I look dubiously at the stern gray cover and its promise of "uncompromising debate."

"Ah, hello, girls. I mean, women." I look up to find Will hovering, flustered in the doorway. I take a quick breath of relief. Thank god, something to distract from the "Brainwashed California Blonds" lecture.

"Hey, Will." I bob up from my seat and go over to hug him hello. "What's up?"

"Nothing new." He unwinds his long, stripy scarf. "How's the campaign going?"

"Pretty good." I nod toward the table. "We've stuffed a ton of envelopes, so hopefully all the board members will have had time to read our pamphlet before the presentation."

"That's great. Is there anything you need me to do?"

"Thanks, but I think we're all set." He's so cute, offering to help.

"Well, in that case . . ." He produces two tickets from the pocket of his navy jacket with a flourish. "They're showing a great film at the Playhouse in half an hour. I stopped by to see if you wanted to come."

"That sounds cool." I grin, leaping at the chance to escape the group before Carrie starts another rant. "Let me just get my stuff."

I bundle up and say my good-byes, that angry feeling gone as quickly as it came. I can't really hold it against them for thinking drunk American party girls are evil tools of oppression. I mean, it's not like they've ever actually met one of them. Aside from me, of course, but that's different. They have no idea I'm one of the girls they keep trashing, and I don't want to think about what would happen if they did.

"So how's the Scrabble master?" I tease as we head down the cobbled street. Lights are threaded through tree branches, twinkling in the dark. "Made anyone cry today?"

"No." Will gives me an evil grin. "But I did beat my sister by two hundred points this morning online."

"Dude, she's fourteen!" I shove him playfully.

"So, this way she'll learn about losing and good sportsmanship."

I laugh. "I forgot to ask, what's this movie about?"

"It's Russian," Will begins. My heart sinks. "An experimental film in black and white about the futility of existence and—" He suddenly cracks up and starts laughing. "You should see your face!"

"What, you mean you're kidding? Will!" I shove him again.

"Sorry, I couldn't help it!" His dark eyes are sparkling. "Your face sort of freezes up whenever somebody mentions subtitles."

"That's because they're totally boring," I exclaim. "I go to the movies to have fun, not read a freaking novel."

"Well, you can relax. They're showing *Rocky Horror*. I thought it would be fun."

"Oh, yay!" I clap my hands together. "Can we stop for ice cream first?"

Will stares at me in disbelief. "It's practically freezing out."

"So?"

"So, I don't understand why you eat so much ice cream. You're always complaining about how cold it is!"

"Whatever. It's like a basic good." I draw on my rudimentary econ skills. "My demand isn't affected by external factors."

"Fine, we'll go to G&D's." We detour down a narrow

side street to the local ice-cream chain. Inside, I drool over the display of pie and candy.

"One cup of blue ribbon and a cup of double chocolate brownie with chocolate topping," Will orders for the both of us.

"Thanks." I beam, linking my arm through his as we exit the store. To tell the truth, it's the first time since grade school I've been good friends with a guy, and just good friends. I mean, I have guy friends, but in the back of my mind, I always know that they want to hook up with me or that I want something to happen with them.

And even though technically that's what's happening with Will, it feels different. He's happy just to hang out and let me be myself, no demands or anything. I wish it was so easy for me: sometimes I have to sit on my hands to keep from reaching over to him or pushing that hair out of his eyes, but so far I've stayed strong. This is too good to mess up.

Chat request from totes_tasha.

Connecting . . .

totes_tasha: yo, em!

EMLewis: Hey! What's up?

totes_tasha: look at you, all americanized :-) next thing you'll b sayin "dude" and "awesome."

EMLewis: :blushes:

totes_tasha: no, it's way cute. anyway, u know any 2-letter words beginning in "x"?

EMLewis: Hmmm.

EMLewis: Xi? That's all I can think of. You know, there are sites online for this.

totes_tasha: but that would be cheating!

totes_tasha: sigh, don't worry. i'm losing by, like, 100 points already.

EMLewis: Will again?

totes_tasha: will again.

EMLewis: . . .

totes_tasha: nothing new to tell. it's driving me crazy.

totes_tasha: aaaaaaaarrrrrrrrrrrrrrrggggggggggghhhhh-
hhhhhhhhhh!

EMLewis: Awww. Hugs!

totes_tasha: thanx :-) anyway. how's the film going?
killed ryan yet?

EMLewis: Not yet.

EMLewis: He's actually been so much better to work
with. We've got the last stretch of filming left, then
it's editing and then, argh, the final screening.

totes_tasha: at the end of the semester, right? save me
a copy—i want to see this masterpiece.

EMLewis: Will do!

totes_tasha: so any plans for your big birthday?

EMLewis: How did you know about that?!

totes_tasha: lil thing called the global exchange info pack :-)

totes_tasha: so, any crazy parties planned? i bet morgan will fix something awesome.

EMLewis: Actually . . .

EMLewis: I sort of haven't told her.

totes_tasha: ??

EMLewis: She was threatening something about State Street and tequila for Lexi's birthday, and I don't really want any of that.

totes_tasha: ha smart move. i don't remember half of what happened on my 19th.

EMLewis: I'll be keeping things low-key.

totes_tasha: just b sure 2 have fun!

EMLewis: Will do.

EMLewis: Listen, do you know if . . .

totes_tasha: ?

EMLewis: Never mind. I better get going. I'm due for class.

totes_tasha: xoxo

EMLewis: Bye!

Emily

I told Natasha the truth; with the whirl of classes, filming, and Morgan's hectic social calendar, I barely notice my birthday until the day arrives. March 5. Nineteen years old. I didn't gave much thought to how I'd celebrate this year, but I would never have pictured being here, doing any of this. In fact, if anyone even mentioned film studies, blond hair, and denim miniskirts, I would have classified them as clinically insane.

"You got some packages." Morgan wanders in with the mail. She's still dressed in her nightwear of ultra-short shorts and a skintight vest, but that doesn't seem to stop her roaming around our apartment block. "Anything special?"

"Probably just books from home," I answer breezily.

"Oh." Her face falls, and she drops the parcels on the counter. "God, I wish I didn't have to go home this weekend."

"Mm-hmm," I murmur noncommittally, speed-reading a textbook.

"I mean, it's just their twentieth wedding anniversary." Morgan keeps whining as she pulls on a jumper. "And everyone knows my dad has had, like, tons of affairs."

I try not to roll my eyes. After the Psi Delt man-snatching show, I've tried to keep a little distance from Morgan. With our shopping trips and tanning sessions, I've been lulled into thinking we could be friends; now I see how she treats Brooke, I'm not so certain that's something I want.

"OK, so I'm heading out now." The announcement demands attention, so I look up from my book.

"Have a wonderful time." I try to smile. Morgan beams back, pulling on a baseball hat and clutching her pillow. Apparently her "wandering around the apartment" outfit is also suitable for travel.

"Call me with gossip," she demands, hugging me good-bye, then hoists a huge duffel bag out the door.

"Will do!"

I wait by the front window until I see her convertible drive away before I turn to my presents. Soon the brown paper and padded envelopes are peeled away: Mum sent money, Elizabeth sent a concise legal dictionary, and my dad has given me an expensive-looking fountain pen set, complete with calligraphy nibs and ink. I lay them out on my desk. Looking at them—sitting beside my sunscreen and a stack of DVDs—I feel a strange pang I can't quite decipher.

My mobile rings, and I answer to find an unfamiliar

American squeal echoing down the line. "Happy birthday!"

"Who is—wait, Natasha?" I ask, pushing the gifts into a drawer.

"Who else!"

"Oh, wow, hi!"

"It's weird, talking in person, right?" She laughs. "You sound just like I thought!"

"You mean, English?" I tease.

"Hell yes, though I can hear some American coming through . . ."

"No way!"

"See?" I hear background noise of people and traffic, and picture Natasha freezing outside a library. "So," she continues as if she's known me forever, "has Morgan sprung a party on you yet?"

"No, it's all still top secret. I don't think anyone but Carla knows."

"Even so, you've got to do something special. Remember your whole plan—loosen up, have some fun? I'd say your birthday is the perfect time."

"Maybe . . ."

"Definitely! Anyway, I've got to run, but I wanted to say 'Happy birthday' in person."

"That's so sweet," I say, touched. "What about you, how are you doing?"

"I'm great. I'm just heading out to meet Will; we're going on a quest."

"Really? That sounds . . . adventurous."

"Seriously! If you don't hear from me again, send search parties, OK?"

"OK." I laugh. "Have fun!"

"You too!" She rings off, no doubt to embark on her wild adventure. I can't help being slightly envious. Of course, the reasons for her trip to England are awful, but Natasha has taken to her new identity in Oxford with such ease, it makes me feel a little pathetic. She's off saving the women's health center and winning over Carrie and Co. while I'm just trying to relax.

A small noise makes me turn back to my computer. I click through to my email, wondering if it's more birthday wishes and—

Sebastian.

I don't move for a moment. I just sit there, frozen in front of my screen. I can't believe it. Now he chooses to get in touch? After all this time? Now, when finally the emptiness in my chest has gone, when I don't replay everything he said?

Now, when I'm over him?

I click through to open the message and scan the few short lines.

Happy Birthday, Emily—remember how we celebrated last year? How are things? I'd be really glad to hear from you.

—Sebastian

No apology, no "I miss you," just a clutter of words that strip away all that wonderful time and space I've put between us. I haven't thought of him in weeks, but those few lines take me right back to a year ago, before we were a couple, when he and I held our own private birthday party. He copied me the whole series of *West Wing* for my gift, and we'd stayed up all night in the student common room, snuggled deep into the old armchairs. It was the most fun I'd ever had on my birthday, and the first time I began to think we could ever be more than just friends.

I stay frozen for a moment, until a voice breaks through my thoughts.

"Hey, what's up?"

I blink. Carla is standing in my doorway.

"Hope you don't mind, but it was open." She's dressed for the beach, in shorts and a lime-green T-shirt.

I nod slowly, part of me still back in Oxford in that student lounge.

"Happy birthday!" Carla tosses me a heavy bag. She's grinning, with a worrying gleam in her dark eyes.

"Thanks," I say slowly, pulling out a pile of dark rubber material. I look back at her in confusion.

"It's a wet suit, dumb-ass!" Carla takes it from me and shakes it out to reveal the shape.

"Umm, thanks?" My eyes flick back to the screen. Back to Sebastian's message.

"We're going surfing. Well, you are. I'm just going to watch. And laugh." Carla pushes my laptop screen closed and spins my chair around until I'm facing her. "It's your gift. I mean, you can't be a real California girl until you hit the waves."

"But I've never—"

She cuts me off. "Which is why my friend Nick is giving you a lesson. C'mon, let's go."

Carla collects my beach things and drags me to her car. We're meeting her friend at an "awesome" surf beach farther down the coast, so I let her talk all the way onto the freeway, her voice a soothing chatter as I rest my head against the cool window and try to recapture my California calm. As strip malls and dry brush speed by, I think about how Sebastian chose to contact me. MySpace. One step up from a Facebook wall posting, but far below email. Or, god forbid, an actual letter.

Did I not even deserve a bloody email?

"OK, spill."

I snap back to the present and find we're parked off-road in front of a long expanse of golden sand. The water stretches, vivid blue, all the way to the horizon, and I can see other surfers already bobbing in the shallows.

Carla turns off the radio and stares at me, worried. "This is the anniversary of your birth, and you're sitting there looking like your dog died." She frowns. "He didn't, did he?"

"What?"

"Your dog. Die. OK, obviously not." She pulls her hair back into an electric blue tie. "But something's wrong, right?"

I get out of the car and begin to pull on the wet suit, but she keeps fixing me with that concerned look. "It's my ex," I admit eventually. "He emailed. Today. No wait," I quickly correct myself with a wry smile. "He sent me a MySpace message."

"Ouch." Carla exhales. "You still into him?"

"No!" I exclaim quickly. "That's just it, I'm not." I tug harder at the wet suit, stuck around my thighs.

"Asshole," Carla declares, pulling on her sunglasses.

"No . . ."

"Asshole," she insists, taking pity on my flailing limbs and pulling the wet suit over my shoulders. "Seriously, it's typical. The minute you get over someone, it, like, triggers an international beacon. 'Warning: she's happy! Red alert!' and just like that, he gets back in touch."

I manage a smile, just imagining the sirens. "Like the bat signal."

"Exactly. Don't even think about it," she orders me. "Today is about having fun, not angsting over your selfish jackass ex."

"Yes sir!" I mock salute her.

"Damn right." She adjusts my zipper and stands back, surveying me proudly. "There, you're ready."

For something so beloved by slackers and beach bums, surfing definitely takes a lot of work. After jumping into an upright position on the sand for what seems like hours, Nick finally takes me to the shallows to try it properly.

"Remember, you've got to feel for the wave. Be a part of the ocean!" He's standing knee-deep in water in a pair of red trunks, his dark hair buzz-cut short and a string of beads around his neck. In short, he is a walking surf stereotype.

"Part of the ocean," I repeat, sitting astride the surf-board. With Nick calling instructions (and Carla lounging on the sand), I cautiously paddle farther out.

"Now wait!" he calls.

"For what?" I yell back.

"You'll feel it!"

Well, that clarifies things.

Squinting at the horizon, I sit, bobbing gently on the tide. Nick says that when the right swell comes along, I'll just know. I'm glad someone has faith in my instincts, because I'm not so sure about them myself.

Sebastian.

Just the memory of him makes me angry. Carla is right: contacting me now like that is a completely bas-tard thing to do, but the more I think about it, the more typically him it is. Sebastian hated conflict, hated me get-ting stressed or anxious. Whenever I was worried about an essay or deadline, he'd always just slip away. "You need some space to deal with this," he'd say, and I'd work through everything alone. So of course he'd stay well away when I was upset, only to reappear when he thought I was fine, wanting to be part of my life again.

But I don't have to let him back in.

I taste salt on my lips, that one thought surrounding me as I rock and sway with the tide. *I don't have to let him back in.* So what if he sent me a message? I don't have to reply. I don't have to think about him, and I certainly don't need to pretend that I'm fine with how he treated me.

I can just be finished with him.

I smile, finally feeling loose-limbed and tension-free

the way I'm supposed to be. Another set of breakers is rolling in, and Nick starts to yell from the shore. "This one, this one!"

I see Carla leap up, cheering me on. Here's my cue. Angling my board away from the waves, I lie forward and begin to paddle, faster as the swell approaches. My heartbeat begins to quicken as the wave rises under me, just like Nick said, so I take a breath and leap into position, my feet unsteady on the slab of board. For one second, maybe two, I'm there: rushing toward the shore as if the wind itself is carrying me, and then I feel my balance go and I tumble over into the water. The wave breaks around me, loud and fierce, and then I surface, knees in the sand and salt water streaming from my nose.

"Way to go, Em!" Carla whoops, running down to hug me.

"You're joking." I cough, wiping water from my eyes. "That was terrible!"

"Yeah, but it was a start." She grins. "Now get out there, and stay on this time."

I laugh, still feeling that incredible surge of adrenaline in my veins. "You know, you should consider a career in the army."

Carla pretends to think about it. "I don't think they'd go for the pink hair."

"Probably not." Hauling myself up, I turn back to the sea, my smile fixed and determined. If I can feel this good staying upright just a few seconds, imagine how I'll feel when I get it right. "Now, let's try that again . . ."

Tasha

"We're so lost."

"No, we aren't!"

"I swear we passed that gate half an hour ago." I stop in the middle of the winding country lane and cross my arms. "Seriously, we're lost."

"We didn't and we're not." Will unfolds his map again and consults the small print. "Look, we took the 57 bus to Upper Higgledown, cut across that field, took the road toward Farleigh Wallop, and now . . ." He stops when I begin to giggle. "What's so funny?"

"Come on." I laugh. " 'Higgledown,' 'Wallop'—who comes up with these names?"

Finally, Will allows himself a grin. "They are rather silly."

"And totally impossible to find," I say, nudging him with my elbow. We're bundled up in totally unfashionable jackets and scarves, but there's nobody except the cows to see us. "If you admit you haven't got a clue where we are, I'll shut up. It won't diminish, like, your masculine prowess, I promise."

"Perhaps . . . I could have taken a wrong turn," he admits as we pass another identical field.

"See? That wasn't so hard." I survey the stretch of trees, grass, and cute cottages around us. When I joked to Emily about search parties, I wasn't expecting it to come true. "I think we should keep heading in the same direction. I mean, we know it's not back there."

"Whatever you say, Natasha." Will makes this dramatic little gesture and hands me the map. "I hereby relinquish all navigational duties."

I laugh, mimicking his tone. "Why thank you, kind sir."

We walk in silence for a while. The weather is finally thawing out now that spring is almost here, and I felt this urge to get out of the city for the day, take a break from all that studying. I even managed to speed through most of my reading for this week, so here we are: strolling through the countryside like we're in one of those BBC America period dramas. I even have my very own chivalrous companion to protect my virtue, except, you know, it's kind of late for that.

"So what is this house we're looking for?" Will asks with a grin. "I'm guessing it's pretty special to get you out on a hike."

"Hey!"

"And you've only complained about not having a car, oh, five times today."

"I wouldn't have to complain if you English people realized cars are basic human necessities. I still can't believe most of the kids at Oxford don't drive."

"There is a little something called the environment," Will teases. "And people who actually want it to last."

"Whatever," I drawl, reaching down to pick a daffodil from the side of the road. "You think a few less SUVs are really going to make a difference? And I thought my math was bad!" Will looks like he's going to fight me on this one, so I change the subject back. "We're looking for Alma Mayall's house. Well, I guess it was her father's—yay, archaic property laws. Anyway," I continue, "she was this pioneering feminist of her time, back in the eighteen hundreds. She wrote all these essays on voting rights and equality, and there are even rumors she had this totally scandalous affair with J. S. Mill."

"Like, omigod!"

I push Will into a hedge. "Chauvinist pig."

"Femi-nazi."

We grin at each other.

"Is that it?" He nods over my shoulder. I spin around.

"Yes!" The cottage is thatched, with whitewashed walls and a little plaque on the gate. It's the cutest thing I've ever seen.

"Then we weren't lost," Will says, smug as hell.

"Oh whatever." I push him again and head for the

front gate. "See? '1824 to 1896, Alma Mayall.'" The front yard is overgrown, flowers dotted around in bunches and a tangle of shrubbery over the door. "Isn't it adorable?" I sigh, clasping my hands together at the total picture-perfectness of it all.

Will just looks at me, loosening his striped scarf. "You're becoming such an Anglophile."

"Says the guy who downloads, like, ten different American TV shows every week." I check my leaflet. "OK, so this place should be open to visitors...." Cautiously, I push the door, half expecting to walk into somebody's actual home. Inside, the hallway is silent and totally deserted, papered with a tiny rose print.

"Gone for lunch," Will reads from a note on the antique-looking desk.

"Cool, we can just wander around. I hate having those guided tours; they're always so dull and—" A side door opens and a woman comes out. She can't be more than forty, but she's dressed in this dowdy flowery blouse and a tweed skirt, with a button on her lapel reading, TOUR GUIDE. She glares at us.

"Umm, sorry." I blush while Will tries to hide his laughter.

The woman keeps looking at us suspiciously, until Will steps forward and shakes her hand.

"Hello there. We've come from Oxford University. We were hoping to take a look around, but, of course, if you're busy ..." His polite thing works like a charm; in an instant, the disapproving expression switches into a smile. I don't blame her.

"Students, of course." She lights up. "It's always nice to see the young people take an interest in Alma's life."

I let out a slow breath of relief.

Will nods along, an angelic look on his face. "Well, she was a pioneering feminist of her time." As he steers the woman down the hallway, he throws me a wink. "Now you must tell me about her relationship with J. S. Mill. . . ."

The house is perfectly preserved, with all Alma's old decor and things, and by the time I'm done looking through her letters (for any hint of that scandalous affair), Will is seriously in need of feeding. Luckily, that tour guide still totally adores him, so she directs us to a nearby pub for lunch.

"Ah, food!" Will bites down hungrily on a wedge of sandwich. "I thought I was going to die of starvation back there."

"And we haven't eaten since, what, that late brunch three hours ago?" I throw a chip—sorry, "crisp"—at him. The pub has tables outside, so we're sitting in the sun by the riverbank. It may not be warm enough to actually take my jacket off, but leaving my gloves behind? Major improvement.

Will doesn't say a thing until his plate is nearly clear. "Did you get enough material for your essay?" he asks, sweeping up the last of his crumbs.

I sip my lemonade. "It wasn't required for class. I just wanted to take a look around."

He looks at me admiringly. "You really are dedicated to your work."

I blush. It's getting harder to resist Will's general cuteness, even though the end of the semester is in sight. I can tell myself "no dating" all I want, but then I'll catch him looking at me with those dark brown eyes and something in me just melts. It's not just the way he looks; it's how he sees me. Like I'm worth something. I hope our friendship can last.

"Are you looking forward to going back to California?" Will says, as if reading my mind. "You must miss your family and friends."

I wait to answer, clearing our things aside and hopping up to sit on the tabletop so I'm looking out at the river. Will moves to sit next to me.

"Yes, and no," I say slowly. "I'm fine without my parents. We're kind of not talking right now," I admit. "And I miss my friends, but all the same . . . I feel like I've changed. I don't know how that will work out when I'm home."

"Changed? How?"

His face is so open and sincere, that right now I'm almost tempted to come clean. I could just tell him everything, hot tub and all. I mean, he's my friend, he cares about me, so maybe he'll understand and—

He takes my hand.

I freeze, just feeling his skin against mine. I can't even look at him for a minute. I'm too busy freaking out. What is wrong with me? I've done this before. Hell, the whole internet knows I've done way more than this before, but here, now, with Will? This *matters*.

"Err, Natasha." He clears his throat, and I finally pull myself together enough to look at him. Oh boy, he's got his puppy-dog look on, the one that reduces stern old women—and me—to marshmallow. "You know your friendship means a lot to me, and I wouldn't want to do anything to affect that. . . ."

I can tell he's rehearsed this, he looks so nervous.

"But you have to know . . ." He pauses, blushing. "I . . . Well, that is to say, we . . ." His words fade out, and then the next thing I know, he lunges forward and kisses me.

Maybe if I was a saint, I would have pulled away right then, but I can't help myself. I've wanted this for so long. I kiss him back. It's soft, and sweet, and nothing like the sweaty make-out sessions I've had back home. He touches my cheek, gently, and I want nothing more than to just fall into it and forget everything . . .

But I can't.

"Will." I pull away, already hating myself. "I don't—"

His eyes widen and he jerks back. "Oh. Sorry, I—"

"You're a really great guy!" I say quickly as he scrambles down from the tabletop and stands there, awkward. "But . . ."

What can I say to him? I've been secretly hoping for this all along, but now it's finally happening, I just can't follow through. How could I even explain: *"But . . . I can't do this without telling you the truth"*? *"But . . .*

*I don't know what you'll say if I come clean"? "But . . .
I'm not brave enough to risk losing what we've got, or
that person you think I am"?*

No, it won't work. I'm not ready to go back to being
Tasha, not yet.

". . . I kind of just got out of something. Back home,"
I say, avoiding his eyes. I swallow, feeling like the biggest coward in the world. "I'm sorry, it's just . . . I'm not
ready."

"Oh," Will says again. "I'm sorry. I shouldn't have—"

"No!" I interrupt. "It's not your fault. I mean, it was
nice, and I wish . . ." I sigh. Boy, do I wish.

"It's all right, Natasha." Will sends me a quiet look.
"Really. You don't have to explain."

"But we can still be friends?" I ask, desperate. "I don't
want to lose you."

"You won't." Will seems to pull himself together,
standing up straight and fixing a thin smile in place.
"We'll be fine."

I look down, wishing I could just take us back in
time.

"Come on, we better make a start back to Oxford."
Will hooks his thumbs in his jacket pockets and nods his
head toward the front gate. I slowly loop my scarf back
around my neck and follow him out of the garden. "And
this time, no complaints about the hike, all right?"

He's looking at me, trying to act normal, so I laugh
along. "No complaining," I agree, my chest feeling hollow inside. "I promise."

. . . .

oh em, i couldn't do it. there he was, totally amazing & sweet & cute and i just couldn't tell him the truth. there's a chance he would understand, but how can i know for sure? guys get weird over this stuff, they just do. i couldn't bear it if he started looking at me different. he says we're fine, but i haven't seen him since the trip and it's been four days now . . .

i guess it's a good thing, right? i mean, we're going home in 3 weeks, and getting involved with him now would just make it harder to go home. and now i can focus everything on my classes and the presentation to the board and oh em, it's such a mess!

xoxox

. . . .

Maybe you need to give him the benefit of the doubt. He sounds like a decent boy, and if you don't trust him, then you'll never find out. Or not. Whichever you think! I'm in no position to give relationship advice—I may be over Sebastian for good now, but that just means I've got all this romantic energy to channel in the wrong direction!

I've got to run, the time slots for the editing suite are like gold dust, and Ryan will kill me if I miss our spot. Don't worry!

xEmx

Emily

After spending three days locked in the editing suite with Ryan, I break. Squinting at a screen all day making minute changes to scene length and order may be the way to earn an amazing mark on our final project, but it's not the route to mental health, happiness, and that sense of carefree California well-being I'm determined to maintain. I insisted on taking Thursday off, to have one whole day of "me time." One blissful, glorious, stress-free—

There's a light tap at the front door. I roll out of bed, pull on my fluffy robe, and cautiously crack it open.

"Ryan?" I step backward, surprised.

"Umm, hey." He takes in my clothing. "I didn't wake you, did I?"

"Oh, no." I pull the robe tighter. "Come in." He slowly edges into the apartment. "Morgan's out," I reassure him, and watch his whole body uncoil.

"Cool." He nods, jamming his hands into the pockets of his dark jeans.

"So . . ." I perch on the edge of the sofa and wait.

"Oh, right." Ryan smiles sheepishly at me. "You weren't answering your cell. I was thinking of heading down to L.A., just taking some time to drive and hang out. Do you want to come along?"

"I thought we were having a little time-out."

"Right, from editing." Ryan slowly frowns. "Did you mean—?"

"No!" I jump up. I'd planned out my whole day, but I need to be more spontaneous. Scheduling my spare time is just another manifestation of those control-freak tendencies I'm trying so hard to shake. "L.A. sounds great. Just give me a minute to get dressed."

"I'll be in the car."

Ryan is horrified to discover I've yet to experience a road trip.

"But you've been here more than two months already. They're like a mandatory national experience!" he exclaims as we speed down the freeway. It's another clear, sunny day, and he's rolled all the windows down, the breeze whipping my hair into a terrible tangle. I don't care. There's something exhilarating about the speed, the movement, the fast song currently blasting from the stereo—as if this is really a part of my life, instead of just a vacation moment.

"I haven't had any reason to go anywhere," I shout as the drum kicks up a notch for the pulsing rock chorus.

"And back in England, well, we just take the train if something's more than a couple of hours away."

Ryan shakes his head. "I guess it's up to me to educate you. Oh wait." Wrenching the wheel violently, he suddenly spins us into another lane. I squeal and grip the seat as we speed down an exit ramp. "Sorry!" he says breathlessly. "But I figured you needed an authentic diner stop as part of your American visit."

"I also need to stay alive!"

"C'mon." Ryan laughs. "You'll forgive me when you taste their cheeseburgers."

He's in a better mood. Whatever weight has been dragging him down these past weeks seems to have lifted.

We only drive another few miles before pulling into a car park in front of an old-style diner, like the ones I've seen on postcards. It's long and low, with a flashing neon sign announcing "Angie's" and peeling paintwork. I hop out of the car.

"Oh, I wish I had my camera. I keep missing all the best things."

"Got it covered." Ryan waves his mobile phone at me and pushes me over to the sign. I stand self-consciously. "You can do better than that!" he urges. I begin to pose, awkwardly at first, but soon I manage to fight my way out of my own head and find myself mugging for the camera— blowing kisses and jumping around.

"I look ridiculous." I giggle, leaning over to see the snaps.

"That's the point." Ryan grins, pushing open the

heavy diner double doors. Immediately, I'm transported into a 1950s tableau, complete with long counter and faded-looking waitress in a pink uniform.

"Wow!" I grin. "It's so . . ."

"Touristy and kitschy," Ryan finishes, leading me to a corner booth upholstered in red leather. "But they do awesome disco fries."

"What are they?" I slide into my seat and look around, enrapt.

"You'll see." Ryan rummages in his battered gray wallet for quarters. "Now, if this is the Americana scene, we need the right soundtrack. . . ." He punches a few numbers on the mini-jukebox next to us, and after a moment, familiar chords begin to play.

" 'Dancing in the Dark.' " I smile slowly. "I love this song."

"The English rose likes Springsteen?" Ryan looks surprised. "Hmm. I didn't see that coming."

"What, it wasn't in your character outline?" I tease, only half kidding, as the waitress comes to take our orders, dark roots showing through her platinum perm. "I'll have one of the famous cheeseburgers. And a chocolate malt whip shake." To hell with healthy.

After Ryan orders, he takes a sugar packet, thwacking it against the edge of the table in time with the song.

"You do that a lot," I note. His restless energy doesn't drive me insane the way it did a month ago, but it's interesting the way he can never simply sit still. "And that scene thing . . ."

"Huh?" Ryan pauses.

I slouch down in the booth, regarding him thoughtfully. The knowledge that I only have two more weeks here makes me feel a little reckless. "Just the way you said we needed a soundtrack. Do you do that too—see things as scenes, like they're on film? I'm not saying it's a bad thing," I add. "I'm just curious."

"What is this, Analyze Ryan Day?" He laughs, but I can see his eyes get hard. I shake my head.

"Relax. It's not as if I'm any better, with my penchant for schedules and order," I joke, trying to relieve the tension. He sits back, making room for the vast plate of chips that is placed between us, smothered in gravy and cheese. "So these are the disco fries," I say lightly. "My sister would be lecturing me about cholesterol by now."

Ryan takes a fry and eats it slowly. "I don't mean to see the world like that. I guess I just get too deep in film, in narrative, you know?" He looks at me for a second before continuing, "Sometimes I feel like I'm trapped in director mode, always looking for the right angle or line, even when it's real life and not a movie."

"Real life is never that simple," I agree. "There's no story arc for one thing or third-act dramatic climax." I scoop up a glob of melting cheese. "And as for resolution . . ." I meet his eyes again. "As if we'd be so lucky."

"Right." He smiles, relieved. "I guess it's my way of trying to get a little control over everything."

"Like me and my timetables." I nod. "The only reason I do it is because there's so much I can't even begin to control. If you just stop and think about how much of your life is totally out of your hands, it's incredible." My voice begins to rise. "I'm not even talking about things like global warming or famine or politics, just normal everyday things. Whether or not your examiner is in a good mood when they mark your paper, or if your application gets filed underneath the person they choose." My eyes are wide. "Ninety percent of your entire existence occurs through luck or accident. Just think about that!"

"Pretty scary," Ryan agrees. He has a slight smirk of amusement on his lips, and I realize I must have got carried away.

"Sorry," I say, deflating a little. "But I get it: wanting to be the one in charge of the scene."

He shrugs. "But it doesn't work that way, right? You can't write everyone's part for them."

He looks sad for a moment, and I remember what Lexi and Morgan said in the salon. "We can do it today," I suggest with a smile. "Pick the soundtrack, stage the scenes. Cut from the car park to the diner interior to . . ."

"Santa Monica boardwalk," Ryan finishes for me. He nods slowly. " 'Emily's Big Adventure.' "

"You make me sound like an animated pig."

"Don't complain, or I'll make it so you don't get home," he warns me with a dark grin.

"And then who would do last-minute rewrites? Face it, you need me."

We spend the rest of the day creating that perfect fun montage you find halfway through every romantic-comedy film.

Tourist photographs at the Walk of Fame; people-watching on Sunset Boulevard; arcade games and candy floss on the boardwalk. Ryan even insists we rent Rollerblades, for that quintessential California experience, and although I can tell he's still watching us through that director's filter in his mind, I'm having so much fun that I don't really care.

"So this is what life is really like for you people." I take tiny gliding steps forward, arms outstretched to keep my balance. I'm covered in an array of crash pads, but I still don't feel particularly stable as we edge down the wide pedestrian path. "Sun and sand, all day every day."

Ryan gives me one of his twisted half-grins, skating circles around me with irritating ease. He's filming me on his digital camera, and I dread to think what I look like. "Not exactly. It's the same living here as anywhere else. Except with better scenery."

"That's not true." I gingerly pick up speed. The boardwalk traffic is thinning as the evening breeze begins to cool, and I feel a rush in my blood that has nothing to do with the skating. "People are so laid-back here—it's like you have Prozac in the water system!"

"You're not doing too bad." He pushes me carefully out of the way as another girl hurtles past—as trussed up in protective clothing as I am but clearly out of control. I feel marginally better about my own Rollerblading prowess. "You haven't checked the time all afternoon."

"Yay me!" I mimic the California-girl squeal.

He laughs. "Don't go changing too much; they won't recognize you when you get home!"

I miss my footing and begin to fall.

"Whoa!" Ryan grabs my elbow and drags me upright. I cling to him for a minute, trying to get my balance back. "You OK?"

I nod, suddenly breathless. I'm not sure if it's Ryan's body pressed against mine or the sudden thought of home, but I feel a sharp clutch beneath my rib cage. "I'm . . . I'm fine." I straighten my legs, he releases me slowly, and we skate on.

The sense of giddy sickness lasts through an old John Hughes screening and the drive back to Santa Barbara. I curl up, sleepy in the passenger seat, while Ryan hums along with the sweet chimes of an indie-rock song on the stereo. My body is tired but relaxed, with a potent soft buzz of endorphins.

"You've gone quiet."

I look up to find we're back at the apartment, waiting in the dark car park. "Oh, sorry. I was just thinking about . . . home," I lie. "I can't believe I'll be going back soon."

"Just when I was getting used to you."

I ignore the wistful pang in my chest and quickly pull my jacket on. "You'll find someone else to keep you on the shooting schedule. Anyway, thanks for today. I had fun." I open the car door, but he turns off the engine.

"Wait, I'll walk you up. It's late."

"Oh. Thanks."

I fill the space between us with project talk all the way into the lobby and up to my corridor. Edits and pacing are safe ground: details that won't belie anything other than professional interest in his opinion. Still, I swallow nervously as we reach my room. The whole day has been one long facade of a date, even though I know it's not real.

"So, I had fun," I say again, stupidly. Ryan looks as awkward as I feel, shifting from one foot to the other in the empty hallway. I unlock the door and push it open to find an empty flat. Morgan is still out. "Oh, do you want that book I mentioned?"

"Sure."

I flick the lights on and he follows me in. "It's here somewhere. . . ." Browsing the stack on the bookshelf, I find the title — a critical look at comedy conventions. "It's not due back for another week."

"Thanks, I'll make sure to get it to you in time." Ryan takes it and scans the back cover before tucking it under his arm. There's a long pause.

"Back to work tomorrow, then?" I say, and immediately want to kick myself for stating the obvious.

"It won't be more than another two days," Ryan offers. "You must be getting sick of me by now."

"Surprisingly, no." I try to sound lighthearted, but when I glance up, he's looking at me with an expression that's almost unreadable.

Almost.

My heartbeat begins to speed as I look into his eyes. Because I know that look, the type of fierce intensity. It's how Sebastian would stare at me when we came up for air: as if I'm the only other person in the world.

I take a quick breath. In a split second, it's as if I'm

outside myself, racing to make a decision. I know that moments like this pass, and that if I don't act now, it will be over and he'll leave and nothing will happen between us. But if I make a move . . .

I take a step forward. In a fleeting thought, I wonder if perhaps those random party hookups were just practice for this, so that when it really mattered, my body would know what to do, even if my mind was still paralyzed. And then I close the last few inches between us and stop thinking.

His lips are cool and soft, and as I bring my hand up to his face, I can feel the slight scratch of stubble against my palm. For one panic-filled moment I stop, waiting for some reaction, but then he pulls me tightly against him and I melt into the kiss.

We fall backward onto the sofa: hands tangling in hair, legs twisting together, and tongues searching, hard and hot and, god, so delicious. I lose track of time, of everything—my mind shuts down.

Finally, I pull away, gasping for air. I'm lying beneath him, Ryan's body pressing me into the bed with a weight that's strangely satisfying. "Oh, wow," I say before I can stop myself. I blush, but Ryan only laughs, propping himself on one elbow and carefully pushing my hair off my face.

"Yeah, that's about right." He looks down at me with a warmth that goes straight to my stomach. "I didn't know if . . ."

"Nor did I," I agree, still breathless. I lift my face and kiss him again, softly, almost to check that this is real.

It is.

"You didn't say—" The words die on my lips as I hear a rattle of keys outside the door. Ryan and I freeze. "Oh god, Morgan," I gasp, but the footsteps move on and then the hallway is silent again.

I collapse backward, my heart racing in double-quick time. That was far too close. "You've got to go." I begin to pull myself out from under him. "She could come back. We can't . . ."

Ryan sits up slowly and pulls his shirt back on. He glances over to me. "But you're OK with this. . . ."

"Yes!" I lean in and kiss him again, savoring the feel of his skin on mine. "I just don't know how I'm going to tell Morgan." I pause. "Or even if I need to tell her at all." Something tells me I don't want to spend the rest of the time sleeping in a confined space with a girl bent on revenge.

"OK." Ryan gives me a melting grin. "I'll see you tomorrow, in the editing room?"

I nod, shooting another anxious look at the door. "Tomorrow."

I'm in such a hurry to get him out of the building before we're discovered that it's only when I'm alone again with nothing but a handful of ticket stubs and a diner menu to show for our day that I realize just what I've done. I kissed Ryan. Morgan's Ryan.

And I don't regret it at all.

Tasha

The day of the big board meeting finally arrives, and I'm nervous as hell. Even a quick call with Em running through her ten-point public-speaking guide didn't make me feel any better. See, Carrie and Uma decided it would make our case stronger if it looked like we had a "coalition of the willing," whatever that is, so they roped me into presenting a section of our case: talking about all the international schools that offer women's services as a given, and how Oxford doesn't want to look backward or sexist. I get that they want to bring up every possible reason to keep the center open, but I really doubt all the potential foreign students out there will be flipping through their prospectuses thinking, "Harvard, the Sorbonne, Oxford—no wait, they don't have a women's health center. I'll go to MIT instead!"

Either way, I'm part of the team, so that means come noon on Thursday, I'm hanging out in the cold stone hallway outside the meeting room with the rest of our group. I made sure to dress super-smart today, in a crisp blouse and tweedy style of skirt that could be right out of a Hitchcock movie, but that still doesn't stop me from feeling totally out of place. I figured I'd shaken my outsider instinct by now, but something about the importance of the meeting is bringing it all back again.

These girls are depending on me.

"Have we got the backup disc?" Carrie is fussing with our stack of materials. "What about a spare cable, in case the projector plays up?"

"Check and check," DeeDee answers, a small smile on her face, like she's happy to see Carrie getting so worked up. I'm not. I've never seen her anything but casual and confident, and if our fearless leader is having some kind of panic attack, then that so doesn't bode well for the rest of us.

"You've been quiet, Natasha." Louise nudges me. "You're going to be OK with your part?"

"I think so." I'm clutching my notes tightly, hoping my sweaty palms won't smudge the writing.

"You know, you look rather pale." She studies me. "Don't you think, Uma?"

"I'm OK," I protest, but now the rest of the group is staring. "Well, maybe I'm kind of nervous," I admit. "I'm not great with public speaking. Being the center of attention and all."

It's crazy. I'm happy dancing on tables and parading

around in my panties for charity runway shows, but put me in front of a panel of stern professors, and I'm reduced to jelly.

"You'll be amazing." Louise gives me a supportive hug. "Don't worry." I nod slowly, just as an older woman sticks her head out the door and beckons to us.

"We're ready to begin now."

"All right." To my relief, Carrie gets her game face on: totally focused and in control. "Let's go. Remember, the women of Oxford are relying on us."

Way to pile the pressure on.

We file into the long room and take a row of seats near the front. There's a long table facing us at the head of the room, which I guess is for the board members to rule over us from, but to my surprise, the rest of the room is quickly filling up too—students and adults packing the rows of folding chairs and looking expectantly at the front.

At where I'm going to be standing.

Oh boy.

"I didn't realize there'd be so many people," I tell Carrie in a hushed voice.

"Great, isn't it? And the *Oxford Student* is coming out this afternoon with a big article too." She's beaming. "I talked to one of their reporters earlier in the week, and he seemed really interested in the issues. Maybe that will help sway them."

"Uh-huh," I murmur, running through my notes again. It's only a tiny part of our presentation, but I don't want to be the one to screw up, not when so much is riding on this. I may be flying back to my private health insurance in a couple of weeks, but I still remember Holly weeping in that bathroom stall and what could have happened if the center hadn't been there.

"Oh, here we go." Carrie falls silent as that stern woman from the hallway takes her seat with the others at the long table and bangs her gavel. As she runs through a welcome and agenda, I take a quick glance at the panel who'll be deciding our fates. It doesn't look good. The guys are old, white, and serious, with that kind of pink-cheeked paunch that comes from drinking too much port. Out of the eight of them, only three are women, and they're the pinched librarian kinds who are wearing baggy cardigans and seem to have an average age of, like, sixty. I can't imagine the last time they ever needed contraception.

We're so doomed.

"Ready for battle?" Professor Elliot leans over from the seat behind me. I turn, surprised to see her—and a bunch of Raleigh kids packing the room. Holly gives me a thumbs-up sign, and I think I see Will sitting in a place by the back.

Now I'm *really* nervous.

"Absolutely!" Carrie answers. And then Stern Librarian Lady No. 1 must have said something, because Uma and Louise get up and I have no choice but to follow them all to the front of the room.

"Thank you for giving us the opportunity to talk to you today." With a respectful nod at the board, Carrie begins. "We feel that an issue as vital as women's service provision must be debated in more detail before any cuts in funding are made. . . ."

As she launches into her opening remarks, I force myself to look up from the floor. Bad idea. There are only about fifty people in the room, max, but it seems way more when they're all staring in my direction. Right now I'm kind of hidden behind a group that has great distracting props like charts and PowerPoint presentations, but soon they'll all be looking at me.

Just me.

I kind of blank out the next part of the meeting, trying not to panic, until I snap back into the room and find that Uma and Louise have said their parts. They've read the personal testimonies, shown the running cost breakdowns, and thrown a bunch of statistics about emergency contraception and sexual assault at them. That means there's only me left.

". . . so next, we'll hear an international perspective. Natasha?" Carrie gently pushes me to the front.

I take a deep breath and ignore the crowd. "Oxford has a reputation as being a world-class college," I begin, trying not to let my notes shake in my hand. "But it's also seen as being stuck in the past. By ignoring women's rights and health issues in this way, the university risks appearing archaic and"—I hear a rustle and then a low whisper from the audience—"alienating a more diverse student intake."

There's another sound from the crowd, almost like laughter. I keep talking, but carefully reach down and make a slow sweep of the front of my body, making sure my shirt is buttoned and the skirt hasn't bunched up around my thighs. I saw the original *Parent Trap* once, and I swear, ever since I've been terrified of standing up and finding the back of my dress missing.

Nope, everything's where it should be.

"So the women's center is more than a health issue." I can feel myself speeding up, rushing to be done. The whispers have turned into low murmurs, spreading across the room. I turn to Carrie, but she just shrugs and motions for me to keep talking. I swallow. "It could also be seen as a PR issue too, making sure Oxford can be associated with modern, forward-thinking campuses around the world."

"Can we have some order?" one of the board members interrupts. There's an outbreak of giggles, quickly covered with super-fake-sounding coughs. I don't understand what's happening, but the sooner I'm done, the sooner I can get the hell out of this room and away from these people. I finish the speech on autopilot, blushing and stumbling over my words as my mind races to figure it out. The way they're whispering and laughing takes me right back to when the video broke, when I couldn't even walk into a room without feeling people's eyes on me, judging me and—

No.

Suddenly I can't breathe. I force the final sentence out, scanning the room for some sign that I'm crazy, that I'm paranoid. Any sign at all. But then I spot two girls in the front row staring at me, wide-eyed with that lip-curling mean look that can only mean one thing: major gossip.

And then I know.

"What's happening?" Carrie hisses at me. I shrug blankly.

One of the librarian ladies bangs the gavel again. "We'll take a short break now. I hope that this disruption won't be repeated when we resume." She glares over her glasses.

"Come on." Carrie drags me down the aisle and out into the hallway, the rest of the group following close behind.

"What the hell's happening?" Mary exclaims, closing the door behind us.

"I don't know." DeeDee shakes her head. "It was all going so well, and then Natasha started her speech and . . ." She turns to grill me. "Do you know anything?"

I shrug. My insides are tangled in a terrible knot, squeezing everything so tightly I can't breathe.

"Go find out what's happening." Uma sends Louise back into the room. I sink back slowly against the wall. It's cold, but I'm already numb, so I guess it doesn't matter. I guess nothing I do matters anymore.

"Now you're really pale." Carrie looks at me carefully. "Don't worry, it's not your fault—whatever's going on. You did fine."

We wait there, the fluorescent light strip flickering above us. To me, it's like waiting for my execution. Melodramatic, I know, but it's kind of true. Soon Natasha will be dead, and I'll be Tasha again. Drunk, slutty Tasha who can't keep her pants on. Maybe I was dumb to think

I could get past her with nothing but a change of clothes and a few thousand miles, but I thought it had worked. I thought I was done with her.

And then Louise comes back out, Professor Elliot fast on her heels. Their faces are full of disbelief.

"Natasha?" Louise looks at me in confusion. She holds out a newspaper, the *Oxford Student* logo clear on the front. I take it, because there's nothing I can do to make this go away.

"Tasha?" she repeats, and I wince at the name, sick. I haven't been Tasha for months.

"What is it?" Carrie takes the newspaper from me and unfolds it, and everything stops.

WOMEN'S CAMPAIGN UNDERMINED BY CELEBRITY SCANDAL, the headline reads. And underneath, the photograph I know by heart: my bare top to the (hidden) camera as I straddle Tyler in the hot tub, so clear you can see that harmony tattoo on my hip.

It's over.

Emily

I lie awake most of the night, analyzing our kisses from every possible angle. I can still feel Ryan's hands on my body and his mouth on mine, my veins sparkling with a fierce heat I've never known before.

And I know for certain that Sebastian was wrong.

I don't have a problem with intimacy or issues with physical commitment. I'd thought that everything he said was true, but in the end, it was only true with *him*. Hours ago, I'd been tangled up in Ryan's body wanting more, not caring about rules or limits or lines that could be crossed. I'd been free, my internal monologue finally quiet. For the first time in my life, there had been nothing but me in my body, feeling every touch without that constant filter of disconnection.

I lie still between my sheets and feel a slow smile spread across my face. The dull fear I've been carrying in the back of my mind for months slips away with every exhaled breath. Sebastian was wrong—I keep repeating it to myself. I'm not doomed to a life trapped inside my own mind. I can feel and act without thinking. I can just be.

I drift back and forth between sleep for a few more hours until my mobile begins to vibrate violently on my nightstand. I pick up, wondering for a moment whether it could be him, but I can't decipher a single word on the other end of the line.

"Hello?" I kick off my covers and stretch. "Who is this?" There's nothing but a muffled snuffling sound, and then I hear a voice.

"Em?"

I pause. "Natasha? Is that you?"

There's a sob, and then, "They hate me. They all hate me!"

"Shhh, it's all right. Just calm down and tell me what's wrong." I sit cross-legged on the bed in my plaid pajamas and try to make sense of her tear-soaked voice. "Natasha? It'll be OK. What happened?"

"It's over," she says, with such resignation in her voice I know that something is terribly wrong. "They know."

"About . . . ? Oh god!" I gasp.

"The *Oxford Student* ran an exposé," Natasha continues, "right before the board meeting. Everyone says I've ruined the campaign!"

"That's not true!" I protest hopefully. "I'm sure it won't make any difference."

"But it has! They all totally despise me now. God, Em,

you should have seen them. Carrie wouldn't even look me in the eye, and Professor Elliot..." Natasha begins to cry again.

I wait, picking at the bedspread until her tears seem to have subsided. I know how much her escape meant to her, how important it was to start fresh where nobody knew about the scandal. And now...

"If it makes you feel any better, I'm completely screwed too," I offer in a whisper. "I kissed Ryan last night."

"You and Ryan?" Natasha's voice lifts a little. "You mean...? No way!"

"I know." I sigh. In the early dawn light of the morning after, my moment of reckless abandon is edged with fresh guilt. "I'm a terrible person."

"That makes two of us."

"No!" I insist firmly. "You've done nothing wrong."

"Not according to Uma. She says now the board can just write off the center as something just for irresponsible sluts."

"She said that to you?" I blink. "Natasha, that's awful."

"That was only the start of it, Em. They were all going on about, like, reinforcing gender stereotypes and setting back the women's movement. You'd think I repealed *Roe versus Wade*!" She tries to laugh, but her voice is still hollow.

"Well, they're just narrow-minded, self-righteous bitches!" I say fiercely. I never had a problem with Carrie and her crusades before, but listening to Natasha sound so alone is heartbreaking. "Don't pay attention to a word they say."

"I wish I could, but . . ." Natasha wavers. "What if they're right? What if I have wrecked the campaign? All that work and—people need that center."

"The board won't pay attention to stupid gossip, trust me."

"But what am I supposed to do? The group, they were my friends, but now . . ." Another sniffle. "They never want to speak to me again."

"Then that's their loss." I hug my toes to keep them warm and try to think of something, anything, to make her feel better. "You're worth ten Carries, hot tub or no hot tub."

"You don't have to say that."

"I know, but it's true. Look at what you've managed to achieve—you went to Oxford! You've been getting firsts in your essays; you contributed to a great campaign." I try to make my enthusiasm cross the continent between us. "You're the bravest person I know, Natasha. All I've had to do is dye my hair and turn up late a few times, and even then I managed to mess up."

"Don't you start." She sniffles, a slight smile to her voice. "Or we'll both be a wreck."

"Score one more for team Global Exchange."

"So come on, tell me what happened with Ryan." I hear the sound of movement, as if Natasha is shifting around in her room. "Morgan sure won't be happy."

"Which is why I'm not going to tell her," I say in a hushed voice, ever mindful of the short hallway separating our rooms. "Can you imagine? I think she'd cut off my hair in my sleep or something."

"Good move," Natasha agrees. "She swears she switched some girl's conditioner for hair removal cream when she hooked up with her boyfriend."

"I better buy new products," I mutter darkly.

Natasha laughs. "So you'll keep it on the down-low for the rest of the time? There's only another two weeks left, thank god."

"Two weeks," I echo slowly. It's crept up on me so gradually, I've hardly seen it coming.

"And? Ryan? I need details to distract me from my misery, remember."

I snuggle deeper under the cover, happy to change the subject. "There's nothing much to tell," I begin, a little coy. I'm not used to girl confessionals. Or, in fact, having anything to confess. "We were kissing—finally—and then I realized that Morgan could walk in at any moment. I haven't heard from him yet, but we're supposed to be working on the edits all day."

"He'll call," Natasha says with a confidence I wish I shared.

"You don't know that." Part of me hopes he will, but the other side knows it'll just make things more complicated.

"Sure I do. I'm surprised he took so long to make a move, but now that he has, he'll totally follow through. He's one of the good ones."

"Wait, you saw this coming?"

"Well, duh!" She laughs. "Honestly, Em, I could tell

from the way you got so mad at him that something was going to happen."

I blink, wondering how it could be so obvious to her when it caught me utterly by surprise. "Thanks for letting me know."

"You guys had to do your own thing."

"You mean like you and Will?" I draw out his name. She sighs.

"I haven't heard from him tonight. I saw him at the meeting, but by the time the group was done yelling at me, he was gone." Her voice gets quieter. "Do you think he'll hate me too?"

I let out a long breath. "I hope not."

There's silence.

"You know the funny thing?" I muse, leaning my head back against the wall. "I thought I'd feel worse than this. I know she's supposed to be my friend, and I do feel guilty about everything, but, well . . . I sort of think it was worth it."

"I can tell from your voice. Don't I get any details?"

I can't stop the grin that spreads across my face just thinking about Ryan and his arms and his mouth . . .

"No." I pull myself together. "Sorry, but I don't kiss and tell."

"That means it was hot. You would have so told me details if it wasn't hot."

"Maybe . . ." I feel myself blush.

"Ha, that's awesome, Em." Natasha sounds genuinely pleased for me.

"It's not! I stole Morgan's boy."

"You didn't steal him," Natasha reminds me. "And Morgan is . . . Well, if she didn't care enough to keep him, you shouldn't beat yourself up, OK?"

I pause. "I thought she was your friend."

Natasha sighs. "She was, back then, but . . . I don't know. I feel like I don't know her at all. Or she doesn't know me, or something. Anyway, you have nothing to be sorry about."

"And you need to take your own advice," I add. "They're not right, Tash. You don't deserve any of what they're saying."

There's another pause. "I'm sorry," she says softly, "for dumping all this on you. I didn't know who else to call."

"It's fine, honest. You know you can call anytime."

She sniffs. "You're the only one who understands what I'm going through, trying to be somebody else."

"Trying to be a different part of yourself," I correct, but she doesn't seem to hear me.

"I have to go now. I have work I've got to do for tomorrow's class. Oh god," she says. "Professor Elliot. She was there; you should have seen the way she looked at me!"

"Shhh, it'll be OK."

"Yeah, well . . ." Natasha swallows. "I guess it's only two more weeks, right?"

"Right." I bite my lip. "Two more weeks and then we're home."

I let myself back into the room with that thought still heavy in my mind. Just two more weeks, and then it's back to reality—to study schedules and dense philosophical arguments, to my parents, to the old Emily Lewis. Only two more weeks. It should be a comfort, but now I'm really not so sure.

I arrive late after selecting the perfect outfit of effortless chic, and by the time I reach the editing suite, my stomach is fluttering with nerves. All morning I've been running through scenarios in my mind: what if he regrets it or never wants to speak to me again . . . ?

I gather my strength and finally edge into the room. Ryan leaps up, his polo shirt a flash of maroon against dark baggy cords.

"Em, hi." There's an awkward pause, and I attempt to smile.

"Ryan. Hey." I swallow. The room suddenly feels far smaller than it was yesterday. Barely six feet across and stacked with audiovisual equipment, there's absolutely no possibility of avoiding his cloudy eyes. Or not touching.

"Hi," he says again, and when I turn back from closing the door, he's only inches away. Softly, he reaches out and cups my cheek. I don't move, my heart suddenly racing. And then he leans in and kisses me, slow and gentle and everything I'd spent the night reliving.

I relax a little into his arms, and we stay that way for a glorious moment: close but barely moving, his lips light on mine.

"So we're OK?" he asks, breath warm in my ear. I shiver slightly.

"We're OK," I echo, practically glowing. So much more than OK.

"'Cause we've got a ton of work to do." Drawing away with a grin, Ryan scoots a chair in close to the screen and moves a pile books off the other for me. "This has to be perfect for Friday."

"How about we just settle for brilliant?" I perch next to him, close enough for our thighs to touch. I can't believe it, but I'm hyperaware of his body, even through layers of cords and my skirt.

"I could live with that." He reaches for a laminated sheet. "Now, according to your schedule, we need to finish act two today."

"You're using that?" I ask, surprised. I haven't seen my planner in weeks—since I decided it was far more stress to try to keep to the plan than just give up and let him work at his own pace.

"Of course." He grins. "It's got everything worked out. And color coded. And spill resistant." I blush. "No, it's great! I'm usually a mess by now, but you've really kept me on track."

"Well, thank you. I'm glad my control-freakery is good for something."

"You're not a control freak." Ryan's eyes are soft and sincere. I look away. "No, listen to me, you're not. So, you like to plan." He shrugs. "It's just part of who you are. And it's great for some things: producing, editing, writing scripts. You talk like it's such a bad thing, and maybe you take it too far sometimes, but you shouldn't try and ditch it altogether."

I nod slowly. "It's just a slippery slope, you know? One minute I'm working out my study schedule, and the next I have everything planned—right down to bathroom breaks and sleeping. I find it hard to just let go."

"You don't say," Ryan kids. He strokes my hair and leans in to drop a quick kiss on my forehead. "We'll get you to that happy medium, don't worry."

"In fourteen days?" I ask, reminded yet again how close I am to the end.

"No problem."

Tasha

The day the video broke online, I was more embarrassed than anything. I mean, celebrity sex tapes always seemed kind of tacky, and there I was starring in my very own Parental Advisory show. But Morgan insisted we go celebrate my claim to fame, and by the time she and Lexi had dragged me to every bar on State Street, I figured she had the right idea. Hell, Tyler was a legit Hollywood hottie, my body looked awesome, and most of the action was hidden under the foam. What was the problem? In a few days, nobody would care less what some random college chick did. I know girls with way more scandalous pics lingering on their exes' hard drives.

And then I woke up the next day to find Shannon had a breakdown on *Good Morning America*. One minute she's pimping the DVD box set of *5th Avenue* and her plans to launch a pop career; the next she's weeping into a handy Kleenex. And I don't mean a real face-screwed-up, nose-dripping crying jag; nope, this was a single precious tear gleaming under the studio lights.

"What I don't understand," she says in her soft Southern drawl, sniffling, "is how a girl could set out to seduce him like that." Pressing a perfectly manicured hand to her chest, she gazes forlornly into the main camera. "Where I come from, there's something called sisterhood."

Cue outraged nod from the host. Cue supportive applause. Cue *US Weekly* cover.

And just like that, I was the enemy.

Slinking into Professor Elliot's study for class the next morning, it's as if I'm back at square one. See, usually the most exciting thing that happens around here is student government corruption or, like, a Nobel Prize; give them a sex scandal by a "crazy feminist protestor" and it's front-page news for sure. That *Oxford Student* article read more like something from the *National Enquirer,* so it's no surprise that Carrie is glaring at me with death-ray eyes, Edwin has that look like he's picturing me naked, and Elliot is wearing this expression of total disdain.

"You're late," Elliot remarks coolly. She jerks her head at the free corner of the couch and picks up her conversation with the other two. I swallow and edge past Carrie, who doesn't make room or even move her books. Slowly, I shift the stack onto a side table and sit down, already full of nervous dread. I figured they would have cooled down by now.

I was so wrong.

"We were just talking about political principles and integrity." Carrie turns to me with a mean smile. "What do you think?"

"I . . . umm." I look down, flushing.

"Because I think that hypocrisy is the worst thing of all. In politicians, I mean. It shows weak character and duplicity. Don't you think so, Susanne?"

I swallow again, shooting a desperate look at Professor Elliot in the hope she'll shut Carrie down and just get on with the class, but instead she nods.

"I agree. And what you have to take into consideration is that these people represent their groups. Their actions can taint whole movements." Her eyes flick over me.

"Right." Carrie's lips are thin. "I don't know how they live with themselves."

I sit, numb, already shrinking into myself. I used to have defenses against this kind of thing: after a couple of weeks of taking crap back in California, I toughened up. I ignored them. But now I've gone soft. Their words cut me, just the way they want them to, and it's all I can do not to cry. Again.

"Why don't you read for us, Natasha?" Elliot says, in a voice that makes it clear that's not a suggestion.

I pull out my pages and try to clear my throat. My essay sucks, I know it does. Nothing Em said on the phone could make me feel any better, so what made perfect sense in the week became these confused, rambling paragraphs. It wasn't my turn to read, so I figured I'd get away with it. I guess I should have known I can't get away with anything.

"You did complete the assigned work, didn't you?"

"Yeah . . . yes." I swallow again, trying to keep it together. Fixing my eyes on my paper, I begin to read. I struggle to block everything out, but the words stick in my mouth and I stumble over the sentences, making it sound even worse than it is.

"You know, some of us actually put work into this topic," Carrie says when I'm done, her voice bitchy. "You shouldn't get to take advantage of that. I mean, where do you start with an argument like that?" She snorts, her face suddenly thin and mean like I've never seen it before. "It would be a complete waste of time to even bother."

"Now, now, Carrie," Elliot stops her. "Let's remember that Natasha hasn't been with us very long." She pauses. "The Oxford way of doing things sometimes just isn't . . . suitable for everyone. No need to be so hard on her."

It's seems like she's defending me, but I know better. Elliot has gone back to that "lost cause" thing she was pulling on me at the start of the semester—like I'm not even worth treating as an equal anymore.

Like I'm less than them.

I spend the rest of the hour slowly dying inside. It's not just that they hate me; it's that I finally thought I'd made a new life for myself—a whole new identity. This time around, Natasha Collins was someone people liked, even respected. But now I know the truth, that I can never get past what happened. It doesn't matter how far I go or how hard I try, I'm stuck with it. As long as Tyler and Shannon are out pimping themselves to every celebrity tabloid in town, I'm screwed.

Streaming video lasts forever.

I grab my bag and head for the door as soon as class finishes, but I'm still not fast enough to lose Carrie.

"I want to talk to you." Her chunky boots echo after me in the narrow stone cloisters. I keep walking. "I said—" She catches up with me, grabbing my arm and pulling me around to face her.

"Don't." I hate it but my voice breaks on that single word. I can't hold it together much longer.

Carrie stares back, unflinching. "I hope you realize what you've done. The board should have backed us up right away, but instead they're taking some time to think about it." She snorts. "What am I saying? It's not as if you even care."

"I care," I say quietly. "I do, I—"

"Yeah right," Carrie drawls, mocking me. "As if someone like you could ever understand. You're too busy fucking any boy who shoves a drink in your direction to even think about somebody else."

And with a final glare, she stalks away.

I spend the rest of the day holed up in my room, splitting my time between triple-chocolate chunk cookies, vintage *Gilmore Girls* downloads, and crying. I can't bear feeling this way again, but the only thing I've got on my side this time around is time: just fourteen days left now until I can get the hell out of here. I never figured I'd think of

California as a blessing, but being old news back home totally beats being the scandal of the week here. In California I'm just a stupid slut; here I'm a betrayal of the feminist cause.

It's ten thirty and I'm thinking about rolling into bed when there's a soft knock at my door. I stay slumped on a heap of cushions on the floor and wait for them to leave.

"Natasha?" I hear Holly's voice. "Natasha, are you there?"

With a sigh, I pull myself up and open the door a couple of inches. "Hey," I say listlessly. She's dressed up to go out, in cute pumps and a fitted magenta top over jeans. I avoid eye contact. "What's up?"

"We had plans, remember?" Holly's staring at me expectantly. I blink.

"But . . ." I can't believe she acting like nothing's changed.

"But nothing." Her tone is gentle but firm, and before I can stop her, she's pushed past me into the room. "I've been looking forward to this all week. You're coming, no questions."

"No way." I cross my arms. "You can't seriously expect me to go out."

She begins to riffle through my wardrobe. "I'm not letting you wallow in here alone. Have you even left the room today?"

"Yes." I pout. "I went to my tute, and it was just . . . I can't."

"Even more reason to have some fun." Holly pulls out my favorite blue dress and tosses it to me. "You've got ten minutes, and then I don't care if you're still in that tracksuit."

I sigh. "Holly." She looks at me. "It's cool you're doing this, really. But . . ." I give a weak shrug, already feeling tears well up again. "I don't know if I can face them."

She's at my side right away, pulling me into a hug. "Of course you can," she reassures me, her small frame solid, holding me up. "And if it's awful, then we'll leave, all right? But you have to try. You can't let them win."

"But I'll be out of here soon." I sniffle, feeling super-pathetic. "Why should I even bother?"

"Because I won't let you stay like this." Holly's eyes are usually sweet, but right now they've got steel in them. "You made me face what was happening to me; now it's my turn to do the same for you."

"You totally won't leave me in peace, will you?" I realize, already reaching to switch on my flat iron. Holly gives me an impish grin.

"Not at all."

The club is a short walk from Raleigh, set up over two floors with a tiny bar upstairs and a dark cavern of a dance floor down below. I feel eyes on me as soon as we walk in, but Holly just takes my hand and drags me through the crowd to a free spot by the bar.

"There," she announces. "Not so bad, don't you think?"

I don't answer, slowly taking off my coat and scarf. I wonder how long I can go before making my escape. Fifteen minutes? Ten, maybe? Holly spots some girls from her crew team, and I wind up standing silent while they babble about practice and race times. She keeps turning to check that I'm OK, her face all sympathetic and concerned, so I just fake a smile and nod along. It's not her fault I can't be saved.

We've been there maybe half an hour when I see a familiar floppy hairstyle looming above the crowd. My heart catches. Will. He winds through the crowd after a couple of other kids in my direction, and I feel like collapsing with relief. He came, like we planned. Even though he must have seen the newspaper, he still came.

"Hey!" I cry out, beaming. He pauses, seeing me for the first time, and then his face twists. He looks away. "Will?" I say, already feeling a sharp pain punch through my chest, but he just lowers his head and keeps moving, passing me and quickly loping down the stairs. I sag against the bar stool, trying to remember how to breathe.

No, not him.

And then my body is moving like I don't get a say, following him down the stairs and around into the unisex bathrooms. The tiles are dark with strips of mirror, and I wait by the sinks for him to emerge, shaking with nerves. Maybe he didn't see me. Maybe he just really needed the bathroom. I gulp.

There's a flush, and then he comes out of a stall right in front of me. He looks up and flinches.

"Will?" My teeth are clenched tight to stop me from crying. He steps around me and begins to rinse his hands. "What's going on?"

"You tell me." His voice is quiet, and he's still not looking at me.

I swallow. "You haven't called me back."

"No." Now he's taking a paper towel and carefully drying each hand like it's some kind of ritual.

"So what's . . . ?" I choke. "Why are you being like this?" The door swings open and a blast of music follows a couple of girls in. I ignore them. "Will, talk to me."

"What is there to say?" Everything about him is shut off: blank stare, hard jaw. And then he softens, just for a moment. "Unless it's not true. It isn't, right, Natasha? It's somebody else. They got it wrong."

He's looking at me hopefully, brown eyes wide. But I can't lie to him.

"What happened, with the newspaper and Tyler . . ." I try to explain. "It was a long time ago, and I didn't say anything because I didn't want you to think . . ."

But Will's face has shut down again, and I can see the hurt, so clear.

"Think what, Tasha, that you were some kind of fame-hungry whore?"

I freeze.

"Or maybe you didn't want me to know you were leading me on, just using me."

"This wasn't about you!" I cry, but he won't listen.

"God, when I think what a fool I've been . . ."

"Please, Will—"

"You must think I'm so pathetic not to even date me." His eyes are like ice. "I mean, you're happy to fuck anyone else who comes around!"

253

I gasp. This isn't Will—this is some kind of stranger. I don't know this guy.

He goes to leave, but then turns back for a moment, and when he speaks, every word is dripping with contempt. "You know, I'm glad we never got together. Who knows what I would have caught?"

I stumble back against the wall as he disappears out into the club. I can't move. I can barely even breathe. My reflection is just a daze of skin and hair and teeth, and, god, I can still hear that last shot.

Who knows what I would have caught.

I lurch into a free cubicle and fall onto my knees, but there's nothing but dry heaves. I'm shivering, alone, and nothing matters because this is how it's always going to be. Every guy, every time.

It hurts too much to stay there thinking, so I stumble out and back up to the bar. A cute boy with stubble appears to take my order like he can read my mind, and within ten seconds I have a vodka in front of me. And another. The burn makes me shudder after so long, but then it brings a numbness down my body and I know I'm on the right track. Screw my pledge, screw changing, screw Will. I may as well enjoy what they think I already am.

I find Holly on the tiny dance floor with the crew girls and quickly get into the beat. All I care about is escaping the sharp pain lodged inside my chest, but the drinks and the heavy bass aren't working. I can still feel it. I can still hear Will's voice. I dance harder, throwing my body around as if I'm just a few steps away from numb oblivion, but still I know deep down it won't work.

Then I feel a touch against my arm. I turn, half hoping it's Will, come back to apologize and make things right, but it's only a blond boy, hair ruffled in the way they do here; dark shirt; jeans. I swallow back my disappointment and turn away, but he's dancing closer, moving his body to try and match my beat. I let him. He's looking at me with interest, attraction, and maybe if I focus on that, I'll forget the way Will's eyes were so cold.

His arms reach around my waist, and now I'm pressed against him, my dance moves grinding my hips into him. His body is hot, and I wonder if it could melt away this ice. Face against my cheek, lips breathing by my neck. I feel myself responding without a thought.

It's been so long since I've been touched like this.

When he tugs me off the dance floor, I don't resist. I'm dizzy but still sober enough to follow him into the dark corner, through a door. My back is pressed up against a wall, and his lips are on mine before I realize I'm back in the bathroom, just inches away from where Will destroyed me.

I close my eyes. Hands on my waist, my hips, my ass. He's pressing into me, hard, inching my skirt up with one hand on my bare thigh, the other pawing at my chest.

I don't feel a thing.

Bending his head, he begins to kiss and lick at my neck. I stay, motionless, blinking back the tears in my eyes. I catch sight of us in the mirrors: dirty graffiti, dim lights, and my own blank face. It's empty, hopeless.

And then I snap.

"No." I push him back. He reels, surprised, but comes

right back in, hands on me again. "I said no!" I shove at him, harder, and wrench myself away.

"What the fuck?" He narrows his eyes, breathing heavy.

"I'm done," I tell him, a weird calm settling over me. This won't make anything go away. I'll just hate myself in the morning.

"Don't tease." He crinkles his eyes up in what I'm guessing he figures is a smile, reaching out to stroke my cheek. I slap his hand away. His eyes darken. "Come on, stop playing. I know you're up for it."

"Changed my mind," I say coolly, making to push past him, but the boy grabs my arm.

"No way, you're that girl, the one from the video." He's still trying to be charming. "You were hot."

"Thanks," I say, but he doesn't get the sarcasm.

"So, how about it—wanna make a sequel?"

And that's when I get it, taking in his drunk eyes and slurred voice. Tyler was different from this; I actually wanted to be with him, for *him*. He was cute and charming and kissed like a dream, and maybe he wasn't worth the cost I'm doomed to keep paying, but at least I hooked up with him out of real desire and not this angry ache to make the world go away.

So I go.

"Bitch."

I've already turned to go when he swears, and I don't bother with a reply, striding out of that place with way more dignity than I had going in. I find Holly and let her know I'm leaving early, grab my coat, and head back to

Raleigh. It's damp and windy on the dark street, but I don't feel the cold. Something major just happened, and I need to think it through.

I'm worth more than this.

The boy, the drinks, the way I just gave up and figured I should be the girl they think I am — it's all beneath me, and I don't think I got it until now. With cold splatters of rain spiking my face, I finally figure it out. Fooling around with Tyler wasn't wrong or bad, no matter what everyone tries to make me feel, but if I let their dumb preconceptions rule my life, then I'm acting like they're right.

It won't ever go away, but I can get past it. I am past it. Sure, there are people like Carrie who can't deal with the fact I wanted to be there — to make out with a guy I wanted, to fool around because it felt damn good, not because I'm brainwashed or damaged — but that's their problem, not my fault. Will still cuts me and it hurts, but now the pain is dulled with disappointment because I know that the guy I thought was so great is just weak. Holly stood by me, Emily propped me up even though the girl's never met me, but the one person I figured knew me better than anyone now couldn't take it. He bailed.

I'm stronger than them. It's a crazy thought after spending the past twenty-four hours on the constant verge of a breakdown, but as I cross into the Raleigh quad, I know in my bones it's true. Will can't handle the idea that I have a past, Carrie can't deal with me not fitting her vision of a "real" feminist, but I'm the one who's kept going. Emily was right: I'm braver than I ever knew. I came to Oxford, I made people see me differently, I scored top marks on my essays, for god's sake, and they can't take that away from me no matter what mean things they say.

I let out a slow breath, pausing a moment to take in the old stone buildings and soft golden lights spilling out over the grass. I'm strong enough to take this.

And just like that, it hurts a little less.

Emily

By the end of the week, I'm overwhelmed with emotion: excitement over Ryan, nervous anticipation for our big screening, growing unease about my return home, and a final layer of guilt about hiding the truth from Morgan. In short, I'm a mess.

"What do I do?" I appeal to Carla for the hundredth time this week. "Surely I have to say something?"

"Why bother?" Casting a critical eye over my now-uniform denim skirt/polo shirt combination, she pulls a black dress from her wardrobe and passes it to me. "It's your premiere night—go sexy for once."

I take it without complaint and turn, quickly stripping down to my underwear and pulling it on. "But I'm lying to her—all the time!"

"So tell." Carla doesn't seem bothered by the moral ramifications of my situation. "Just get ready for a world of drama."

"Oh god, you're right." I pause, imagining yet again how my roommate would react—with tears and tantrums, no doubt. "I just have to keep quiet until the end of next week. Then I'm gone and everything will be back to normal again." The words sound reassuringly rational as I turn to assess myself in the mirror. The dress buttons up the front in a military style, but the cut hugs every one of my barely-there curves. "Isn't this sort of . . . tight?"

"That's the point; Ryan's going to flip."

"Oh, well . . . all right." I look at myself again, secretly warming to the idea of any boy flipping over me. "You're sure it's all right for me to borrow?"

"You're still going to lend me the party government papers?" I nod. "Then we're cool." Carla carefully applies a layer of bright scarlet lipstick and blots. "Let's go. Your big debut awaits!"

Professor Lowell has organized for all the class film projects to be screened in the auditorium as if it's a proper premiere, with a student audience seated on the tiered red seats and drinks afterward. The room is already full when we arrive, and I hunt through the crowd for a glimpse of Ryan.

"I'm nervous," I whisper to Carla, who's looking around the collection of film students and drama kids with all the focus of a hunter seeking out her prey. "What if it's awful?"

"Then you'll feel like crap," she says matter-of-factly. "But it won't be; it'll rock. I mean, is it really going to be any worse than *their* movie?" Carla nods toward the clique of gum-snapping girls who have sat passing notes and copies of *InStyle* in the back of every class.

"Good point." I try to relax. "And besides, I've only been studying film for two months. I'm never going to be as good as the others."

"There you go." Carla grins. "It's all about perspective."

"And rationalizing the bad things away," I agree, before being swept up into an enthusiastic hug. "Ryan!" I catch my breath as he releases me.

"Ready for battle?" he says. Then his eyes widen as he takes in my outfit. "Wow. Uh, I mean . . ." He swallows. "You look great, Em."

"Thanks," I say breezily, but inside I'm dancing. Somehow I don't mind being objectified when it's Ryan — and he's doing it with such blatant admiration. "You're looking rather dapper yourself."

"Why thank you," he jokes, adjusting the smart jacket he's wearing over that favorite Thermals T-shirt and jeans. "I figured I'd better make an effort. You know Lowell's invited industry guests, right?"

"What?"

Ryan nods, glancing around. "People he knows from studios, some agents." He's trying to sound nonchalant, but I can sense nerves radiating from his body. I slip my hand into his and squeeze it gently.

"We'll be fine."

"Sure you guys will," Carla agrees. "I mean, your obsessive film-geek perfection plus Em's planning. How can you fail?"

My grip on Ryan's hand grows tighter as we sit through the other films. Some are terrible, some are fun, and although privately I think ours is far better than any of them, I can't help but wonder if I'm blind to the reality of the situation. After all, somewhere along the way, hundreds of people thought that *Blonde Ambition* should get a theatrical release. What if this is our *Blonde Ambition*?

Oh god.

Finally, I see our opening credits flash up on-screen. Ryan's entire body goes tense, and I find it hard to breathe. It dawns just how important this project is to me. For what must be the first time in my life, I don't care about my class grade, only about everybody around me. I want them to love it the way I do, to believe in the story I worked so hard to create.

I mean to keep watch on Carla's face and study her reactions, but before I know it, the scenes are flying past on that big screen and then it's over. I can hardly believe it: two months of work for just those few minutes in the spotlight, our piece over quicker than it takes to cook a bowl of pasta or give my computer a thorough clean.

"Well?" I hear Ryan's low whisper.

"I don't know," I breathe back, dazed, as the audience bursts into applause. I twist around in my seat to try and gauge the general reaction. They're smiling and clapping, but is it sincere? Are they just being polite, the way I applauded some of the terrible films? I can't tell, but when I force myself to look over at Carla, she's beaming.

"You guys!" she exclaims. I gulp.

"Really?"

"Seriously." She nods, eyes sparkling. "Would I lie to you? Wait, I would, but I'm not, I swear!"

I slowly exhale. "That was . . ."

"Terrifying," Ryan finishes from my other side. We sit in silence for a moment, adrenaline still dashing through my bloodstream. "Come on." He finally gets up. "We still have to face the real critic."

My pocket begins to vibrate. I check the caller: it's my father. "I'll catch up with you." I push Ryan down toward the front of the room, then retreat through the crowd to the hallway outside.

"Dad, hi!" I exclaim, overflowing with happiness. "They liked it—our film! We just had the screening, and it went really well, I think. I hope!" I know I'm babbling, but I want him to understand that this is a success. My time here hasn't been the waste he thinks it is.

"Of course it did, Emily." He sounds more relaxed than usual. "Well done."

"I didn't think we'd get it done in time." I keep talking, the fluorescent-lit beige corridor striking me as the wrong place to celebrate such a victory. "But we've been working all week and—"

"That's wonderful," he interrupts. "But I've got even better news. You got a letter in the post this morning, and I'm sure you can guess what it says."

"You opened my mail?" I try to keep up, but I can't

263

help glancing back toward the auditorium, wondering what Lowell is saying.

My father laughs. "I knew you'd want to hear right away. You got it!"

"Got what?" I watch two of the gum-snapping girls from my class stalk out of the doors, obviously displeased. "What are you talking about?"

"Your internship, silly. With Sterns, Cahill, and Coutts. I'm sure you'll get other offers, of course, but this is the big one."

"The big one," I echo, only half listening.

"It looks like my time on the golf course with Giles paid off, eh? Not that your sterling record didn't have anything to do with it, but every little bit helps. Now, I've already started looking into flats you can rent for the summer, something in the city, I think, perhaps Pimlico or Marylebone. Perhaps even buy outright if the price is right; you'll be needing somewhere after you graduate, and if I cosign your mortgage . . ."

I listen to him ramble about property-value appreciation and the right neighborhoods while I try to take the news in. So I did it, after all. The prized internship is mine, and I'm one step further along in my five-year plan. California hasn't ruined my chances: I'm still set for a summer beavering away in the offices of one of the most prestigious law firms around, and after that they're almost certain to offer me a job.

The future unfolds before me in that corridor: certain, secure, and clear as if I'd mapped it out on my miniature whiteboard with indelible ink. Summer, then my final year in Oxford, then a move down to London and that well-located flat Daddy is so intent on buying. Everything is just as I planned.

"That's wonderful," I say, a new sense of satisfaction mingling with the elation from before. Everything is just as I planned. "It all worked out."

"Of course it did! It's like I always told you: you've just got to follow the plan." He's so proud, I can hear it beaming in every word.

"Thank you." I feel a weight ease, that creeping discomfort that's loomed whenever I think about going home. Now I know how everything will be, I don't have to panic. I don't have to worry anymore.

The doors slam open again, and I look up to see Ryan barreling toward me, a huge grin on his face.

"I have to go, Daddy," I say quickly. "But it's great news, it really is."

"I'll call when you get the other offers, and we can go through them all."

I hang up and turn to Ryan with a smile. "I've got some news," I start, but he puts a hand to my lips.

"Me first!"

He's so full of excitement, he's practically bouncing up and down. I giggle and thread my fingers through his. "All right, you go."

"Lowell loved it," he announces, pulling me to him and punctuating each sentence with a kiss. "He totally loved it. And that's not all: Julian Morton is here."

"The director?" I exclaim.

"They go way back." Ryan laughs, slipping his arms

tightly around my waist and leaning in, trapping me against the wall. "So Morton saw it and loved it too. He wants to mentor us!"

My mouth drops open. Ryan closes it with kisses while my mind reels until at last, I come up for air.

"But . . . What does that mean?"

"It means we've got jobs!" Ryan squeezes me tighter. "His new movie starts shooting in June, and he wants us to intern! Paid! We'll be total slaves, I know, but we'll get to learn about script writing and direction and a real-live production!" I gasp, swept along by his enthusiasm. "Can you believe it, Em? The whole summer on set together."

And then I remember.

"Wait, Ryan, I can't—" But he's kissing me again, and whatever I need to say can wait. Gripping my waist, he brings my hips hard into him, and for a moment there's nothing in my mind at all, just the feverish pull of hot mouths and racing blood and—

"Omigod!"

A familiar voice splits through my oblivion. Ryan wrenches himself away and I blink, still dizzy.

"Em?" The voice becomes a screech, and I turn to find Morgan gaping at me in disbelief, Brooke and Lexi flanking her with equally stunned expressions. "What the hell are you *doing*?!"

From: totes_tasha
To: EMLewis
Subject: just an idea . . .

. . . .

hey,

so, the end is nigh, but i was thinking, we totally need to hang out. what do you think about a tiny detour before we head home? spring break in florida is, like, a rite of passage. you could fly in for a couple of days before going on to england, and i could do the same in the other direction. how about it? i could really use a vacation before facing everyone back home, and there's no way we can go home without meeting in real life!

xoxo

From: EMLewis
To: totes_tasha
Subject: re: just an idea . . .
. . . .

Oh, boy, sign me up. Things have got *really* complicated here—I'll need a holiday whatever happens.

Talk soon,
Em

Tasha

I don't bother with my preppy Oxford uniform after that last, awful class with Professor Elliot and Carrie. There's no point—everyone knows who I really am, so why should I be universally loathed *and* unfashionable? But even though I figured I'd switch right back to my old Uggs and miniskirts, I find I'm holding back from the full-on look. It all seems kind of . . . obvious now. So, instead, I mix it up: working the Hitchcock skirts with casual layers; blending crisp shirts with my distressed denim. It's not like the other kids here, but it's not like Tasha either, and when I look in the mirror every day, I feel like what Emily says is true. The girl I've been here is part of me too. She's not just this character I've been pretending to play; she's another side of me—as real as the girl who tears up the clubs and can find every sample sale in Southern California.

Maybe I need to find a way to be both.

Once the dust settles, the last days of my stay creep by pretty much how they started: on my own. Holly hangs out when she can, but her schedule is manic as hell, so most of my final week passes quietly, in libraries or tucked away in my old corner of Starbucks with a book. But instead of being lonely or frustrated like before, I'm weirdly at peace. I have just one more paper due for Elliot, and as another way to make me feel bad, she's assigned a discussion of modern feminism and an essay question that asks: "Can submitting to male-created standards of sexuality ever be compatible with feminist values?" There's no way I'm letting her take me down again, so I'm clocking up some serious reading time in my quest to make this my best paper yet—which is why I'm back in an armchair in Borders past nine on Wednesday night, iPod plugged in and a triple-shot macchiato at my side.

Despite the peppy pop soundtrack I've got playing, it's tough going. The reading list is full of books like her own: passing judgment on girls who sleep around and undermine the feminist cause. But the more I read, the more I realize that there's this gaping void in Elliot's thesis, in what Carrie and the girls all say. They may be right about the whole "raunch culture" thing being kind of sleazy, all that stripping and soft porn, but there's one thing they're not talking about. Desire. It's like their view of the world is totally sexless, like they've never felt that pull of lust low in their stomach or longed for the feeling of somebody's body hard against theirs.

Sure, I might make mistakes trying to figure that side

of myself out, but at least I'm trying, instead of feeling like it's sinful and wrong. Isn't that a good thing? And their stupid superiority kick ... Is it any wonder none of my friends back home would ever look into feminism, when people like Carrie do nothing but look down on us, like we're somehow less than them? Maybe if they stopped being so damn judgmental, we'd start realizing it's not just a straight choice between waving placards and making out with five guys a night on a dare.

I know, it's not rocket science, but finding another way that Carrie and Co. don't have it all figured out only makes me feel stronger. And gives me more material for this paper.

I'm deep in my notes when I become aware of somebody standing over me. At first I just ignore them, figuring it's someone hovering to try and take my comfy seat, but when they don't move, I finally look up.

It's Will.

I feel that blade in my chest again. He's looming awkwardly, striped scarf thrown around his neck and hair falling in his eyes the way it always does. Slowly, I reach up and take out my earphones.

"Can we talk?"

His voice is low and uncertain, but just the sound of it takes me back to the club bathroom and all the awful things he said. I swallow.

"Do I want to hear what you've got to say?" I fold my arms carefully and try to glare.

He hunches his shoulders. "I really just want to—"

"So you're talking to me again?"

"Please." His eyes meet mine, and they're forlorn enough to make me soften.

"Whatever. Talk."

"Here?" He looks around. The corner is full: a large old man in glasses is reading the paper, and on my other side a thin-faced woman sneaks cookies from her bag and sips a cup of tea. I don't care what they hear.

"It's all you're getting."

Will moves to the chair next to me, stumbling past a low table and the stacks of books littering the space. I don't move to help him. I feel stiff with anger, but part of me can't help wishing he'll say something to make this right.

"So?" I ask when he's sitting down. I've got my book still in my lap, like I could ignore him whenever I want. I grip it to hide the fact that my hands are shaking like crazy.

Will swallows. He toys nervously with the cuff of his jacket. "I'm sorry," he says at last. "And, ah, I didn't mean it—what I said. I'm sorry." He looks at me and I see he means it. He knows he's wrong, he's sorry, and it's everything I wanted to hear, but . . .

But it doesn't matter.

I blink.

"I was awful, I know, but I was just so angry." He's still talking, still looking at me with those dark brown eyes, but the metal in my chest doesn't melt away. I don't hurt any less. "I know you hate me. I'm just . . . sorry," he finishes, miserable, and stays there, watching me hopefully.

"I don't hate you," I say, closing the book. My hands aren't shaking anymore. I know how this is going to end.

"You don't?" His expression picks up.

"No," I say, just damn tired of it all. "I'm disappointed. You let me down."

He nods quickly. "I know I did."

"No, you don't get it." He thinks all it takes is some apologetic words and we'll be cool again, but I know now it's not enough. "You bailed. You made this about you— everything was falling apart, and all you cared about was what? The fact I didn't fuck you?" My voice is low but ice. He flinches.

"Tasha—"

"My name is Natasha," I interrupt coolly. "And the things you said to me, you totally meant them." I sit up straight. Proud. "So this won't work, OK? I can't have people in my life who are too weak to step up and deal with who I am."

He doesn't argue. He just sags back in his seat, and I know I'm right. If he really wanted me, he'd fight. If he really didn't care about Tyler and the video, he'd show some damn backbone, instead of just watching while I grab my stuff and walk away.

Alone.

Even with all the drama since the board meeting, I still haven't forgotten the real reason any of this matters, so after I print my paper and leave it in Professor Elliot's mail cubby the next morning, I head over to the cold stone buildings that house the Oxford admin staff. A stuck-up secretary won't let me near any of the board without an appointment, so I wait an hour in the dreary gray lobby until one of them comes by.

"Excuse me." I leap up the minute I see a familiar face exit one of the offices. It's one of the librarian-type women, wearing the same baggy cardigan from the meeting, or one exactly like it. I don't pause on why someone would buy one, let alone two, of those ugly things and race after her. "Do you have a minute? I really need to talk to you."

"I'm sorry." She barely looks at me. "I'm terribly busy."

"But this won't take long." I plant myself in front of her. "Please."

Her eyebrows lift, and I can tell she recognizes me. Those thin lips purse even more.

"Please," I say again, pouring everything into that one word, and something must have slipped past that iron shell around her heart, because she finally relents.

"Well, all right. But just a minute."

"Thank you!" I follow her eagerly back to her office. It's as drab as she is, with worn green carpet and faded watercolors. There are a couple of fancy diplomas on the wall, and I snatch a quick glance as I pass to catch her name. Dr. Alison Aldridge.

"Take a seat." Dr. Aldridge gestures at a hard, tall-backed seat. I obediently take it. "So, Natasha." She finds a pair of wire-rimmed glasses and puts them on, looking at me over the top of the rims. "What can I do for you?"

"Umm." I'm suddenly nervous. Going face-to-face with someone from the board seemed like a good idea back in my dorm room, but now that I'm here, it's pretty daunting. "I was wondering what you're planning to do, about the health center."

"The board will announce their decision shortly." Dr. Aldridge folds her hands primly.

"I know," I apologize. "I just had to come and make sure . . ." I gulp, my mouth dry. "I don't want what happened to make a difference to our case."

"What happened?" She arches her eyebrows again, like a challenge, and I realize I can't dance around the issue anymore.

"With me." I take a deep breath, looking at her dead-on. "The video and the newspaper story. I need to know it won't affect your decision. Because it shouldn't." I lean forward, stressing every word. "Everything in our presentation was true: the girls here need that center. It's a matter of principle." Her lips twitch, so I sigh. "I know, right? You're probably thinking I don't know the first thing about principles, and that's OK. But what you all don't seem to get is this is the real world. The girls here are in college, they're legal, they're going to have sex, they're going to get raped. And closing the health center isn't going to change that—it's just going to take away the resources they need to deal with it all."

I let out a breath and stand. "That's all I had to say. Thanks for the time, I guess."

I'm halfway to the door when I hear her clipped voice behind me. "We'll keep funding it."

"What?" I turn back.

"The center. Tomorrow we'll announce a continuation in funding." Dr. Aldridge nods slightly. "I appreciate your coming to see me." She pauses. "It seems Professor Elliot was wrong about you."

"Elliot?" I repeat.

A smile is playing on the edge of her lips. "She talked to me, you know. After the meeting. Urged me not to let the actions of a . . . well, we don't need to go into that," she corrects herself. "But I see now she misjudged you."

There's another pause, and I wonder just what Elliot said about me.

"I was one of the first, you know," Dr. Aldridge adds.

I look at her blankly.

"The first women at Oxford to be admitted to the real colleges." Her eyes take on a new glint. "Oh, they let us in before, but only if we kept to the new women's schools. They all said it would be the end of the institution, that girls didn't have the character or intelligence for the rigors of a *male* education." Her lips twist into what I swear is a smirk. "I suppose we proved them wrong."

"We?" I repeat slowly.

"You're on a semester abroad, undergraduate, I think it was?" I nod. Dr. Aldridge opens a drawer. "Perhaps you'll consider coming back to us. We run summer programs and even master's degrees. I don't do a lot of teaching anymore, but I'm sure I could find time to supervise you."

Mouth open, I walk back to the desk and take the papers she holds, outstretched. "Something to do with feminism and the media, maybe." And then she winks at me, so fast I think I'm imagining it.

"I . . . Thank you," I breathe, clutching the sheets. She nods again, curtly, and stands.

"Now, I really do have other appointments."

And just like that, it's over.

I spend the rest of the day packing in a daze. The health center is safe, and I have a maybe-invitation to do a master's. At Oxford. The ideas dance around my head like some kind of promise, and it's nearly time to meet Holly for a good-bye drink in the bar when I realize I have one more stop I have to make before I can be done here.

Light from Professor Elliot's study filters under the door into the cloisters, so after a quick knock, I walk in. She's at her desk with a stack of papers, and her whole face tightens when I walk in.

"You missed our tutorial," she says with this icy voice.

"I know," I reply, calm. She may not think I'm worth anything, but I know now she's not the only one who matters. "I figured I could miss another attack on me and my terrible morals."

Her eyes narrow. "So what can I do for you?" Her tone is like the least helpful thing ever.

"I came to collect my paper."

"Oh, yes." Lifting a folder from the edge of the desk, she holds it between her finger and thumb like it's contagious. "It was certainly an interesting perspective, but hardly up to *Oxford* standards." She smiles but it doesn't reach her eyes.

"I'll bet." I take the file and don't even bother looking at the grade. I know it'll suck, but that wasn't the point.

"I'm sure you'll have fun back at home."

"I'm sure I will." I'm at the door before I turn back to her. It's the same as this morning with Dr. Aldridge, but this time I'm the one who's getting the final word.

"You know, you're the one who's supposed to be the adult here." I make sure every word carries, not caring when her mouth drops open in a tiny "o." "I really respected you. I mean, you were so helpful and supportive; it was like my opinions mattered." I stare at her, this woman who made me feel so smart and so dumb all in the space of one semester. "But you're just as hypocritical as the rest of them. The minute it looks like I'm not one of Carrie's little clones, you act like I'm totally worthless." I shake my head. "That's not good teaching, but more than that, it's crappy feminism."

I don't stick around to hear if she's got anything to say. It wouldn't mean anything to me, anyway. Besides, I've got a good-bye celebration to get to. There's only the two of us, but who needs a crowd?

Emily

I spend the next two days after our premiere inhabiting the delightful state of denial. I sleep on Carla's floor to avoid Morgan's wrath, refrain from answering my phone to avoid Ryan's enthusiasm, and throw myself into studying for finals to avoid thinking about the end of my stay and my impending return to Oxford.

I am nothing if not a multitasker.

"Put the poor guy out of his misery." Carla points a highlighter at me as my mobile begins to vibrate again. "That's, like, the sixth time tonight."

"I can't." I look up from my textbook and press "decline call." "I don't know what to say to him."

"What is there to say?"

"Um, 'You know that summer job you're so excited about us doing together? I'm not taking it, I'm going back to England, and I'll probably never see you again.' Yes, that's just perfect." I sigh, reaching for my aspirin. Ever since my life exploded into drama, I've had the most terrible headache.

Carla rolls her eyes. "So take the job."

"You know I can't."

"Because of your dream internship, yeah, I know." Carla fixes me with a stare. "If you're switching back to the old you, what's with the outfit?"

I look down at my powder-blue polo shirt and denim skirt and shrug. "Habit, I suppose. Don't forget, half my things are still at Morgan's."

"Which you need to get if you're going to pack in time," Carla reminds me.

"What's the point? She's probably burned them all by now."

"True."

I think of Morgan's drama-queen routine and wonder if I can do without all those trivial possessions. My laptop, for example. Or my passport. "It's all right. I doubt I'll need Uggs in the offices of Sterns, Cahill, and Coutts."

"For something you swear is the perfect job, you're sure not enthusiastic about it."

I stiffen. "Because I feel terrible about letting Ryan down."

"Sure, sure." Carla glances back at her notes. "If I didn't have a killer history final tomorrow morning, I'd be grilling you right now."

I sit back in my seat, looking around the busy study section full of panicked last-minute crammers and take-away coffee cups. If only we hadn't kissed. My life would be so much simpler if we just hadn't kissed.

"And even if I did want to come back for summer, which I don't," I muse, "I couldn't give up my dream for Ryan. What kind of girl would that make me?"

"Julian Morton's personal protégée?"

"No! I'd be one of those girls who sacrifices all her own ambition to fit around a boy's plans." I cross my arms firmly. "And I hate those girls."

"That's true." Carla shrugs. "But..."

"No 'but.' There are no 'buts' involved."

She laughs. "What if you really do want to take the L.A. job, but you're refusing to even think about it because of Ryan? Isn't that still making your decision based on a boy?"

I narrow my eyes at her. "You're not helping."

"Hey, I was just putting it out there." She holds her hands up. "But if you want to let the chance of a lifetime slip by, just because it happens to come with a summer of hot make-out action as a bonus..." Carla's expression is supremely dubious.

I sink my head onto the table and groan.

"I had a plan!"

She pats my head gently. "Plans change, Em."

"Not mine." I sigh wistfully. "My plans come with built-in contingencies and backup insurance and special allowances for unexpected variations. The plan itself never changes."

"So think of this as one of those unexpected variants."

I smile sadly. "It doesn't fit. Summer working on a

film in L.A. . . . How does that get me any nearer to my law career?"

Carla shakes her head. "Get it together. So you spend the summer in L.A. or London; either way you have to talk to Ryan."

"No, I don't."

"Yeah, good luck with that." Carla's eyes flicker over my shoulder, and I turn to find Ryan fifteen feet away, his battered black sneakers approaching fast.

"Oh, crap."

"Em." His face isn't happy, and I can't blame him. If he'd kiss-and-run the way I did, I would be an angry, raging mess by now.

"Hi." I try to smile, but he simply towers over me. My stomach tightens.

"Let's go talk somewhere."

"I'd really love to," I say limply, "but I have finals and—" He takes my hand and looks at me with those cloudy dark eyes. "I suppose I have time," I finish in a whisper. He nods and walks away, out of the side library entrance and toward the small memorial garden.

I follow slowly, apprehension growing with every step. I'm not usually this way, shrinking away from difficult conversations as if I'm scared of confrontation. In fact, I've often been the one urging friends to face challenges head-on, rather than let them grow out of all proportion. And here I am, dreading every word because this time it all seems to matter so much more.

But I can't delay the inevitable. Soon I'm standing next to the arrangement of shrubbery, just inches away from Ryan, his hurt expression making me regret being such a coward.

"Um, hi," I start.

"Are you OK?" He's angry, it's obvious, but his first question is to see how I am. I feel a pang. He really is one of the good ones.

I swallow, avoiding his eyes. "I'm fine."

"I was worried. I thought Morgan might have"—his lips lift slightly—"killed you. Maimed, at least. You took off so fast after she found us."

"Death by lip gloss," I try to joke, but my words just hover awkwardly between us. "No, really I'm fine."

"Look, I know you must feel guilty, like you betrayed her or something." Ryan takes my hands and forces me to look at him. "And I get that, you're too nice sometimes, but you can't break things off, just because she—"

"That's not it." I can't bear it any longer. He thinks I'm doing this because I'm a good person, not because I'm putting myself first. I swallow. "This—us—I don't know how it'll work. I'm leaving in a few days, and then I'll be thousands of miles away."

"But you'll be back for summer." He tries to pull me closer. "That's only two months away. We can email and talk—it'll be no time at all."

"I'm not coming back." I feel something inside me break as I say it. All this avoidance has been to delay those words; as if saying it out loud makes my decision final. This really was just a brief escape from my real life.

Ryan frowns. "I don't get it." I slowly detach my hands from his.

"The job with Julian Morton, I'm not taking it."

"What?"

"I got an internship offer, the one I told you about." Ignoring the confused look in his eyes, I keep talking. "I'll be working in a law office all summer, so I won't be coming back. And after that, it's my final year, so I'll be studying through my holidays." I try to keep my voice steady. "So it just won't work with you. If we're not going to be spending time with each other, what's the point in pretending?"

He's quiet for a moment. I can't bring myself to look at him, so I study the leaves shivering slightly in the breeze.

"You've already made your mind up, haven't you?"

I nod. "You know how important this is to me. I can't just throw it away for a fun summer on some movie."

Ryan exhales, his whole body going still. "So all that stuff you said about letting go and being happy was just bullshit."

I flinch. "That's not true."

"So why won't you even think about the internship?" Ryan grabs me again, pulling me into him until I can feel his body against me, so I can't help but look up into his eyes. "Just think about it."

"I have! But I can't change my life around for you."

"No, not for me." He shakes his head. "For you, for what you really want to do. You've loved this movie, Em, you know you have. The writing, the production. Admit it."

I stay motionless in his arms. "Of course I've enjoyed it, but—"

"But nothing! Do you have any idea how many kids would kill for this chance?" I don't answer. "So why are you so scared to give it a shot?"

I wrench away. "I'm not scared! You don't understand. I've worked my whole life to get on this path. This is what I want!"

Ryan looks at me, his expression slowly closing off. I know I picked this, but still it hurts more than I expected.

"Well, this is good-bye, I guess." He clears his throat. "You fly back to England on Friday?"

"To Florida," I say, digging tiny half-moon prints into my palms. This is worse than how it was with Sebastian. "I'm going to meet Natasha. Then home."

"Right." He nods slowly. "I'll drop by a copy of the movie before you go; you should have one. You did a great job."

We did a great job, I think. But saying that would be useless, so I just nod. "Oh. Thanks. I'd like that."

"So . . ."

We stand, awkward.

"Good-bye," I say softly. Ryan tilts his head slightly in acknowledgment. Part of me wishes he would keep fighting, kiss me, say anything to convince me to stay, but we don't have somebody writing this scene for us, and life doesn't happen like that.

I just walk away.

Tasha

God, I've missed the sunshine. After Em and I meet up, we dump our bags in the hotel and hit the beach right away. The moment we step out of the lobby, I turn my face up to the cloudless sky and sigh. "Ahh . . ."

Em giggles. "You had sun in England!"

"That was so not sun." I close my eyes and try to absorb the warmth into my bones. "That was, like, this pale weak glow pretending to be sun. *This* is the real thing."

"Did you bring sunscreen?" Em asks, checking her tote. I only met her an hour ago, but already I know she totally wasn't exaggerating about her organizing kick. We sent digital pics so we would recognize each other coming off our flights, but it's still a trip to see her with all that honey-blond hair, a cute little pink shirt—and such a crisp accent.

"Chill." I grin, pulling my big tortoiseshell shades on. We're based right across the street from the sand, and the water is sparkling at me like an invitation. "I'm, like, immune to it, remember?"

"Whereas I've gone through about three bottles of SPF thirty since I've been here." Em waits for the cross light to turn green, oblivious to the group of college boys who are totally checking her out. "Do you think it'll be warm enough to swim?"

"Swim, lounge, whatever . . ." I spy a gap in the cars and grab her hand, pulling her into the street.

"Tash!"

"C'mon, you don't understand: I've been dreaming of the beach since the day I left!"

Em laughs and follows me across the street, and soon we're sprawled under that glorious hot sun. "See, this is what I'm talking about." I kick off my sneakers and bury my toes in the bleached sand. A sense of total peace sweeps through me. Screw therapy—we should just send stressed people to a tropical island for a couple of weeks. It would wind up costing the same, I'd bet, and there's none of that "tell me about your parents" crap. "You keep your stuffy libraries and cold cobbled streets—I'll take sun and ocean any day."

"You don't have to convince me." Em flops backward and stretches, her shirt riding up over her already-golden stomach. "I'm a convert. Oh, I'm dreading getting back to the cold."

"Sucks to be you," I agree. She laughs.

"I still can't believe this is the first time we've met! I feel like I've known you forever."

"I know!" I exclaim, stripping down to my navy bikini. "I was scared this would be totally awkward. I worried all the way on the flight I'd hate you."

"Me too," she confesses, peeling off her skirt. "Or that we just wouldn't click, and then we'd be stuck in a hotel room together all weekend."

"Watching pay-per-view and raiding the minibar just for something to do," I finish. Then I look at her scarlet bikini and shake my head. "I still can't get over how different you look. There were photos of you up on the Raleigh website, and now . . ."

"I know." She blushes. "But I think I like it. People treat me differently now; they don't just assume I'm serious and boring."

"Right! And now guys act like I have an actual brain instead of just breasts." I pause. "Or, at least, the ones who haven't caught the video do."

"Oh, Tash." Em reaches over and squeezes my hand. "Will was a bastard, but they're not all like that."

I shake away all thoughts of him. "Say that again."

"Bastard? Oh, not you too!" She makes a face. "Ryan loved making me swear. I don't know what it is about my accent." Her eyes get kind of sad, but she keeps talking before I can say anything. "Anyway, is Tash OK? Or do you prefer Natasha?"

"Natasha is best," I decide. "Or Tash. But Tasha is

like someone else now. It's weird, how it just stopped feeling like my name."

"I think it's great." Em lies down, a hand shielding her eyes from the sun. "You get to reinvent yourself, how other people see you."

"And what about you—is it Em or Emily?"

She pauses. "I don't know if I'll get a choice, but for now I like Em. Em's the girl who has the fun, spontaneous adventures."

"Like taking off for spring break in Key West." I hold up my hand for fake high fives. She whoops and hits my palm.

"Spring break, baby!"

We fall back down, giggling.

"But seriously"—Em props herself up on one arm—"what exactly are we doing here? It seems rather extravagant just to take a holiday."

"But we need it," I insist. "I need the time to recover, and you need the time to figure out you've got to take the internship in L.A."

"Tash!" Em's eyes cloud over again. "We've been through this. I want the law job!"

"I know." For somebody so smart, she sure is being dumb. "But that doesn't mean you don't want the film gig too." And I have forty-eight hours to convince her, before she goes back to Oxford and snaps into old Emily mode. I have a feeling I wouldn't like old Emily much.

"You of all people should understand," she scolds me.

"I can't pretend to be somebody I'm not. That was never the point of all this."

"I know," I repeat, my voice totally sweet. "Which is why you need to admit you want to explore the film thing more. So you're not lying to yourself."

I wanted this vacation as breathing space for me, but the minute Em filled me in on her career crisis, I knew I had to do something. She may not see it yet, but this weekend could set her whole path in life. It's up to me to make sure that path leads to happiness, cute boys, and creativity, and not a nervous breakdown by the time she's twenty.

I fix her with my best knowing look. She doesn't budge. "Whatever." I roll over and make like I don't care. "But you're the one who keeps telling me about how this switch makeover thing is about finding new sides of our identity and, like, not letting other people's expectations define our identities." I'm quoting her own emails back at her, and she totally knows it. "So I'm just going to chill here, and then we're going to dinner and maybe a club. But if you feel like emailing Lowell and telling him you've changed your mind, just let me know."

Em scowls. "I won't."

"Whatever you say." I hide a grin. She's totally going to crack—I can tell.

I bust out my blue dress again for our night out, safe in the knowledge that what was kind of trashy by Oxford standards is practically a nun's habit when it comes to Key West.

"And, anyway, who gives a damn about being sexy or not," Em declares, linking her arm through mine and pulling me into the bar with nothing more than a quick flash of our fake IDs. "It's not like we're going to pick up a guy and take him back for a threesome!"

I giggle. "Tell that to them! Drunk college dudes aren't exactly rational."

We blink, adjusting to the dim light. I figured the bar was kind of upscale, in sleek blue and silver, but still it's packed with rowdy groups of guys downing shots and girls stripped to bikini tops gyrating on the dance floor.

I pause, the noise and loud hip-hop beats overwhelming me. Everywhere I look there are flashing lights and drunk, squealing girls. "Maybe I should have rethought this whole spring break thing." I was only away a couple of months, but somehow I forgot it was like this. Guys looking you up and down so blatantly, girls glaring at the competition. I gulp. "We could do that pay-per-view thing and—"

"No way." Em pulls me firmly toward the bar. "We're reacclimatizing you to your old habitat."

"We're what?"

"This is the horse, and you're getting back on it."

I should have figured Em wasn't to be disobeyed; she has us perched at the bar with a couple of drinks in under ten seconds.

"Nonalcoholic," she yells at the campiest barman I've even seen. His shirt is sheer and stretched so tightly across his chest you can see every ridge of muscle. Em turns to me. "No offense, but this isn't the sort of place I want to get drunk in."

I clock at least three jocks in football shirts looking at her hungrily. "Good call."

"So what shall we toast to?" Em looks at me over the fruity cocktails, her face flushed and glowing. I'm struck by how far she's come—not far enough, for sure, but still she's got a look in her eyes I swear I never saw in any of those old photos: happy, relaxed.

"The switch!" I exclaim loudly, trying to feel like I can blend back in here.

"The switch!" she echoes, plucking a cherry from the top of her glass and biting into it. "And the strangest three months of my life."

I toast along, but I hear the past tense in her tone. "So . . . You haven't heard from Ryan?"

Em sighs. "Nope, and I doubt I ever will."

"You could call him, you know," I suggest, watching her carefully. "Or email, or even just text."

She shrugs kind of listlessly. "It won't make a difference; there's no point. God, how pathetic am I? First Sebastian, then Sam, and finally Ryan. I'm doomed to be alone."

"Who was this Sebastian guy, anyway?" I take a sip of my drink. "Maybe I met him."

"You would have definitely. He lives right next door to me."

I choke.

"No way!" Spluttering, I reach for a wad of napkins and dab at my streaming nose. "Robin Thicke dude is your ex?"

Em looks puzzled. "I gave him that CD for Christmas."

I laugh, not believing this. "Oh god, honey. You are so better off without him. I hate to break it to you, but he slept with, like, three different girls every week."

Her mouth drops open. "Really?"

"Honest." I shake my head, tears still in my eyes. "And none of them sounded happy, if you know what I mean."

"Tash!"

"I heard everything," I swear. "I wish to god I hadn't, but that's the truth."

She presses her lips together, like she's trying not to laugh.

"What?" I ask.

"Nothing. Just . . . I suppose it was a lucky escape." She finally grins. "That I didn't sleep with him, I mean. If what you heard was true."

We fall about in hysterics, laughing so hard I nearly lose my balance and fall off my seat.

"And I never met him," I gasp, shoulders shaking. "I know what noise he makes when—" I can't even get the words out. "But I never even laid eyes on him!"

"Whoa there." The guy behind me grabs my arm just before I slip to the floor. "Easy does it."

"Thanks!" I gasp, gripping on to the rim of the bar for safety.

"No problem." He flashes a grin at me, blond and cute and eager looking.

I turn back to Em.

"Go on," she whispers. "Back on the horse, remember?" I shrug, but she widens her eyes and kicks me, hard.

"Oww!" I hiss, but she doesn't quit, so with a sigh, I swivel back to him.

"Hey," I start, since it's clear Em won't be happy with anything less than a conversation. "Thanks again for helping me out."

"That's cool." He runs one palm over the top of his head, like he's checking every tuft of bronzed hair is in place. "These places can get way out of control."

"Uh-huh." I nod, immediately bored. I think of Will and feel that clench again in my chest, but Will is an ocean away and out of my life.

"Dude!" Suddenly another guy appears. He's short and stocky like a baseball player, with a beer in his hand and wearing a pale-blue shirt soaked with sweat. "You know who this is, right?" He looks at me, mouth wide open. "It's her. You know, from the video. With what's-his-name."

Blond Boy's eyes slowly spark. "No way, it is you!"

I feel Em's hand on my back. She's already standing, ready to go, but I don't move. I knew this was coming, but I figured I'd be panicked, sick, like I've always been.

No more.

"You liked the show?" I ask, calmly taking another drink. It's strange, but I don't feel threatened or exposed.

"Totally!" They snigger, kind of disbelieving. "Man, you were so hot."

"I played that clip, like, all the time."

"Lovely," I say, totally sarcastic, but they're too busy panting to notice.

"And when you did that twisty thing, with your hips?" It only took a moment for the cute, chivalrous one to become a leering jackass. "I tried to make my girlfriend watch, but she dumped my ass. Frigid bitch."

"Dude, I remember!"

"Ha, I know, right!"

I roll my eyes at Em. She's watching me, all concerned, but I'm fine. Finally.

"So, you, like, up for a replay?" They look at me, only part joking.

"I've got, like, a hundred bucks on me," Jock Guy adds.

I raise my eyebrows.

"I've got another two hundred," Blond Boy says quickly. Like it makes a difference.

"You know what . . . ?" I pause, biting my lip as I pretend to think over their amazing offer. They lean closer.

"No."

And then I take both our drinks and upend the glasses over their heads.

"Let's go, Em." Slipping down from my stool, I take my purse and shoot a look back at the guys. They're soaked, sickly sweet syrup dripping down their fronts, and Blond Boy even has a paper umbrella lodged in his now-not-so-perfect hair. I laugh. "I always like to meet my fans," I yell behind us as Em tows me away.

And then I blow them a kiss.

Emily

We're still laughing by the time we get back to the hotel, tripping over our heels and clinging to one another in glee.

"And the look on their faces . . . !" I gasp, fumbling in my clutch bag for the room card.

"I know!" Tash sweeps into the room and flings herself on one of the beds triumphantly. "And I didn't freak out, not at all."

"You were amazing," I agree, pulling my pajamas from my case and slipping into the bathroom to change. "You see?" I call through the door. "I knew you could adjust to this sort of scene again."

"I guess I can." When I come back into the room, Tash is sitting cross-legged, munching on a handful of extortionate minibar peanuts. She pauses to lick salt from the corner of her mouth, a giddy grin still on her face. "You know who they looked like? Professor Elliot, right after I called her a bad feminist."

I giggle, rummaging in my suitcase for my wash bag. "I still can't believe she slagged you off to Aldridge—and then you got that offer, anyway."

"Totally." Tash beams. "Oooh, is that your movie?" Spying a manila envelope buried among my clothes, she reaches over and takes the small package.

"Oh. That." I feel my elation suddenly begin to ebb away. "Ryan dropped it by before I left. I haven't been able to watch it yet," I admit.

"Let's do it now," she cries. "Come on, I'm dying to see it."

"Well . . . all right," I agree unenthusiastically, but she's already flipping up her laptop screen and opening the envelope.

"Which one is it?"

"Hmm?" I carefully begin to smear moisturizer under my eyes, the way my mother ordered me to at age twelve, "to stave off the ravages of time."

Tash tosses the discs onto my bed. "There are two. And a note!" she exclaims, withdrawing a single sheet of paper.

"I don't want to hear!" My heart drops, just imagining what Ryan would have to say.

"Sure you do." Ignoring my plea, Tash begins to read. *"Emily—I know you've already made up your mind about us, so I won't try and stop you. But please think about the summer job."* At this Tash fixes me with another of her looks. *"Either way, I made this so you remember your time here and everything you managed to be. Have a safe journey home."*

She lowers the letter. "That's all there was. Go on, play the disc!"

I slowly clamber over beside her and slip the DVD into the computer, my insides already twisting themselves into a tangle.

"Look, it's you!"

I watch in silence as a photograph of me fills the screen under the words "Emily's Big Adventure." It's one of the shots from outside the diner: my hair is glossy under the sun, and my whole face is lit up as I blow the camera a kiss.

"So cute!" Tash coos, hugging me, but I just feel a pang. It already feels like that place is a world away. The first still is quickly replaced as new photographs and short bursts of film dance across the small screen. Me working on the script, me lying out on the lawn with a book, me ordering our group around during filming, all set to a familiar soundtrack of Bruce Springsteen, Patsy Cline, and all the other songs Ryan played for me that day.

I watch myself as if in a daze. The girl on-screen is more hesitant than the people around her, I can see. She holds back, visibly assessing each moment, but then there are moments where Ryan has caught me completely unaware: doubled over with laughter on the beach; eyes animated as I explain a line of dialogue.

"That must be Carla!" Tash exclaims happily, as the slide show continues. And then another film clip plays.

I'm Rollerblading on the boardwalk in Santa Monica, begging Ryan to turn the camera off.

"You're not doing too bad." Our banter is a burst of noisy giggles and sarcasm. *"You haven't checked the time all afternoon."*

"Yay me!" I'm breathless and flushed, backlit by the sparkling ocean and sinking neon sun.

"Don't go changing too much; they won't recognize you when you get home!"

The shot freezes on my face in that moment before I started to fall, lingering on the screen in front of us.

"You look so sad," Tash murmurs quietly. I nod. She's right, it's as if a shadow is drifting over my features. Ryan captured me in the very instant that I thought about going home, and what he saw there would be clear to anyone: a fleeting look of panic in my eyes, a fraught tension in my jaw.

The image finally fades away and the disc is finished. I exhale, not realizing I've been holding my breath.

"Are you OK?" Tash looks at me carefully. I shrug.

"Yes. No." I fall back onto the pillows, my voice small. "I don't know."

"Oh, Em." She lies down beside me, our hands overlapping and limbs splayed out like paper dolls. "Talk to me."

But I don't know how to find the words, so we just lie in silence while aching waves roll through me until, at last, I drift to sleep.

I slip out of bed early before Tash awakes and wander across to the beach. Sitting on the cool, clear sand, I watch the light from the rising sun behind me turn the water a brilliant blue and try to find a path through all my confusion.

I'm on the edge of something, I can tell, but even the thought of moving in any one direction is enough to paralyze me. Snuggling deeper into the folds of my new UCSB jumper, I try to organize all my thoughts into a neat, ordered list like usual, but nothing stays in its place. Images from Ryan's film keep jumping into my mind; memories of the past semester; my script; the hours I spent on research and applications for the law internships.

I sigh. I thought I would make the decision and be done with it—that's always been the way it's worked before. I may make lists and weigh up every available criteria and even occasionally plot a spreadsheet of competing values, but in the end, once I reach a (well-considered) conclusion, that's it: over, finished, certain. No regrets, no repeats, and certainly no changing my mind.

But now . . .

I shiver despite the sun, remembering the look on my face in that frozen shot. Things will be the same as they always were back in England, of that I have no doubt, but surely that's a good thing? I missed my old routine: the academic rigor, the satisfying framework of achievement—so why now do I feel such a flutter whenever I imagine working until 2:00 AM on an essay or spending eight hours a day buried in the dusty Raleigh library?

I've tasted something different here—that's the problem. The past three months have been the first time in my life I've stepped out of the hyper-driven rush of school and career planning, the first time I've ever been able to look in on my life from the outside and see myself for what I am.

Stressed. Overachieving. A control freak.

I repeat the words under my breath, and then again, feeling lighter with every whispered syllable.

It shouldn't be this hard.

That's what I've learned on this trip, I realize—besides how to dress like a California girl and fake an excited squeal. That my life shouldn't be this hard. I'm nineteen years old, buried in activities and work, and I'm acting as if one wrong move will throw me into a downward spiral. Like I'm just a single ruined timetable away from stacking shelves in the village Tesco for all eternity.

I start to smile. A sense of gentle reassurance is spreading through me, as easy as the Florida sunshine on my skin. Because in this instant, I know without a doubt that I'll be all right. No, better than all right—I'll be excellent. But not if I let myself get tied up again in stress and cold fear and the constant Oxford rush to *do more* that put such an awful expression on my face in that shot.

I always thought I was aiming for the best possible kind of life, the one my parents told me I should strive to achieve, but now I know I deserve better than the neat plans I made so carefully; I deserve that trip in my bloodstream that I felt watching our film up on the auditorium screen; I deserve laughter and adventure and the rush of uncertainty that comes from living without a schedule.

I start suddenly as a body collapses beside me on the sand. Tash passes me an open box of Krispy Kremes, oozing custard and calories.

"For breakfast?" I exclaim, my pulse still beating a giddy dance from those revelations.

"Uh-huh," she mumbles through a mouthful of icing. I stop myself from making another nutrition-related comment and fill my mouth with soft fried dough instead. It turns out to be a far more pleasurable option.

"So what are we up to today?" Tash asks, yawning.

"I don't know," I muse, stretching all the tension and worry free from my muscles. The beach around us is filling up as the college kids prepare for another taxing day of tanning, the breeze scented with sunscreen and ocean tang. "I was thinking some lounging, a little more relaxing . . ."

"Perfect," Tash agrees. "And remember, we've got wireless internet in the hotel room if you feel like running over and sending Ryan an email."

I laugh at her tenacity. "Will you ever quit?"

"Umm, no." She gives me a wry grin. "This is what friends do."

"Well . . ." I stretch my lips into a slow smile. "Perhaps I will just write a quick message before we hit the pool."

Tash squeals and grabs me. "Seriously?"

"Seriously." I giggle, and to my relief, the decision really does feel final.

"I knew it!" she exclaims. "I knew you'd break sometime. And I hadn't even started with the movie marathon or the guilt trip about opportunity."

"Gee, thanks!" I elbow her. "I didn't realize this was an intervention."

"Only 'cause you needed it." Tash pushes back. "And anyway, you have to come. What would I do all summer without you?"

"Go clubbing with Morgan and Lexi?" I tease.

"Ew no!" She grimaces. "They're toxic. Oh, wow, we're going to have the best time."

"We will," I agree happily, reaching for another donut.

"And Ryan's going to be pleased . . ." She looks at me sideways. I laugh.

"This isn't about Ryan!"

"I know, it's about identity and autonomy, blah blah." She waves my protest away. "But that doesn't mean you can't have your cake and kiss your boy too."

I pause for a second, reveling in the lightness in my chest. I have no idea whether Ryan will want to get back together with me or how my parents are going to react when I tell them what I've decided, but I don't feel as if I have a single problem in the world. "I'm going to have everything," I say slowly, like a promise to myself.

"Don't you mean *we* are?"

"Absolutely."

And we lie there in the sun together until all the doughnuts are gone.

ACKNOWLEDGMENTS

Thanks first must go to my wonderful agent, Rosemary Stimola, whose serendipity and skills brought this whole project together. Thanks to Liz Bicknell, Kaylan Adair, and everybody at Candlewick, Mara Bergman, and the Walker team—you've all been a debut author's dream.

Thank you to my mum for never telling me to stop daydreaming and get a real job, for all those nights tirelessly helping me "research" Gilmore Girls, and for just being amazing. Thanks to my dad and sister for all their support. Thanks to Lauren Barnholdt—getting stuck in traffic with you that day made all the difference; Stu S. and Ned R. for the generous extension of couch privileges; Narmada T. for reading every draft of everything with unwavering enthusiasm; and finally, thanks to Kate S-B., Veronique W., and Dom P. for assorted fun times and putting up with all the book talk.